# GULF OF LIONS

Paul Weston

www.paulwestonauthor.com

Copyright © 2025 Paul Weston

www.paulwestonauthor.com

The rights of the author to be identified as the Author of this Work have been asserted in accordance with the Copyright, Designs and Patent Act 1988.

This novel is entirely a work of fiction. The names, characters and incidents portrayed in this book are the work of the Author's imagination.

No part of this book may be reproduced, or stored in a retrieval system, or transmitted in any form or by any means, electronic, mechanical, photocopying, recording, or otherwise, without express written permission of the publisher.

Cover picture is a detail from:
'An Ocean Freelance'
by
Mark Myers

Note - Glossary at end for readers unacquainted with antiquated nautical words and phrases

*For my brother, John Weston*

# CONTENTS

Title Page
Copyright
Dedication
Chapter 1 – Captain Wright ... 1
Chapter 2 – The Grapes ... 7
Chapter 3 - Trevennec ... 11
Chapter 4 - Sarah ... 14
Chapter 5 - Wapping Again ... 17
Chapter 6 - Celebrity ... 20
Chapter 7 – Off Again ... 21
Chapter 8 - Lézardrieux and Oleander's Revenge ... 28
Chapter 9 - The Prize ... 37
Chapter 10 - Aber Wrac'h ... 42
Chapter 11- Raz de Sein ... 46
Chapter 12 - The Orchard at Agen ... 51
Chapter 13 - The Basque Roads ... 54
Chapter 14 - Levanter ... 63
Chapter 15 - Palamós ... 66
Chapter 16 - Girona ... 75
Chapter 17 - Arrest ... 83
Chapter 18 - Escape ... 93

| | |
|---|---|
| Chapter 19 - A Plan | 98 |
| Chapter 20 - Fontainebleau | 105 |
| Chapter 21 - Rosa | 109 |
| Chapter 22 - The Gulf of Lions | 112 |
| Chapter 23 - Watching | 118 |
| Chapter 24 - Convoy! | 124 |
| Chapter 25 - Cobs! | 136 |
| Chapter 26 - Westward! | 141 |
| Chapter 27 - The Admiral | 145 |
| Chapter 28 - Stop Him! | 153 |
| Chapter 29 - Renegado | 159 |
| Chapter 30 - Isabella | 167 |
| Chapter 31 - The Strait | 169 |
| Chapter 32 - The English Engineer | 173 |
| Chapter 33 - Salé | 178 |
| Chapter 34 - Béziers | 187 |
| Chapter 35 - Sealed and Delivered | 189 |
| Chapter 36 - Xebec | 199 |
| Chapter 37 - Ready | 209 |
| Chapter 38 - Gibraltar | 212 |
| Chapter 39 - Farewell | 216 |
| Chapter 40 - The Plan | 219 |
| Chapter 41 - Kennedy | 221 |
| Chapter 42 - The Diversion: Daisy at Palavas | 222 |
| Chapter 43 - The Raid on the Malpas Tunnel | 228 |
| Chapter 44 - D'Ensérune Ridge | 234 |
| Chapter 45 – The Diversion: Oleander at Sète | 236 |
| Chapter 46 - Aftermath | 242 |

| | |
|---|---|
| Chapter 47 - Pegasus | 245 |
| Chapter 48 - The Beach at Maguelone | 248 |
| Chapter 49 - Béziers | 253 |
| Chapter 50 - Damaged | 256 |
| Chapter 51 - The French Fleet | 257 |
| Chapter 52 - Gibraltar Again | 260 |
| Chapter 53 - The Dinghy | 262 |
| Notes | 265 |
| Glossary | 267 |
| About The Author | 275 |
| Books In This Series | 277 |

# CHAPTER 1 – CAPTAIN WRIGHT

Lieutenant Snowden, dressed in unassuming civilian clothes, paid off the Thames boatman and climbed the steps which led into an alley between high buildings. He walked along the passageway and into busy Narrow Street, which ran behind the warehouses fronting onto the river. The wharves were crowded with merchant ships, their yards trimmed fore and aft so that they did not break the windows of the buildings, and the street was a confusion of activity, with wagons moving goods into and out of the warehouses, using cranes mounted high on their walls to access upper storeys.

He enquired of a labourer, and saw the location for his meeting, The Grapes, a public house squeezed between two warehouses. As he drew near, a man in nondescript clothes pushed himself off the wall he had been leaning on and fell in step with Snowden. Snowden glanced at the man and started in surprise.

"Captain Wright!"

"No ranks today, Snowden, if you please. If you'd be good enough to follow me, I've engaged a private room."

They went into The Grapes, which was busy and rather gloomy, Snowden following Wright as he pushed his way through the crowd, climbed some stairs, and entered a small dark panelled room. The room's window overlooked the river and was at the same level as the mainyard of a ship which was made fast to the wharf outside the public house. The ship, a collier by the look of her, was aground because of the low spring tide.

Wright indicated a chair and poured two glasses.

"Your health, Snowden. Thank you for coming." Wright's voice was slightly tinged by an accent which Snowden could not identify but which he thought might be Spanish.

"My pleasure, Cap ... I mean Mr Wright. *Oleander*'s at Deptford, and the tide has a few hours of flood left in it."

"A splendid ship, famous, too."

Snowden knew Wright was referring to the pamphlet that had been published about *Oleander*'s recent cruise, written by a member of the ship's company identified only as a 'British Tar'. It had become a public sensation, and Snowden and Signora Bianca, the mysterious 'female Corsican bandita', the heroes of the hour. Snowden admitted to himself that he did not mind the attention it brought him.

"Thank you."

"Yes, I saw *Oleander* this morning as I came up the river. Mine's at the Nore."

"Yours is ...?"

"*Vincejo*." He pronounced the name as a Spaniard might have done. "*Vincy Joe*, the sailors call her, a brig, captured from the Spanish. Not so spectacular as your ship, Snowden, but a very handy vessel."

Snowden had a shrewd idea that any ship commanded by Wright, who was as much spy as sea officer and who had escaped from imprisonment in the Temple with Sidney Smith, was likely to be employed in some covert activity.

"What do you do with her?"

Wright looked at him and smiled. "Not much at the moment, I'm spending most of my time at Whitehall."

"What is this about, Sir – sorry – Wright. Why here?"

"I would have met you at the Admiralty, Snowden, but I fear that our discussions might be observed."

Snowden felt a twinge of unease "Observed, Wright?"

"Yes, and perhaps overheard. I have learned in my career that discretion is essential to success. The fact of our meeting at the Admiralty might be communicated to an agent, or perhaps mentioned to a neutral diplomat, and that could have grave consequences."

Snowden was thoroughly discomfited by now. "Agents, at the Admiralty? What on earth do you mean? I think you should state your business, Wright, without further ado."

"Very well, but I have here a letter which I should like you to read."

He handed over a sealed letter, which Snowden opened and read with a rising sense of excitement. When he had finished reading, he put the letter in his coat pocket and looked at Wright.

"It seems, Wright, that the First Lord has asked me to put myself and my ship at your disposal, and that my duties may include those not usually required of a sea officer. What is it that you want me to do?"

"First of all, Snowden, I must ask for your assurance of complete secrecy."

"Of course. Jervis made that plain in his letter."

"Your ship's bosun …"

"Rubert, Rubert Puyol, Spanish Bob as they call him."

"Yes indeed, but he is not actually Spanish"

"Almost. I think he's from Menorca."

"Really, Snowden, there's a world of difference between a Menorcan and a Spaniard."

"I'm sure there is, but what of him?"

"I was brought up on Menorca, and I have known him for a long time, since I was a boy." Abruptly, Wright started to speak in Italian. "You understand what I am saying, Snowden?"

Snowden replied in the same language, which he had learned to speak with reasonable fluency. "I do, but am at a loss to understand why that is of interest to you."

"It shows an aptitude. To undertake the task that I have in mind for you, speaking Spanish would be a distinct advantage, and your Bosun can teach you."

"What do you have in mind?"

Wright leaned forward. "You are aware of the situation in Europe, the political situation that is?"

"Well, to a certain extent, I suppose." He thought, and laughed, "I have some knowledge of Corsican affairs, though it is all very complicated, but I could not call myself an expert. As to the rest of the continent …"

Wright waved his hand, interrupting. "Come on, man, you have been pretty deeply involved, and have even done a bit of negotiating on your own initiative. Some might uncharitably have called it hostage taking, but you certainly achieved the result you wanted. Taking your ship alongside at the Château d'If!"

Snowden laughed, "We anchored off, we didn't go alongside!"

"But the point is, Snowden, that you saw your chance, kept an ace up your sleeve so to speak …"

"I think the ace you refer to is General Bartoli. Yes, I did put him up my sleeve, as you say, but it was not my idea. The credit for that must go to my ship's master, Kennedy."

"Your ship's master? Well, I think he's one that bears watching!"

"It was completely unexpected. I was about to put the ace, well the gentleman concerned, ashore at Malta, when Kennedy piped up and suggested he might be useful. I'd always thought of him as a simple seaman, but I admit I looked at him in a completely different light afterwards. Promoted now, on Nelson's recommendation no less, and he's now my Acting First Lieutenant. I've no doubt he'll fly through his ticket."

"I hope his replacement is as able."

"Poore, who was Midi and then Mate, will be made up, and a Corsican, Luciani, who joined us at Macinhagiu will be Mate. Merchant seaman, skipper of his father's ship in fact. He's certainly got potential. I'm making a Bermudian, Soares, up to Master's Mate, and we have several Corsican sailors as well."

"And you, Snowden. You know you have some powerful interests working for you now? You have done very well, and I should have thought ..."

"So would I, Wright, and I'm due a Post, but there's this court martial business. You know, Parkinson"

Parkinson was the commander of the squadron that had been just offshore when *Oleander* was fighting a desperate battle to evacuate Corsican recruits from Macinhagiu. The squadron had heard the noise of battle, but Parkinson, despite desperate entreaties from his frigate captains, had refused to investigate. One of the captains had made a public accusation, questions had been asked in Parliament, and it was possible that Parkinson would be court martialled, despite his extensive political connections. Snowden, who had been greatly angered by Parkinson's inaction, had been persuaded not to complain to the Admiralty, and he now had a strong suspicion that his promotion was being held up by Parkinson's friends as a warning not to become involved in the legal proceedings, which could, at least in theory, end with the execution of Parkinson.

"I do know of the Parkinson affair, Snowden, but I think that once you are back in the Med, out of the way so to speak, your time will come."

Snowden smiled. The Med again. "So I have been assured, though I would like to help nail that bastard Parkinson. I've spoken to Jones, the frigate captain, and I have deposited a statement with my lawyers which he can have if he needs it."

He looked at Wright, "So what is it you would have me do?"

# CHAPTER 2 – THE GRAPES

"So, Snowden, that's the gist of it. Tide's still flooding, and I'm for the town. Will you share my boat?"

Snowden decided that he'd had enough of Wright and his schemes for now, but knew that no waterman would, or indeed could, take him back to *Oleander* at Deptford until the spring tide began to ebb.

"I think I'll find something to eat here, and take a boat back to Deptford when the tide turns."

"Very well, I will send word when we are to meet again. In the meantime, please ready your ship. Speed is of the essence."

When Wright had departed, Snowden went downstairs, and sat at a small table near the front of the building, looking at the tide flooding rapidly into the river, carrying with it an astonishing array of craft – rotund colliers heavy laden with Tyne coal, barges with hay stacked high above their gunwales and rudimentary sails rigged on top of the cargo, ships from Scandinavia loaded with timber.

In a mood of retrospection he ate his meal, watching as the ship on the wharf below lifted with the incoming tide and began to nudge gently against her moorings. He had done well, very well, and professional success seemed assured. In the last few weeks he had certainly taken advantage of the openings to society his burgeoning celebrity had given him, but tonight he felt no desire to make his way on the flooding tide to the brightly lit salons 'out west'. Since he had been wounded, he sometimes felt, as he did now, the need for anonymity, to not be 'Your Honour' on the deck of his ship or 'the hero of Corsica' around a glittering dinner table.

He had noticed several people making their way purposefully upstairs, and when he paid his bill, he asked the woman behind the bar if there was a game afoot.

She looked at him closely. "First room on the left as you go up, Sir. Say 'Maria sent you'."

Snowden did as she said, and was soon seated at a gaming table. He played carefully, and well, for a couple of hours, winning modestly, until he felt the first intimation of resentment from some of his fellow players. He pulled out his watch.

"Excuse me, gentlemen and ladies, I must be on my way. Thank you for your company."

A thickset man, probably a reasonably prosperous ship chandler or merchant, who had been drinking steadily, looked at him angrily.

"Leaving so soon? Without giving us a chance to win our money back?"

"I'm sorry, Sir, I must be on my way."

"You've taken my money. I don't know how you've done it, but it didn't seem fair to me. In my opinion you're a ...."

Snowden looked at the man, and held up his hand.

"Stop! Don't say it, Sir, or I guarantee you'll regret the word. I won fairly, and if you'd taken less drink and paid more attention to your cards than to Lizzie here, you'd have stood a better chance."

"He's right, Bobby," said Lizzie, leaning over the man with her hands on his shoulders. "He's won fair and square. Leave him be."

The man subsided, and Snowden made his way out of The Grapes. Light spilled from buildings, making pools of light on the road, but between them the Narrow Street was dark. It was by no means deserted, but the commercial activity of the daytime had subsided. Snowden walked along, realising that he felt much better for spending time concentrating on the game. He was in a dark patch, near an alley between warehouses, when he heard footsteps behind him, half turned, and then felt a tremendous blow on the back of his head. He fell, stunned, the ground rising up to meet him, feeling surprisingly soft against his head.

When he came to, he was lying on his back in the dark, cold stones beneath him. He realised that he had been unconscious only briefly and that he was in the alley. He heard a man speak, and then smelt alcohol fumes and felt hands in his pockets, searching. At least two of them, then. He lay still for a moment, recovering, thinking. They could take the gold he had just won. It didn't amount to much, but once they'd taken it, would they leave him alive? He thought they would, they had had the opportunity to kill him already and he had not seen their faces. The letter, though, Jervis' letter, was important, and he couldn't let them take it that. The familiar thrill ran through him, the thrill he experienced before action. He felt one hand go into the pocket of his breeches, the other hand resting on his chest.

Now or never, he thought, and grabbed the fingers of the hand on his chest with both of his hands, pulling them down and simultaneously twisting. He felt bones break and the man screamed, struggling to get his uninjured hand out of Snowden's pocket. As the man pulled away, Snowden brought his knee up as hard as he could and felt it connect with the man's face. Snowden released the hand and the man fell away. He could hear his assailant breathing in sobs nearby, and, as fast as he could, Snowden rolled to his left, came into violent contact with the legs of the second man, and clung on tightly, rocking the struggling man back and forth until he fell, cursing. Snowden got to his feet, groggily, and kicked hard, as hard as he could, at the sound of the cursing. There was a satisfying crunching sound, and the cursing was replaced with a bubbling groan. Snowden's eyes had grown accustomed to the darkness and he could just make out the man's shape. He knelt beside him, grabbed the man's hair and lifted his head roughly.

"What were you after?"

The man spoke weakly, "Sir, please don't hurt me anymore."

Snowden twisted the man's hair.

"Who sent you?"

"Sir, nobody sent us. We saw you leaving The Grapes, thought you'd won. We were after your winnings, Sir, God help us. We'd taken drink, Sir."

Snowden violently pushed the man's head back into the ground and stood up. He felt for his unresisting hand, spread it on the ground and put his heel above the fingers.

The man, knowing what was about to happen, struggled weakly.

"Sir, for the love of God, no, I won't be able to work."

Snowden seemed to feel the restraining arms of a marine about him and recalled the sergeant's voice, "She's struck, Sir, it's over."

Suddenly overcome with tiredness, he moved his foot from the man's hand, knelt down and pressed a couple of coins in it.

"Don't spend it on drink," he said, and limped out of the alley, his head throbbing.

# CHAPTER 3 - TREVENNEC

Since Snowden's last visit, his parents' house, Trevennec, had been if not transformed, then considerably improved, and the estate was clearly better tended.

The hall did not exactly glitter, but it was well lit, clean and warm, and there were sufficient servants, some borrowed from other houses it was true, to attend to the guests, who included, to Snowden's satisfaction, the Lord Lieutenant of the County. Snowden's parents seemed much less careworn than they had previously, and he was pleased to see that neither drank any intoxicating liquor during the dinner. Snowden was seated next to a very attractive woman, Mrs Sarah Stanbridge, who he had known as a child. In the last few weeks, he had become used to being the centre of attention, but Sarah Stanbridge, though she conversed intelligently with him about his recent exploits, was by no means sycophantic. She was very interested in his account of meeting the poet Coleridge, and after they had both partaken rather freely of the excellent wine, she rather startled Snowden when she whispered in his ear that she had nearly finished writing a novel.

"Have you?" said Snowden, "I have met another lady novelist, Captain Burney's sister."

"You've met Fanny Burney?"

"No, his other sister, Sarah. Perhaps you've heard of her?"

"I have, and have read her book, *Clarentine*."

"Did you enjoy it?"

"Yes, I thought it was pretty good, though perhaps a little contrived."

"I am glad to hear it! She's a very clever lady. Captain Burney is likewise particularly intelligent."

Their conversation was interrupted by Snowden's father, Lord Penzance, who stood and tinkled a spoon against a glass until he had the room's attention.

"I would like to say a few words before the ladies retire, as what I am about to say concerns my wife." He turned towards her and nodded. "With your permission, my dear."

Lady Penzance looked surprised, but indicated acquiescence. Her husband continued.

"Some of you will have read the pamphlet published about my son's recent adventures in the Mediterranean. If you have not read it, I expect that you know the general outline of the story. What you may not know is that the idea of raising troops in Corsica was conceived in this house and came – and I almost feel as though I am dreaming when I say this – from my wife."

There was a murmur of disbelief in the room.

"Oh yes, it is true. And furthermore, Mrs White, who some of you may have met when she was standing in as steward on this estate, and, I may say, standing in most effectively, is the Julia Bianca of the narrative, the 'Corsican bandita' with her rifle and bayonet, the daughter of Pasquale Paoli."

There were more expressions of surprise from the room, but Lord Penzance ploughed on.

"And, what is more, those two ladies went to London, without my having an inkling of what they were up to, and persuaded the government to back the scheme."

Someone started to clap, and before long the guests were

standing, applauding, while Lady Penzance sat back, a mixture of embarrassment and pride on her face.

When the applause had died down, Lord Penzance continued, "Perhaps my son would like to add a few words? Percy …"

Snowden stood, slightly nonplussed. "Yes, firstly I would say don't believe everything you read in pamphlets. Secondly, what my father has said is true. The expedition to Corsica was conceived by my mother, and the quiet Mrs White transformed into Julia, Corsican patriot, who does in fact own a Baker rifle and bayonet. And I would like to propose a toast to these two remarkable ladies …"

# CHAPTER 4 - SARAH

On the morning after the dinner, Snowden and Sarah Stanbridge rode out to the clifftop. The sea shone brightly in the sun, ruffled by a light south-westerly breeze.

They dismounted, and after picketing their horses to a bush, sat on the grass. Snowden watched with professional interest as a large coaster, close inshore, tacked and headed out to sea, the sound of her sails flogging as she went through the wind clearly audible.

"I think he may as well anchor and wait for the tide to turn. He's not going to gain much on that tack."

He looked at the woman, saw her face cloud, and realised that he may have made a mistake.

"I'm sorry, Mrs Stanbridge, that may have been insensitive."

"Don't apologise, Percy, and please call me Sarah. I cannot go through life avoiding all mention of the sea. It was an unfortunate accident, but I am constantly told that time will heal, and perhaps that process has already started."

"I remember your husband well, Sarah, as a child. A strong swimmer, I always thought."

"Indeed he was, Percy, but he sometimes pushed himself too far. And on that occasion …"

Snowden knew that Sarah's husband had been drowned while bathing some eighteen months previously.

Sarah looked at the coaster, now losing ground on the

starboard tack.

"I suppose you find we English women rather insipid in comparison with your Corsican 'bandita', Percy."

"Ha! It's a matter of opportunity, or even necessity. Nobody knows what they are capable of until they are tested. Julia," he thought of the time he had spent with her, "Julia has been tested, often, almost from when she was a girl, and has the confidence that comes from knowing that she has overcome her fears."

"Is it true that she fights like a man?"

"Like a man? I'm not sure about that, but she can certainly fight. I expect that you could as well, but you were not brought up as a Corsican, with all the hatreds and passions that motivate those people. It can be a harsh place."

"Did she kill a corsair? I'm not sure …" She looked at Snowden, who was frowning, and stopped.

"Let's not think about that on this beautiful day." He looked at her. "I wonder if you would be able to emulate one clever thing that she did."

"What is that?"

"Showing Lord Nelson her bruises!"

\*\*\*

The next few days, until Snowden had to make his way back to Deptford, were some of the happiest he had ever experienced, spent mostly in Sarah's company. His headaches, the aftermath of the wound he had suffered in Corsica, became less frequent, as did Sarah's periods of introspection. Sarah had decided not to return to her parents after the death of her husband, and her house, which was within walking distance of Trevennec, was pleasant and well ordered. The garden was her pride and joy, and she owned numerous books on botany and gardening. They spent pleasant evenings together, Sarah sometimes playing the piano, while Snowden sung the sea songs popular aboard ships, often including verses that they improvised.

Snowden returned to Deptford feeling that he had recovered from his wound, and elated by the time he had spent with Sarah and the prospect of taking *Oleander* back to the Mediterranean.

# CHAPTER 5 - WAPPING AGAIN

Giotto Luciani, *Oleander*'s new Master, leaned on her taffrail and watched as Snowden made his way across the quay to a waiting boat. Luciani turned to Kennedy, now *Oleander*'s First Lieutenant.

"Old Man seems happy."

"So he does, Giotto."

"He was very …", Giotto searched for the right word, "very down. The blow to the head, I think it affected him very much. But now …"

"A few days at home, perhaps that is what did it."

"I think it's a woman. I feel happy like that when I've met a new woman."

"From what I've heard, Mister, you must often feel happy!"

Kennedy thought about Snowden's dingy attire. "Off for a run ashore, dressed like that?"

"I think secret business, Lieutenant. Dangerous perhaps. Last time he went ashore so dressed, he came back with his clothes muddy and a cut on the back of his head. He said it was robbers. At Limehouse."

"Limehouse!" In their short stay at Deptford, Luciani had acquired a good knowledge of London. "What was he doing there?"

"I don't know, Giotto, but I feel sorry for the men who attacked him!"

*\*\*\**

Snowden met Wright at 'The Pelican', a rather disreputable public house in Wapping.

Wright gave Snowden his orders, verbally – nothing was written down.

"Jervis' letter will give you all the authority you need, Snowden, without me giving you anything that might be ...," he searched for the right term, "misinterpreted."

Snowden thought that Wright carried secrecy to extremes, although he was willing to grant that imprisonment in the Temple might make one rather cautious.

"You're ready for sea, Snowden?"

"She's on twelve hours' notice, Wright."

Snowden pulled out his watch, looked at the sky out of the window and thought about his ship.

"South-westerly. We can catch the ebb tomorrow morning. We can work *Oleander* to windward down Channel pretty quickly."

Wright held out his hand. "*Bon voyage*, Snowden."

"Thank you, Wright. Will you tell me where you're off to?"

Wright looked about him. "Your old stamping ground, Snowden, southern Brittany."

"My word, Wright. I'll never forget the Vilaine. Go carefully."

Snowden never knew whether or not Wright went carefully, for he never saw him again. *Vincy Joe*, becalmed off the Vilaine, was surrounded by French gunboats which she could not engage with her short-range Carrons, and was forced to strike her colours. In captivity, Wright was separated from the rest of the crew and sent to the Temple for a second time, never to emerge alive.

# CHAPTER 6 - CELEBRITY

Though it had been some time since the anonymous 'British Tar' had published the sensational pamphlet about *Oleander*'s activities in the Mediterranean, an account that did not by any means play down his role in the affair, Snowden's star was still riding high in London.

He knew that the fame was ephemeral, and that before long he would be replaced or disgraced in the public's attention, but he had made up his mind to enjoy it while it lasted. He had an invitation, a very good invitation, for that evening – a ball in London – and though the thought of a last appearance as some sort of celebrity was briefly tempting, he was overcome by common sense, and realised that *Oleander*'s imminent departure meant that he could not attend.

His evening, however, dining with fellow officers aboard a frigate in the dockyard, was by no means uncongenial, and he returned quite late to *Oleander*.

# CHAPTER 7 – OFF AGAIN

As *Oleander* was being warped out of the basin the next morning, Snowden, who was standing on the deck, feeling rather exhausted after last night's events, and who was allowing Kennedy to supervise proceedings, heard a shout from the dockyard foreman ashore and looked up.

"Admiralty Messenger, Your Honour."

The foreman addressed some of the crew handling the sternline.

"New orders, I reckon. Greenland probably. Nice and cold for you."

To a chorus of derision, the Messenger climbed aboard and, in the cabin, handed the letter to Snowden, who signed the receipt. The man turned on his heel and made off.

At the Nore, after a fast trip down the river, Snowden called his seniors into the cabin. He looked at them in turn – Kennedy, the First Lieutenant, steady, experienced and a fine seaman, Acting Lieutenant Poore, and Ensign Watton of the Marines, both of them hardly more than boys.

"We're for the Med!"

The men looked at each other, smiling.

"Coasting work."

"Very good, Sir," said Kennedy. "Prospects?"

Snowden knew very well what Kennedy meant. The last trip to the Mediterranean had been a success by most measures, but they had taken no prizes.

"Prospects, Kennedy. What do you mean?" said Snowden, smiling.

"Um, financial ones, I suppose, Sir."

"I should think we might be in with a chance, Mr Kennedy."

"Very good, Sir. Straight to Gib, is it?"

"No, as a matter of fact it isn't. We received this just before we sailed, as you no doubt noticed." He gestured towards the Admiralty letter. "We're to head to St Peter's and pick up a passenger."

"A passenger, Sir?"

"Yes, not exciting passengers like last trip, but a Breton who wants to be dropped off at home."

Kennedy's face fell. He'd spent long years dodging about in the rocks and tides of Brittany.

"And, gentlemen, Their Lordships are concerned that part of the French fleet has slipped out of Brest and there may be warships in the north Brittany creeks. We're to look into as many as we can, on our way to the Med."

"Dammit, Sir, she's a handy ship, but some of those places are shallow, and she's pretty deep. And it's coming up to springs as well."

"I know, Kennedy, we must do our best."

Later, Snowden stood on the starboard side of *Oleander*'s quarterdeck as she rushed past the South Foreland in the gathering dusk, and the white cliffs of Dover came into sight on the starboard bow.

Kennedy approached him. "South Foreland abeam, Sir,"

he said unnecessarily.

"So it is," said Snowden. It was very good to be at sea again in *Oleander*, even if she wasn't the frigate he deserved, to feel her lifting to the swell as she came out of the shelter of the land and hearing the wind sighing in the rigging. They had had a very good run before from Deptford, making the most of the ebb tide and the south-westerly wind, and Snowden had been in no mood to anchor in the Downs until daylight, or to await a more favourable wind.

He looked at his watch. "We've got a bit of tide left, Ken. Let's lay her on the wind and see if she'll make anything on the starboard tack."

"Aye aye, Sir. I'll hand the squaresails."

"Very well. Don't pinch her up too tight."

Kennedy looked at him. "As if, Sir!"

Snowden grinned, and ducked into the cabin.

Orders were given, the foremast squaresails were furled and when the helm put up, *Oleander* set off eagerly, heeled to the breeze, heading towards the French coast, her progress down Channel helped by the ebbing tide.

The watch changed, and Poore approached, his face split by a broad grin.

"Hello, Mr Poore."

"Sir," Poore nodded. "Tramping along as usual." He dodged a dollop of spray and patted the rail. "Good to be back in *Olly*. My word, Sir, doesn't she move. Like a rat up a drainpipe!"

Through the night and during the next day, *Oleander* beat her way down Channel, Snowden carefully observing his crew at work.

Their starboard tacks took them well offshore, out of sight of land, and the port tacks almost to the English coast. By the evening of the next day they were just off St Catherine's Point on the southern side of the Isle of Wight, and as day broke they saw the dark bulk of Portland emerge from the gloom.

Snowden, leaving the cabin after a long Spanish tuition session with the bosun, looked aft and saw Luciani working with Midshipman Pascoe on the patent log. Snowden walked forward, nodding or speaking as he passed men working on the deck. The ship was heading almost due south now, heeled over on the starboard tack to the brisk south westerly.

Snowden was used to Bermudian informality by now and was not surprised when one of the seamen, Iris, asked him, "We be heading south, Your Honour – Med again?"

"We will be, Iris. Guernsey first, briefly, and then we'll be poking into some of the creeks in Brittany. When that's done it'll be Gibraltar and into the Med. How do you like that?"

Iris smiled. "I like the Med fine. England's too cold for Bermudians, though we not be sure about Brittany."

Snowden walked aft again, hanging onto the rigging as the ship plunged into the waves.

He spoke to Luciani who was standing by the helm, notebook in hand. He looked at the book.

"Ah, Giotto, I see you've copied Pascoe's notebook. A remarkable bit of work."

Pascoe's notebook summarised the results of the sailing trials that the Admiralty had conducted when the ship was new, setting out the most advantageous way of sailing the ship in different conditions, and taking advantage of the patent log which continuously indicated the ship's speed through the water, and a clinometer which measured her angle of heel.

"Amazing, Sir."

"It is. I don't know if anything like it has been tried before, ship handling reduced to a science. Pascoe is an enthusiast for that sort of thing."

"I know, Sir. Earlier I helped him with the patent log, dismantling and oiling it. Based on an invention of the famous Mr Watts, he tells me. When we finished, we checked it against the ordinary log and it was spot on, Sir."

"I don't doubt it. How are you liking the ship?"

"She's a beauty. So fast, and up to windward ..."

"She is a beauty and I'm glad to have her."

Snowden looked up at the straining mainsail.

"We've never gybed her all standing, Giotto."

"I hope not, Sir, a nasty thought. My father's ships are different. Some square rigged, some lateen."

Snowden was very wary of the huge booms at the feet of the main and fore sails. If the ship was gybed accidentally, 'all standing', through a shift in the wind, momentary inattention on the helmsman's part, or a mistaken order, the booms would sweep across the deck, damaging rigging or even carrying away the mast when they were brought up abruptly. The advantage of the fore and aft schooner in being able to work her way to windward was considerable, but the fear of gybing was such that some schooner captains had converted their ships to square rig, sometimes at their own expense.

Just at that moment there was a hail from the masthead, "On deck there! Land!"

"Where away?"

"A point on the larboard bow."

"That'll be the Casquets," said Kennedy, coming up on deck. "Nasty place." The Casquets were a high rocky formation, with an evil reputation. Before long, from the deck they could see the main rock, with the white surf beating against its bed.

Pascoe busied himself with compass, log and chart and said to Snowden, "Another *Oleander* landfall, Sir. Bang on, we are, just about where I thought we would be."

"Yes, Pascoe, well done."

Snowden let Kennedy take the ship through the Little Russell, the rock-strewn channel between Herm and Guernsey, *Oleander* close hauled, but under reduced canvas to allow Pascoe time to take almost continuous bearings, check the log and plot their position on the chart. Snowden recalled his trip with Jack Stone through the same channel in the fishing boat from Lymington – it seemed so long ago.

They anchored in St Peter's in the late evening, and before the anchor had set there came a call from the lookout, "Barge setting out from the quay. Admiral I reckon."

The bosun, Rubert, burst into activity, making sure the sails were furled neatly and the ship and men were tidy. Ensign Watton formed his marines up at the chains.

The whistle piped as Admiral Sausmarez emerged onto the deck, stopped to salute aft, greeted Snowden warmly, and spoke loudly enough for the bosun and the side party to hear.

"A fine ship you have here, Snowden, immaculate order, but I can tell she's a fighter."

They walked towards the cabin and the Admiral said, "I hear you've done some good work with her. Last time you were here you had that Froggie frigate – the one you took off Ushant – and the time before that it was in a damned little fish boat."

(During the Peace of Amiens, Snowden and his midshipman colleague Jack Stone had sailed a fishing boat to France and had made their way by land to Paris.)

They sat in the cabin.

"I know you're off to the Med, Snowden, but we have a difficult situation here which Their Lordships have recognised. There seem to be some French ships missing from Brest, and I've an idea they may be in one of the north Brittany rivers. We want you to have a poke about, see what's going on. Trieux, Wrac'h and so on, you know the places. We don't have anything very handy on this station, but with *Oleander* you should be able to get away if you're spotted. If you see anything worth knowing, get back here and tell me about it."

"I'll do my best, Sir."

"I'm sure you will, Snowden. I say, any news of that friend of yours, the one that owned the fishing boat?"

"Stone, Sir."

"That's the one. A very able young man, very able in my opinion."

"As you will remember, Sir, he was wounded in the affair with the barges, and the Frogs got him. Fouché, you know, Sir, the secret policeman …"

Sausmarez shuddered. "Go on."

"Fouché very much took against Stone and had him taken to the Temple. He got out through the offices of Captain Morlaix – you have undoubtedly heard of him as well."

"I have. Just as well the French don't have a hundred officers with his ability!"

"And he married Morlaix' daughter and escaped to America from the Gironde."

"Extraordinary. I heard he resigned from the Navy."

"Yes, Sir, he is not a man for fighting, though he's uncommon good at it."

The marine guard tapped on the door.

"Ah yes, Snowden, your passenger."

Trezeguet, the Breton Chouan rebel, stepped into the cabin, and Snowden rose to shake his hand.

# CHAPTER 8 - LÉZARDRIEUX AND OLEANDER'S REVENGE

In the gathering dusk, with a nearly full moon rising, *Oleander* slipped past the Roches Douvres, that fearsome plateau of tide-beset rocks. The westerly wind was light, and the coast of Brittany could be discerned ahead. Pascoe, aided by Luciani, was busy with his instruments, marking their position on the chart every few minutes, and from time to time looking at the tidal curve he had drawn on a large sheet of paper. Their destination, the Trieux estuary, was rocky and heavily tidal, a place that demanded the utmost respect. There was no room for mistakes.

With the men tense at their stations, under only the mainsail and a flying jib, with the longboat towing astern, *Oleander* swept silently forward on the last of the flood tide, with a dark rocky island, Bréhat, close to port.

Pascoe gestured ahead, to where an ugly looking rock rose from the water. Snowden could distinctly hear the suck of the sea around its base.

"La Croix, Sir." He consulted his watch and the tidal curve. "It wants an hour to high water. We are just where we should be."

"Well done Pascoe, you've judged it nicely."

As the ship went further into the rocky estuary, Pascoe pointed to starboard.

"Île à Bois, Sir, where we're to drop our passenger."

Snowden turned to Trezeguet who was standing near him. "Are you ready …?"

At that moment, in the distance, they heard the sound of shouting, and a soft call came from the foremast top, a Bermudian voice, seemingly out of place in this dark Breton estuary.

"On deck there, there's fires further up the river, and shouting … Music as well maybe, and shooting I think."

Snowden peered forward and saw the orange glow of fires behind the darkly wooded hills at the side of the estuary.

"Trezeguet, I don't think we'll land you just yet, we'll take the ship a bit further up to see what's going on."

Leaving Kennedy and Pascoe to con the ship, Snowden went forward with Trezeguet to where Luciani was standing on the cap rail, balancing on a forestay. The ship, her sails driving her slowly and silently through the water, was swept up the estuary by the last of the flood tide, the dark wooded bank of the western side very close.

The men at the forward guns, the huge Carrons, ghostlike in the moonlight, sat on the guns' slides, the captains hunched over the barrels, occasionally sighting along them.

Trezeguet said, "The last bend before the town, Snowden."

Iris at the crosstrees, looking over the low headland, called down softly, "The town, all lit up it is. Looks like a party."

"*En fête*," said Trezeguet. "Perhaps a saint's day."

There was another call from aloft, the man, Iris, clearly excited.

"A ship, a big one, moored in the river." A pause. "Seen her before, I reckon."

Snowden leaped for the foremast shrouds and scrambled aloft.

In the moonlight, the town, Lézardrieux, was visible, a few hundred yards from the sea, lit up by bonfires. Standing on the crosstrees he could see people in the wide main street and hear music. Occasionally there were small explosions, he thought probably of firecrackers.

In the middle of the stream, with her bow pointing towards the sea, a ship was moored, her yards glinting in the moonlight. A big ship, a warship.

"You're right Iris, we have seen here before!"

"Where?"

In his best Bermudian Snowden replied, "In de Atlantic, bye, she be *Blonde*."

Snowden's heart raced with excitement. He was in command of a warship, a superb engine of destruction, honed to perfection. He had a skilled and disciplined crew, but he alone was responsible for the ship, and her success largely depended on him. He had been at sea almost continuously since he had joined the Navy as a boy, was a veteran of warfare conducted on a global scale, and the traditional aggression and confidence of the Royal Navy was deeply ingrained in him, as was the Service's lust for prize money. And he was a young man, without the caution that age often imparts.

He slipped down the rigging and ran aft along the deck. The flood tide was slackening and the ship was moving slowly. There was not much time.

"Ken", he said, urgently, "you asked if we had prospects this trip, and there is your prospect", gesturing to the moored ship. "She's the *Blonde*. Remember her? Gave us a mauling off Bermuda."

*Blonde* was a big Malouine privateer, much feared by merchantmen, which had nearly defeated *Oleander* a few days out from her shipyard in Bermuda. Snowden presumed that she had opted to refit in Lézardrieux, rather than St Malo, which was closely watched by the British.

"But Sir", said Kennedy, lust for prize money tempered by caution, "she's a big bastard. Packs a punch too, as I recall. Nearly had us last time."

"They're all ashore", said Snowden with more confidence than he felt, "at the village fête. Here's what we're going to do …"

\*\*\*

The Trieux was narrow, and although the privateer was moored only a hundred yards or so off the town quay, *Oleander* was apparently unnoticed as she passed the darkened ship to starboard.

The river was wider here, but still a tight place for *Oleander* to work herself round in. Everything depended on the next few minutes.

"Now, Ken," said Snowden, almost conversationally.

Kennedy, who had been anxiously awaiting the order, turned and said, "Down your helm, Quartermaster."

Then "Let fly your jibsheets."

"She's answering nice, Sir," said the quartermaster as he watched the ship's bowsprit sweep across the dark background of the land, slowing as her head came into the wind and the mainsail flapped once, twice. For an agonising moment she lingered in irons, the mainsail flogging.

Kennedy, judging the moment, shouted, "Weather jibsheet." Men tramped along the deck, hauling the sail aback. Snowden heard Kennedy urging her round, patting the rail. "Come on, my darling, you can do it."

*Oleander*, as though she heard Kennedy's entreaty, fell off on the port tack, but her momentum had taken her close to the town quay. The noise of the flogging mainsail had obviously been heard ashore, as there were shouts from the land. Snowden could not make out the words, but they did not appear to be hostile.

"Haven't seen the ensign, though it's plain as a pikestaff in this moonlight," said Kennedy softly, and then as the shouts ashore grew in volume, Snowden heard the word '*Anglais*'.

"They have now," he said. "Let's keep 'em honest."

The port Carron fired, immensely loud, sending grapeshot hissing into the water. The orange flash lit up the people on the quay ashore, who ran for cover, though they were safe enough, out of the gun's range.

As the ship slowly gathered way, Kennedy looked at the privateer, black and sinister in the moonlight, judging distances.

"Back her now," he shouted, and as men pulled on the braces, the wind pressed the square fore tops'l against the mast, slowing the ship.

Snowden ran to the rail, where a boarding party of marines and sailors crouched, ready.

*Blonde* was very close now, her hull towering above *Oleander*. Snowden saw that some of her gun ports were open, no doubt for ventilation.

"Marines through the ports," he said to Watton, who stood beside him, his young face white in the moonlight. "Sailors with me to the deck."

*Oleander*'s starboard side crashed into *Blonde*'s port side, to the accompaniment of the sound of splintering wood.

Snowden shouted, "Ken, be gentle with her", eliciting a ripple of laughter.

The great mainsail fell to the deck, the Carron fired again, and Snowden saw grapnels thrown from *Oleander*, hooking over rails on the privateer. He grabbed a rope, tested it, yelled "Come on boarders, up we go", and then he was climbing up the side of the privateer. He reached an open gun port, saw a movement inside and swung himself feet first through the port, just as the gun fired, throwing itself back against its ropes, deafening him and half blinding him with the flash. He felt himself roughly kicked forwards by the next man through the port, landed more or less upright on the privateer's gun deck, fired his pistol at a vague shape, and threw himself forward through the smoke, cutlass swinging, slashing at dimly seen figures, parrying blows aimed at him. Resistance slackened and, vision returning, he saw men around the next gun aft. He ran towards it, uncaring whether his men followed, arriving at the gun as the gun captain was about to put his match to the hole. Snowden shouted "Stop!", the gun crew turned, saw him with *Oleander*'s men around him, and raised their hands in surrender.

He saw no one else on the gun deck as he raced aft and threw himself up the companionway, meeting Watton near the helm. Marines were guarding a group of prisoners, men and women, who were sitting on the deck around the mainmast.

"I thought you were going in through the ports," he said.

"And I thought you were going onto the deck, Sir."

"A fair point, Mr Watton, well done."

Luciani arrived with a group of Corsican sailors.

"Secure below, Sir."

"Very good. Get the hawser on her, men aloft with axes."

"Aye aye."

He turned to Watton. "Guard on the powder room?"

"Already done, Sir."

He looked over the stern of the privateer, where several small boats were tied up.

"Get all the prisoners into the boats. They can make their

way ashore."

"Aye aye, Sir."

Snowden grasped a grapnel rope and swung himself back onto *Oleander*'s deck. Kennedy stepped forward to meet him.

"She's yours, Ken," he said, pointing to *Blonde*. Kennedy touched his forehead in acknowledgement, grabbed a grapnel line and rapidly climbed aboard the privateer. The tide was turning, beginning to ebb, and *Blonde* tugged at her sternline. Snowden knew that in a few minutes the stream would be so strong that their opportunity would be missed. He went to the bow of *Oleander* and shouted over to Kennedy, who was supervising the securing of the hawser to the privateer's bitts.

"I'm getting her underway."

"Aye, Sir, tide's turned. I'll cut the sternline as soon as the hawser's taut."

At that moment there was the sound of a cannon fired from ashore and a ball thudded into *Oleander*'s side

Snowden shouted, "At the flash, Guns."

And then, "Poore, let draw the fore tops'l, get the foresail on her."

The great foresail was raised and sheeted home. *Oleander*'s broadside fired, one gun at a time, but Snowden did not pay attention to the fall of the shot. The shore gun fired again, hitting the bulwark of the privateer and sending splinters whizzing across the deck, and he heard a man cry out, but under the force of her sails and the tide, *Oleander* was moving forward along *Blonde*'s side. Seamen aboard the privateer shouted, bracing the ship's yards round fore and aft, and men scrambled aloft with axes, ready to cut *Blonde*'s rigging free of *Oleander*'s embrace.

He saw Kennedy on the privateer's deck, gradually paying out the slack in the towing hawser, and as it tightened, water squirting from its strands, he saw men hacking at *Blonde*'s sternline and anchor cable. *Oleander*, smaller than *Blonde*, almost stopped as the load came on the hawser, and she turned away from the wind, pivoting round the tow rope.

Snowden shouted, "Let fly foresail sheet, clew up the tops'l. Up with the mainsail, in tight, now."

Men ran on the deck, and cast off and heaved in ropes, while *Oleander* hung at right angles to the estuary, swept down by the ebbing tide towards a reef, the Donan Roc'h, which protruded into the channel. A jolt ran through *Oleander*, and they heard, from deep within the ship, a crashing sound, but the ship did not pause, and her sails gradually brought the ship under control, the huge privateer following dutifully in her wake.

"Donan Roc'h," said Poore. "Nasty."

The Carpenter appeared and spoke to Snowden.

"It was the keel that hit the rock, not the planking, Your Honour, probably a bit taken out of it. It hasn't started any seams as far as I can see, and she's making no water. We build 'em good on t'Island!"

"Thanks, Chips."

The ships continued downstream until Poore pointed to a point of land ahead.

"I saw a glint of something there, Sir."

Snowden looked, saw nothing, but Iris, sharp-eyed Iris shouted from the foretop, "Deck there, gun on the land, two points larboard bow."

The gun ashore fired, but Snowden did not see the fall of the shot, and soon *Oleander* was wreathed in smoke from her own broadside replying, the land rushing past as the tide swept the ships down the estuary.

Pascoe came up, his personal compass round his neck,

chart in hand.

"Sir, there'll be a fierce west-going tide at the entrance. Best to keep her as close to Croix and Bréhat as we can."

Snowden knew there was a danger that the slow-moving ships, almost without steerage way, could be set by the current onto the horrible plateau of rocks on the west side of the entrance.

"Very well, Pascoe, do what you can."

He looked astern towards *Blonde* and, to his relief, saw her fore topsail break out and belly as it was sheeted home, and unthinkingly grabbed Pascoe and turned him to look aft.

"Look at that, Pascoe, Kennedy's getting sail on her."

In a few minutes, *Blonde* was sailing, the strain on the towrope reduced.

"She be steering better, Your Honour," said the helmsman.

Snowden turned to Pascoe, "Where's Poore?"

"He was hit, Sir, that last gun from ashore. Splinter."

The bosun came up to the helm.

"*Blonde*'s sailing, Sir. I was thinking …"

Snowden knew what he was going to ask – should they release the towrope? At that moment, there was a cry from below, and Rubert said, "I think Mr Kennedy has just cast off, Sir, I'd best get that hawser in."

He hurried off, and Snowden saw, in the moonlight, *Blonde* under her topsails and mizzen, a white wave beginning to foam at her bow. Well done, Kennedy, thought Snowden, you'll have your day of glory.

# CHAPTER 9 - THE PRIZE

The two ships forged steadily northward for the remainder of the night, *Oleander* keeping close company with *Blonde*. Snowden knew that Kennedy would be as aware as he was of the proximity of the Roches Douvres to leeward, and towards which the tide would take them when it changed.

One of *Blonde*'s guns fired, and Snowden turned to Luciani.

"Range her alongside *Blonde*, Mister, within hailing distance."

With the ships close together, Snowden picked up his speaking trumpet and shouted across the gap, "Lieutenant Kennedy, you have my attention."

Kennedy's voice, without the benefit of speaking trumpet, was difficult to hear, but Snowden was able to make out "heave to" and "repair aboard".

As he watched, *Blonde* backed her topsails and lowered a boat, and Snowden saw Kennedy in the sternsheets as it was rowed towards *Oleander*, which had also heaved to.

In *Oleander*'s cabin Kennedy spoke without preamble.

"Sir, do you intend to take us into St Peter's?"

"That was my plan, Ken. Do you suggest otherwise?"

"I don't think that's the best course of action," said

Kennedy with considerable emphasis.

"Why not?"

"Sir", Kennedy lowered his voice, rather theatrically, Snowden thought, and said in a soft voice, his eyes glinting, "*Blonde* has cargo, Sir."

"Cargo?"

"Yes, and if I'm any judge, a valuable one. She's a fine ship of course, 44 guns, nearly new, and that'll make us a pretty packet. But …", he paused, "she's loaded, loaded to the gunwales." Kennedy searched for the right word, but gave up and said, "Completely stuffed, Perce."

"Indeed?" Snowden said, his tiredness vanishing. He had spent most of the night trying to compute the likely value of a fine new frigate, as indeed had most of the crew, but this was something else.

"She loaded a cargo, in the States, foodstuffs mostly, but more than that, Percy, there's stuff from the ships she's taken – loot. Come and have a look."

Completely forgetting himself, he stood up and tugged at Snowden's sleeve, and then, embarrassed, said, "Sorry, it's been a long night."

"Never mind that, Ken, I'll come right away."

Snowden sat with Kennedy in *Blonde*'s splendid cabin, a bottle of brandy between them. Snowden sipped from his glass, and smiled with pleasure.

"These privateers live well, or at least they did until we took their ship! My word, Ken, we've been through a lot together, but nothing like this. I can hardly believe it."

Kennedy looked shrewdly at him. "The ship's very valuable, 44, almost new, sails like a witch, but the cargo, well, that is quite something else. If we take her into St Peter's …"

"I think I know what you're going to say, but say it

anyway."

"I think Guernsey is out of the question. There will be fingers in the pie, the Admiral might expect a share, and it's no place to sell a cargo like this."

"You are right, as usual, Ken. I think we should head for Plymouth. It has proper prize agents, I have lawyers there, and there will be a market for the cargo. But we do have our duty."

"Duty?"

"Yes, Ken, I must report to Sausmarez."

"Must you?"

"Yes of course, but here's how we'll do it ..."

As he stood to leave, he noticed a polished mahogany box in the corner of the cabin.

"What's that?" he asked.

"I haven't noticed it before," replied Kennedy.

They went over to it and Snowden opened the lid.

"My word, Sir, look at that. A chronometer." He peered more closely. "Berthoud."

"I think, Ken, this is going to make Mr Pascoe's day."

\*\*\*

Leaving *Blonde* to continue towards Plymouth, Snowden took *Oleander* into St Peter's on the last of the flood tide. *Oleander* hove to in the roadstead without anchoring, and fired a gun. As Snowden had hoped, the Admiral's barge was soon approaching.

As he came aboard, Sausmarez looked at the splintered rail and said, "You've been in a fight, Snowden, what news?"

"It is in my report, Sir. Shall we go into the cabin?"

In the cabin, Snowden said, "We went into Lézardrieux. There was a privateer there, *Blonde*."

"*Blonde*, my word, I hope you beat a hasty retreat."

"We did, Sir, but with *Blonde* in tow."

Sausmarez threw himself back in his seat in surprise. "Do you mean that you cut her out? A great thing like that?" His eyes narrowed slightly. "Where is she now?"

"Sir, she was moored in the river, just off the town. She was just back from a cruise. Probably found St Malo too heavily watched and so slipped into the Trieux. The town was *en fête*, and the crew, or most of them, were ashore. Kennedy has her now, she's on her way to Plymouth."

"To Plymouth? Why did you not bring her here?" Sausmarez thought briefly, and decided to give in gracefully. "Well, never mind that, well done Snowden!"

"Thank you, Sir."

"You'd best be on your way", and, remembering, he asked, "Trezeguet, what happened to him?"

"We chucked the crew who were still aboard off into her boats. We think Trezeguet went with them, though nobody noticed him go. At least, he's not aboard either ship now."

The admiral raised his eyebrows.

"On your way, Snowden, and congratulations, but remember there's the rest of the coast to investigate."

*\*\*\**

Kennedy took *Blonde* into Plymouth, with *Oleander* following close behind, looking very small compared with the privateer. A huge British ensign flew from *Blonde*'s mizzen, above an equally large tricolour and Malouine flag. By the time she was warped alongside, the whole town seemed to be watching, and often cheering enthusiastically.

Snowden sent a messenger into the town, and an hour later Anderson, Snowden's lawyer, was in *Oleander*'s cabin. By the time the lawyer left, Snowden was confident that *Oleander*'s officers and crew would profit as they should from the disposal of *Blonde* and her cargo. Snowden was careful to keep the crew informed of the negotiations, and *Oleander* suffered no runners, and no new crew members were required.

Despite her encounter with the rock in Lézardrieux, *Oleander* did not leak, and, as the dry dock was busy and time short, Snowden and the dockyard concluded that inspection should be delayed.

Snowden's parents, accompanied by Sarah Stanbridge, visited the ship. Snowden and Kennedy showed them round *Blonde*, his father full of praise for his son's bold action, and his mother rather anxious, though she took Kennedy aside and, as he said afterwards, "asked some pretty straightforward questions about what price we might expect for *Blonde*". They promised to remove Poore from the hospital to Trevennec to recuperate as soon as he could be moved, and watched as *Oleander* warped out into the stream, set her sails and disappeared into the rain.

# CHAPTER 10 - ABER WRAC'H

They had 'looked into' Roscoff and the Bay of Morlaix on the previous night, had seen nothing, and now, in the darkness, waiting for the dawn, *Oleander* was a few miles west along the rocky Breton coast, under easy sail in a fresh south-westerly, with all the indications of a stronger blow to come.

They were off Aber Wrac'h, or at least that's where their reckoning put them. In the darkness, above the noise of the wind, they could hear the distant sound of surf crashing onto rocks. As the sky lightened, they saw ahead a low coast emerge from the darkness and, just to off port, a horrible jumble of white water, clearly the source of the noise.

"Libenter," said Pascoe, with satisfaction, as, dividers in hand, he looked up from the chart pinned to a table on the deck. "Just where we want to be."

"You may want to be here, young man", said Kennedy as *Oleander* slid past the Libenter reef, "but of all the nasty places I've visited, I think this is the nastiest."

Snowden smiled, despite the tension. "I agree with you, Mr Kennedy, it is truly dreadful. Let's get this over with as soon as we can." He looked hard at a rocky island. "Tide still seems to be making."

Pascoe pulled out his watch and confirmed, "For another half hour I reckon."

"There's the marks," said Kennedy, a tone of relief in his voice, pointing ahead and moving over to the quartermaster at the helm, indicating the leading marks to him. "Keep her on them, watch her in the tide," he said as the man squinted forward.

"You have her, Kennedy," said Snowden. "I'm going aloft. Be ready to wear or tack."

He went forward, the men ready at sheets, halyards and braces, or crouched over the guns – alert, nonchalantly watching the nearby rocks, whose blackened bases showed stark against the white waves surging against them.

At the foretop he greeted Iris.

"We meet again."

"Good morning, Your Honour," he shivered. "Be a fresh day."

As the ship crept along the channel, the sweep of the estuary, bordered by sandy beaches, came into view from their elevated position.

"Anything, Iris?"

"Nothing, Sir, few little boats."

Snowden agreed. As far as he could see, there were no warships. That was enough for him – he had no intention of pushing his luck again, especially with that fort ...

Iris said, urgently, "Sir, the Froggies be up early."

Snowden saw a huge tricolour raised on the fort, and, almost at the same time, cannons fired from their emplacements.

He shouted down, "On deck there. Take her back out."

Whistles blew, the helm went up and *Oleander* turned away from the wind. Barely under control, the great booms swept across the deck, and Snowden felt the mast under him shake as the gaff at the head of the foresail swung over. Water splashed onto the deck as balls hit the sea around the ship, and he heard one shot pass very close to him as he scrambled back down the ratlines. He ran aft, shouting to the Gunner as he went, "As you bear."

Taking *Oleander* into the Wrac'h had been a gamble, but those were his orders, and he had hoped that an approach at dawn would be unobserved. And now, he knew, he'd been wrong, though the fort had made an error by firing too soon, with *Oleander* at extreme range for its guns.

The ship was hit, once, twice, three times, splinters whining across the deck, but Kennedy stayed by the helm, unmoving, occasionally glancing up at the sails and issuing orders. Snowden watched with fascination as Kennedy and Pascoe discussed the ship's course, each absorbed in his task, oblivious to the balls from the fort which splashed into the sea near the ship. *Oleander*'s rather puny broadside fired in reply, one gun at a time.

The ship heeled to starboard as the sails were sheeted home. A ball crashed into her side, and more scythed across the deck, harmlessly, as the men working the ship had thrown themselves down as soon as the sail handling was over. Now *Oleander* was moving quickly, but there was a crash from forward.

A runner came up. "Your Honour, port Carron's hit. Men wounded."

The next salvo from the fort fell astern of the ship. "Out of range", said Kennedy, with satisfaction, and then, as *Oleander* turned the corner in the channel and headed out of the estuary, "My God!"

Snowden looked and saw a warship, a frigate, come round the ugly Libenter reef from the north. Libenter had become a seething cauldron of white water as the wind rose and the tide fell.

"Get the rags on her, Ken," said Snowden.

The topsails were set and braced tight, and the sea hissed along the lee rail as the schooner responded, but the French ship turned to port, aiming to intercept *Oleander*.

"How close to those rocks can we go, Pascoe?" said Snowden, indicating the breakers to port.

"A bit closer than this, Sir."

"Bring her up a point, Mr Kennedy."

*Oleander* would pass close to the French ship, but she was really moving now.

Snowden saw Pascoe run to the taffrail and look at the patent log. "Fifteen knots!" he shouted, and went back to his table.

The French ship was close now, converging with astonishing rapidity. Snowden knew that the enemy would have very little time to fire as *Oleander* swept past, but also that the schooner's angle of heel meant that her starboard battery could not reply. The encounter, when it came, was almost an anticlimax. The French ship fired, but *Oleander* was not hit, and soon she was out of range, heading west in a wild career, close to the rocks on her port side.

Snowden, elated, said to Kennedy, "That'll do, snug her down. We'll take her outside Ushant, get some sea room."

There was another hail from the masthead. "Two more Frenchies. Starboard bow and abeam."

Snowden looked up. More ships, frigates. They must have been in Morlaix, in the town at the head of the estuary, waiting for *Oleander*. The French had sprung a trap. There was no chance that *Oleander* could make her way between them, north or east. Kennedy looked at him.

"Get her hard on the wind, Ken. We'll take her through The Trade."

# CHAPTER 11- RAZ DE SEIN

Blocked by three frigates from making her escape out to sea, Snowden realised that *Oleander*'s only chance of escape was through the narrow, tide-scoured channel between the island of Ushant and the mainland, the Chenal du Four, or 'The Trade' as it was historically called by the English.

The wind, now west by south, had increased to gale force. He knew *Oleander* was more weatherly than the square-rigged frigates, and that, by pointing closer to the wind than the pursuing ships, she had a chance of escape. Assuming, he thought to himself, that nothing carries away and that no ships come out of Brest to bar our way.

The warrant officers came to make their reports. A man had been killed, a Bermudian seaman, three had been wounded, there was a hole in the hull above the waterline, and the port Carron had been knocked off its mount. The ship was making no water, and repairs were in hand.

The ship was stood down from quarters and the men fed. Snowden went to visit the wounded, ate quickly, and, as he knew the coast well, sent Kennedy and Pascoe below to eat and rest, taking the watch with Luciani.

"A frightful place, Sir," said Luciani. "I will not miss these tides when I return to Corsica."

"They are very useful, if you know how to work them."

When the huge rock of the Four was abeam, they could just about make out the topsails of the pursuing ships from the deck, but they were a good distance astern and to leeward. *Oleander* was moving quickly, well reefed down, hard on the wind in what was now a full gale, and swept along by the south-going tide. Kennedy and Pascoe were back on deck, the latter having moved his chart table under the break of the poop, to protect it from the continuously driving spray. Between them, they navigated the ship through the rock-strewn channel as she swept southwards, past Kermorvan and Le Conquet, constantly taking bearings on landmarks and making small course corrections.

The ship was reefed down to scraps of sail, but her progress against the backdrop of the Breton shore was very rapid.

"Point St Matthew" shouted Pascoe above the moan of the wind in the rigging, pointing over the port bow, where a high headland with a tower atop it was visible through the spray.

Snowden beckoned to Kennedy and they went into the cabin, blissfully free of the wind.

"What will we do, Sir? Outside of The Saints? I'm not sure we'll make it in one tack."

Once *Oleander* passed Point St Matthew, they would be in the Iroise, the long bay that led to Brest, with The Saints, a low island on its south side, and Ushant to the north. There was a narrow channel, the Raz, between The Saints and the mainland, but it was dangerous and narrow, rock strewn and with fantastically fast running tides. Snowden was about to answer when there was a knock on the door and Pascoe ran in.

"Ships, Sir, to windward. A lot of them, battlers. Frenchies going into Brest I reckon, but there could be some of ours behind them, chasing them, Sir."

There was no question of *Oleander* taking on the French

men o' war. She would not even be able to slow them down. The confines of the Iroise would make it difficult for *Oleander* to manoeuvre past them, so Snowden had only one choice – to escape.

He looked at Kennedy. "I think our minds have been made up for us. The Raz it is."

The leading French ships, 74s and frigates, were quite close, but they showed no interest in *Oleander*, concentrating only on running the blockade and getting safe into Brest. Snowden knew this would change if he attempted to take *Oleander* seaward, past them. One choice, he thought without enthusiasm, the Raz it was.

It was about twenty miles across the Iroise, and the tide was still south going when the lookout sighted an island on the starboard bow. Before long they could see it from the deck, dark and forbidding, shrouded in spray from the waves smashing against its base.

"Trévennec," shouted Pascoe into Snowden's ear.

"My house," replied Snowden.

Pascoe looked at him, wondering.

"Never mind, Pascoe, I'll tell you later."

The surface of the sea was almost completely carpeted in foam. The waves were enormous, Atlantic rollers sweeping in from the west, with huge breaking crests. *Oleander*'s design emphasised speed, almost to the exclusion of everything else, and to keep her hull as light as possible, her freeboard was low, the main deck only a few feet above the waterline. The consequences of this now became obvious – she was a very wet ship. Occasionally a wave crest hit the ship, sending solid water foaming across the deck. She would stagger, heel and then free herself, water pouring from the freeing ports. Lifelines had been rigged, and men caught out by the waves leapt for them, scrambling atop them so that they were clear of the waves. The galley fires had been put out and the whole ship was cold and wet.

Despite her reduced canvas, a staysail and heavily reefed main, *Oleander* made good progress with the tide under her. Snowden slid across the sloping deck from handhold to handhold to where Kennedy crouched by the wheel.

Snowden shouted in Kennedy's ear, above the screaming of the wind in the rigging. He pointed ahead to the seething cauldron of the Raz de Sein.

"Get all hands below except Luciani."

Kennedy shouted an order and Luciani came up to the wheel.

"You and the Lieutenant take her, I'll con the ship. Lash yourselves to the binnacle, I'm going to the rail." He pointed, uphill, to the port side.

Lashed to the rail, Snowden could see, ahead, the famous Raz de Sein, where the waters of the English Channel were pouring, driven by the tide over rocky ledges on the seabed, against the wind, through the narrow gap between the mainland and an off-lying island, The Saints, into the Bay of Biscay.

The Raz was a demented mass of churning white water. Waves of incredible steepness curled and broke and smashed against each other, combining to send huge white peaks into the air. To port there was a huge rock, the Old Woman, grim and black against the white waves crashing into it, and to starboard the low island of The Saints surrounded by evil reefs. There was no way to avoid the Raz, they had to go through.

A breaker reared and Snowden ducked behind the bulwark as the wave broke onto the deck, the water so deep that for a moment his head was submerged and he felt the incredible power of the sea trying to snatch him from his lashings. He looked up and saw the deck of the ship emerge from the foam, struggling to free herself from the weight of water. She had slewed violently to port and he saw Kennedy and Luciani pulling at the spokes of the wheel to get her back on track. He held his arm out to show them the course.

There was a moment's respite and then another hissing roller threw itself at *Oleander*. Above the shriek of the wind, Snowden heard splintering and saw the remains of the ship's boats entrained in the foaming water that poured over the ship. But she rose, to Snowden's relief and astonishment, righting herself, freeing herself from the tons of water that submerged her deck. Again, Snowden, his teeth chattering, pointed the way, and Luciani and Kennedy hauled at the spokes, bringing her slowly round onto her course.

And then, blessedly, she was through, into the Bay of Biscay. The wind screamed, but it seemed more moderate, and the rollers, still huge, were at least regular. Snowden untied himself and slid over to the helm.

"That", said Luciani, "was not nice!"

# CHAPTER 12 - THE ORCHARD AT AGEN

Morlaix sat beneath the shade of a plum tree in the orchard of his house at Agen, the air full of the scent of flowers and the hum of insects. He felt if not content then at least not entirely discontented, despite occasional twinges of pain from his right leg, a leg that, from below the knee, was no longer there. He was far from Paris, far from Napoleon, and in Agen the war seemed remote. Napoleon, proclaimed Emperor but thirsting for glory, still had his *Armée d'Angleterre* in Boulogne, waiting for an opportunity to cross the Channel to England. Morlaix knew of Napoleon's ignorance of sea power and was not sure that the opportunity would ever come. England, prosperous and with her formidable Navy, might well frustrate Napoleon's ambition, even if the Emperor was successful on land.

A splendid army, though, he thought, and if he cannot use it against England, what will he do with it? He won't keep it idle in Boulogne for long. Well, it was not his problem ...

He heard the house door open and close, turned his head, and saw his wife, Odile, walking towards him. He waved, knowing that she would encourage him to exercise, walking on his wooden leg around the track the gardeners had mown in the orchard's grass. She paused halfway towards him when she heard the sound of a horse on the gravel from the front of the house and the jingle of accoutrements as a rider dismounted. She went back into the house, returning after a few minutes in the company of a young man in naval uniform who saluted smartly.

"Lieutenant Crouzet. I presume I have the honour of addressing Captain Morlaix?"

"Indeed you do, Crouzet."

"Sir, I have a letter for you. From Paris."

He handed over a sealed letter, which Morlaix opened and read.

"What is it, my dear?" asked Odile.

"Promotion, Odile."

"Admiral Morlaix!" Odile's face clouded "But will ...?"

"I don't think I'll have the opportunity to hoist my flag to the masthead of a ship, Odile, at least for the time being" he collected his thoughts "can we offer this young man some refreshment?"

As the servant was clearing away the remains of their lunch from the table in the garden, Morlaix asked the lieutenant, "What naval news from Paris?"

The young man, who was still rather in awe of the great Captain (now Admiral) Morlaix, answered hesitantly. "The damned English are everywhere, as usual, Sir. We are hopeful of breaking out, and I am sure if we do we will beat them."

*I wouldn't bet on it*, thought Morlaix gloomily. At St Malo, he had seen the way the English had handled their ships and their rate of fire. *Rather you than me, Lieutenant.*

The lieutenant looked at Morlaix, perhaps saw the scepticism in his face, and continued, "The damnedest news came in just as I was about to leave Paris. An English ship, a schooner it is said, quite small, went into the estuary at a place called Lézardrieux in Brittany."

"I know it very well," said Morlaix. "Difficult place, full of rocks, and very tidal."

"Yes, Sir, well, this schooner, a remarkable looking ship they say, apparently went right up to the town, miles up the river, on the tide, and there was a big privateer there, a St Malo ship, *Blonde*, 44 guns, moored in the stream. They had just arrived from a very successful cruise, and went into Lézardrieux because the English were at St Malo. Anyway, the crew were ashore, celebrating, and …"

"Don't tell me any more, Crouzet, let me guess."

Morlaix imagined himself on the deck of the schooner, creeping up the dark estuary, the excitement, and then seeing the prize! It was the sort of thing he was made for.

"They cut the ship out and made off with her," he concluded.

"Yes, Sir, that's what they did."

"There'll be a few disappointed privateers I imagine, and some happy Rosbifs. A schooner taking a frigate!"

"Yes, Sir, but that's not the only strange part of the story. We think the ship is the *Oleander*, the one that was in Corsica, you know, she took on a regiment of Cuirassiers. Her captain, Snowden …"

Morlaix held up his hand. "I know, he was the one that burned my barges."

"Odile, I must start for Paris!"

"*We* must start for Paris," replied his wife

# CHAPTER 13 - THE BASQUE ROADS

The night was wild and seemed never-ending, but eventually, as it always does, the sun rose, and its thin watery light illuminated a desolate scene. *Oleander* was out of sight of land, alone on a wild ocean, with the wind, though more moderate, still blowing strongly. As the morning wore on, the wind veered to the north-west, making a return to the north round Ushant exceedingly difficult.

"We'll find some of our ships around the Basque Roads," said Snowden to Kennedy as they sat in the cabin, referring to the area of shallow water near La Rochelle, sheltered from the Atlantic by the isles of Oléron and Ré. The Royal Navy kept a close watch there because ships entering or leaving the French naval base of Rochefort had to pass through the Roads.

"I'll lay off a course."

"Let's be cautious until we've got some sights, Ken. I want to be well clear of Penmark" he said, referring to a notorious Breton headland. "We've had enough surprises recently."

"That we have, Percy. Penmark's a nasty place."

As the following day broke, *Oleander* was under easy sail. Snowden's innate cautiousness had stopped him from storming through the entrance to the Roads, the Pertuis d'Antioche, solely on the basis of Pascoe's lunar sights.

When the call came from the masthead "Land on the port

bow", Pascoe was crouching over the patent log. He stood up, ostentatiously pulled out his watch, and looked up at Snowden.

"Very good, Pascoe. You've done it again."

There was another shout from the tops: "On deck there. Ship astern. Big. Man o' war, I reckon", and immediately afterwards, "and another one, smaller."

Snowden started. If the ships were French, *Oleander* had to get some room or she could be trapped between the warships and the land.

"Put the helm down, Mr Luciani."

"Aye aye, Sir."

"Get her on the port tack, close as she'll bear."

The ship came on the wind, heeling in the breeze, which as always seemed to become much stronger as the ship turned and it blew from ahead.

"Pascoe, up and have a look at her."

"Aye, Sir."

A few minutes later Pascoe shouted from the foretop, "Ship of the line, and a frigate."

Snowden tensed, and then relaxed as Pascoe yelled "*Indefatigable* perhaps, I can make out the colours."

"Master", said Snowden, "tack her round and take us to meet them."

*Oleander* took station astern of the 74 and her accompanying frigate as they went through the disturbed water between the Islands of Oléron and Ré, listening to the sound of the surf breaking impressively on the Whale Rocks at the northern end of Oléron.

The squadron anchored in the northern part of the Basque Roads. Except for the dinghy, all of *Oleander*'s boats had been destroyed in the Raz de Sein, and Snowden waited until a boat was sent from *Indefatigable* and repaired aboard her.

He was met by a rather elderly man who introduced himself as Lieutenant North. North conducted him across the immaculately maintained deck, sparkling with brasswork, and paused at the break of the poop. To Snowden's surprise he said in a soft voice, "I advise you to keep calm, Snowden."

Snowden had no time to reply as he was shown immediately into the spacious cabin, but understood the reason for the warning when he saw that the officer who rose from the chair at the desk overlooking the stern gallery was Commodore Parkinson, the man who had failed to come to his aid in Corsica.

Snowden, his voice shaking, began his account of *Oleander*'s findings in north Brittany. He had not been speaking long when he was interrupted by Parkinson, who, without looking Snowden in the eye, said, in a flat and expressionless voice, "Unfortunate to lose all of your boats, Snowden."

Snowden's voice steadied. "Yes, Sir, we were swept stem to stern, twice, in the Raz."

"What, pray, were you doing there?"

"Well, Sir, we went into Aber Wrac'h …"

"You went into where?"

"Aber Wrac'h, Sir, it's a creek just near l'Île Vierge …"

"I know very well where it is, Snowden, my question was rather why you went there."

"My orders, Sir, to see if there were any men o' war."

"Men o' war, in Aber Wrac'h? It's a very small place as I recall. Whatever next!"

"Bigger than Lézardrieux …" Snowden was about to say *'but there was a man o' war there, or at least there was until we cut it out'* – but the gambler in him realised that he might as well hold his ace back, and he caught himself in time and said, "Orders, Sir, but we were fired on by the fort."

"Did you not know the fort was there?"

Snowden looked at the Commodore but did not reply.

"I asked …"

Snowden held up his hand and the Commodore stopped speaking.

"I heard you", he said, not bothering to conceal the contempt in his voice "Sir, I knew of the fort, but I considered that we might remain undetected long enough to account for the shipping in the place."

"Well, you did not, did you?"

"No, Sir, we were not undetected, but we did establish that there were no men o' war in there."

"And why did you take your ship inside Ushant? Surely a dangerous thing to do."

Snowden's hand, unconsciously, drifted to his sword hilt. Out of the corner of his eye he saw the elderly lieutenant, who was behind Parkinson, raise his hands palms downwards in a calming gesture. Snowden collected himself and replied, with studied composure.

"When we came out of Aber Wrac'h there were three French men o' war blocking our way, so we went through the Four."

"I see, Snowden, but it does seem remarkable sloppy to be ambushed by the fort, and then to be surprised by the French on the way out."

Snowden said with exaggerated politeness, "Indeed, but sometimes, Sir, I have found that taking risks advances the cause, and indeed, Sir, duty sometimes requires us to put ourselves in peril."

Parkinson winced, discomfited, and the elderly lieutenant behind him smiled and nodded.

"And then, Snowden, you went through the Raz? In a gale?"

"Yes, Sir, we did. We had no choice. We met a French squadron in the Iroise, making for Brest, pursued, I believe, by some of His Majesty's ships. We could not beat out past them."

"You saw French ships, pursued by our own, making for Brest, and you made no attempt to interfere?"

The lieutenant was shaking his head, and Snowden said, in a display of meekness. "No attempt whatsoever, Sir."

"Well, Snowden, I need scarcely say that this will be included in my despatch."

"North, please show Lieutenant Snowden", he emphasised the word 'Lieutenant', "off the ship."

"Very well, Sir", said North, "I'm sure he'll be eager to get away and back to *Oleander*."

On the deck of the great ship, in the cold wind slicing across the quarterdeck, the elderly lieutenant stopped and said in a low voice "What a bastard. I thought momentarily you intended to run him through!"

Snowden laughed. "I fought hard to control myself. He's not in the Med anymore, then?"

"No, Nelson wouldn't have him there, and they don't want him back in England, political connections or not, so he's here. And when I say him, I mean us, we're all damned by association."

He thought for a minute. "Well done, Snowden. Our barge will take you back to *Oleander* directly, and if you send a crew back with the barge, we'll find a boat for your ship."

*\*\*\**

Snowden was very concerned about *Oleander's* vulnerability, anchored for the night so close to the French coast, but he had no choice as he did not want to beat out to sea through the Pertuis d'Antioche in the dark. He made sure that a sharp lookout was kept, rigged boarding nets, and stationed a man with an axe ready to cut the anchor cable.

*Indefatigable* was moored several cable lengths ahead of *Oleander*. The crew stood down from dawn quarters, and as daylight spread across the choppy surface of the Basque Roads, they noticed strange activity around the 74. Men swarmed up the rigging and took station in the tops. The ship's boats were lowered and began to row around the ship.

"Man overboard, I reckon", said Kennedy to Snowden, and then, "look, she's signalling. I don't recognise that one."

Pascoe arrived, looked at *Indefatigable*'s signal hoist, and disappeared to find the signal book, reappearing moments later.

"Commodore's missing", he said in an astonished voice, and then, "I'd better check that."

"Mr Kennedy can do that, Pascoe. Get the new boat out and take me to *Indefatigable*."

Snowden boarded the battleship, almost unnoticed, and saw the elderly lieutenant, North, in conversation with a tall thin man who he realised must be the commander of *Indefatigable*'s accompanying frigate. He went up to them and the lieutenant looked up.

"Good morning, Snowden. This is Captain Tennant of *Hebe*," indicating the frigate moored close at hand. "Captain Tennant, Lieutenant Snowden of *Oleander*."

Tennant nodded and turned to Snowden. "I think we should repair to the cabin."

In the cabin, sat at the table, Lieutenant North looked nervously at Snowden and Tennant.

"The Commodore is gone."

"Gone? When?" said Tennant in a tone of disbelief.

"In the night, we don't know when."

"You've searched the ship of course?"

"We have, twice. He's not aboard. He's ..."

In a flash of sudden realisation, Snowden knew what had happened, and said gently, "Over the wall?"

"Yes, Snowden, that's what he's done. From the stern gallery." He swallowed hard. "There's a nine pound ball missing from a pile at the starboard quarter chaser."

"Poor devil," said Snowden, remembering the anger and barely concealed contempt he had displayed at yesterday's meeting. "Was there ..."

"Yes, there was." Lieutenant North, looking even more elderly than usual, went to the door and called, "Atkinson, if you please." He turned to the men at the table. "Atkinson's the writer."

Atkinson came in, bearing several letters. "He left these on my desk", he pointed to a desk at the side of the great cabin, "in the night. They are addressed to you, gentlemen."

He handed a letter each to Snowden, Lieutenant North and Captain Tennant and made towards the cabin door. As he reached it, he paused, turned to the men at the table and said, "He just didn't have it in him anymore."

A steward appeared and set a bottle of brandy and glasses on the table.

Tennant poured. "A thoughtful man, your writer, North." They drank, and opened the letters.

Snowden read:

*'My dear Snowden, I have wronged you, and for that I apologise. I should have come to your aid in Corsica, but I did not because I have become a coward. I was formerly a brave man, as my record shows, but courage has deserted me. I treated you very ill this evening. I did not know at the time that you had cut a frigate out of Lézardrieux, but even so I should not have spoken as I did. To be*

known as a coward, to be in command of a squadron in which every man holds me in contempt, is more than I can bear.

Yours

Parkinson'

Snowden watched as the other officers finished their letters.

"Poor bastard," said Lieutenant North, looking even older. "It's my fault. I never spoke a civil word to him, after Corsica. I felt such shame. I did my duty, but it was grudgingly done. Nobody in this ship has ever spoken a cheerful word to him since then. The men were insubordinate, in his hearing, but I did nothing about it. He tried to speak to me, sometimes, but I cut him off. My God, what have we done?"

Snowden felt a great weariness descend upon him. "It's not your fault, North. I was pretty horrid to him last night."

"He had no right to speak to you in that way," replied North. "He was attempting to intimidate you, in case there was a court martial."

"He was", said Snowden, "but I was … Oh, I don't know …"

"The worst thing was", said North, "when the boat crew came back from your ship, they were all talking of your cutting out the frigate. I need not have done it, but I went into the cabin last night and told him the story. He took it … he took it very hard. He dropped onto the settee and said, 'I've done that boy wrong, twice', but I turned on my heel and left him. There was no pity in me."

Captain Tennant interjected, "I was no better. I felt shame as well, and anger after Corsica. He would signal me to repair aboard *Indefatigable*, and sometimes I would not even acknowledge his signal. I would hang back when we were supposed to be keeping station. When I did meet him, I said as little as possible."

He downed the contents of his glass and winced. "Early for me. Look here, Snowden, you know what it's like in command. You are on your own. I pride myself that my people do not hold me in contempt, but even so, it is lonely work. With the scorn of everyone around it must be hard beyond compare."

# CHAPTER 14 - LEVANTER

*Oleander*, alongside in Gibraltar, was noisy with the sound of dockyard workers repairing the damage caused by enemy action and weather. Under Kennedy's watchful eye, the work was progressing well, and Snowden hoped that the ship would be ready to sail the next morning. The issue at present was boats – boats to replace the ones *Oleander* had lost when she was swept by breakers in the Raz de Sein. *Indefatigable* had given them one boat and the dockyard had provided several more, but Snowden wanted something that had a more Mediterranean appearance, and he had sent the boatswain ashore to scout around the port for something suitable.

He saw Rubert approaching along the wharf, and when he was aboard, addressed him in Catalan: "Did you find anything, Bosun?"

"Yes, Sir," Rubert replied in the same language. "A tartan, Sir, eight oars, and a lateen sail."

"Light? Expensive?"

"I think not too heavy, but strong enough for a swivel. The owner is a rogue, though. He realised I was from the Navy and adjusted the price accordingly."

"Very good, Bosun, thank you. Perhaps you could go with Mr Pascoe and his boat crew and sail her back."

"Aye aye, Sir", Rubert paused, "and Sir, your Spanish is

improving."

Pascoe and his crew spent the remainder of the day practising with the new boat, with its unfamiliar lateen sail. By the time the boat was hoisted aboard and stowed next to the other two new boats, they were adept in handling it.

***

In the early morning, as *Oleander* slipped out of Gibraltar, Kennedy stood at the rail with Luciani.

"The Levanter, up to windward again, Mister."

The Levanter was the name of the east wind, and Luciani looked at the cloud over the Rock. "The Levanter cloud is touching the Rock, so the wind will not be very strong. I think it will be no problem for our *Olly*, Sir."

"I think not, and at least we'll be moving. Last time we came this way we were becalmed and met with Corsairs."

The Corsican grinned. "I wouldn't mind meeting the Moors in *Oleander*!"

When *Oleander* tacked, just off Ceuta on the African coast, there was no sign of Corsairs, but, despite Luciani's prediction, the easterly wind had become strong, and the ship heeled to the wind, her decks wet with spray.

Pascoe, now Acting Lieutenant, went about his duties with enthusiasm, and though Kennedy and Snowden checked his work, they could in truth hardly keep up with the constant stream of calculations and updates on the ship's progress which appeared on the chart. There was now implicit faith in Pascoe's mathematical skills, and he had become, *de facto,* the ship's navigator.

They had tacked the ship in the night, and now, as dawn broke, she was at quarters, slipping slowly along under reduced sail. Pascoe looked up from the sounding machine as a cry came from the foretop.

"Deck there. Land ho! One point on the larboard bow. A city, big church."

"Malaga," said Pascoe, with quiet satisfaction to Snowden. "Should be a league distant. I suggest we tack her now, Sir."

By the morning of the third day, *Oleander*'s company had had quite enough of working the ship to windward, but with the high castle of Alicante visible in the distance, they tacked once again and pointed her head in the general direction of Africa. They passed close to the high rocky island of Ibiza, and six days after leaving Gibraltar, at dawn, they took her close enough inshore to confirm that they were off the Catalan port of Palamós.

# CHAPTER 15 - PALAMÓS

In the evening, after a day of idling out of sight of land, they worked *Oleander* slowly back into the coast, towing *Rosa*, the lateen-rigged boat they had acquired in Gibraltar. There was a headland to the east of Palamós, Cap Gros, and behind it was a bay, with a small village almost on the beach at its head. To the east of the beach there was rocky shoreline with a low cliff above it, reasonably protected from the wind, and this was where Snowden intended to land.

The ship's company were tense at their stations, and Pascoe and Kennedy conversed in low tones, intent on navigation, Kennedy occasionally giving directions to Luciani.

"Twenty fathom," called out the man at the sounding machine. They could hear the suck of the waves on the rocky coast, see the dim outline of the cliffs against the starry sky and the village nestling behind the beach.

"Bring her to, Mister," said Kennedy to Luciani. "Get the boat alongside" and "Pascoe, man the boat."

Snowden was elated at the prospect of action. He and Rubert were dressed in clothes they hoped would be inconspicuous, yet sufficiently naval to deflect accusations of spying. Snowden spoke to Kennedy.

"Ken, you have her. Mind you treat her kindly!"

"Indeed I shall, Sir."

The swell was breaking white in the darkness as Pascoe steered the boat through the offlying rocks. Her keel bumped heavily on the shore, and men jumped out to hold her steady and pull her up a little so that Snowden and Rubert could disembark dry shod.

"Best of luck, Your Honour," said the bowman as he helped Snowden ashore, his Bermudian drawl, as always to Snowden, sounding out of place in this Mediterranean setting.

"Thank you", said Snowden, "I feel in the mood for a little walk."

The man laughed and turned to help get the boat off the rocks.

"Well, Rubert, we're on our own," said Snowden in Catalan to the boatswain, who was examining a steep path up the low cliff.

"I think we can get up here," replied Rubert.

They scrambled up the cliff and were soon on the headland. Far below, in the dim light, they saw the boat making its way out to sea. *Oleander* was nowhere to be seen.

Snowden thought of the detail of the map that Wright had given him, so long ago it seemed, in Wapping. In an effort to memorise the map, he had copied it out many times, as had Rubert. He was glad now that he had gone to so much effort, as its details were clear in his mind. He glanced at his compass and they set off, soon finding a path that led away from the coast through the fragrant pine trees. They came to a corner and Snowden stopped to look at his compass, bringing it up to his face so that he could see it in the almost complete darkness. Rubert had walked a little further on, and suddenly, to Snowden's horror, he heard a shout and a conversation in Catalan, too rapid for him to make out the detail of what was being said. Moving quickly, he drew his sword and worked his way quietly through the woods to the side of the path towards the sound of the voices.

A man lay face down on the ground, speaking in a pleading though rather weak voice, the reason for which was clear – Rubert was kneeling on his back, with his knife pressed to his neck.
Snowden called out softly "Rubert."

The boatswain looked up. "I nearly bumped into this man."

"Who is he?"

"He's from the village of Margarida, you know, the one on the beach," Rubert pointed south-west. "He says he was out hunting. It is not his land, but he hunts for his family."

Snowden had no wish to harm the man, and said, in Italian, which he knew Rubert understood, "Tell him we are French. We do not want to harm him, as France is a friend of Spain, but he must not tell anyone of this meeting."

Rubert relayed this to the captive, who responded, unwisely, "French? You must be with the sailors."

"What do you mean, the sailors?"

"Sir, please! The sailors that are camped at Palamós. The ones that you French guard."

"Sailors at Palamós? It is a port, there are sure to be sailors."

The man was silent for a moment, clearly thinking.

"You are not French. Are you English? I think you are English. I have heard Englishmen speak, when I used to go to the port with my wagon, when trade was good."

"Tell me about the sailors. Are they from a ship?"

"No, Sir, please. These sailors are walking, they are Spanish. They have walked a long way. It is said they are from Cartagena, but I do not know. They are going to France, and the

French are with them. The men are not happy and they would like to go home, but the French guard them."

"Are there many sailors, at the camp?"

"Yes, Sir. I do not know how many, but a great number, hundreds."

The man struggled ineffectually under Rubert's weight, crying out in pain as the boatswain's knee pressed into his back.

"Go easy, Rubert," said Snowden. "Let him stand, but keep hold of him."

The man stood, shaking, looking in horror at the unwavering barrel of the pistol in Snowden's hand.

"Your name, please."

"Enrico Martinez, Sir."

"I will remember that. Listen very carefully, Enrico," Snowden reached into his pocket and drew out a silver dollar, holding it up in front of the man's face. "English or French, I am a humane man, but I do not want this meeting spoken of to anyone."

"No, Sir, I will not speak of it, on my honour, but please let me go."

"I will, but if I find out that you have betrayed us, my ship will return." He turned to Rubert "And it is a big ship, is it not, Rubert?"

"A very big ship."

"With 74 great guns. If we hear of treachery, the ship will return, and we will bombard Margarida. In a few minutes, every building will be destroyed. Every building, do you understand?"

"Yes, Sir."

"And then, many soldiers and sailors will go ashore from the ship and burn what is left. Houses, boats, wagons, everything. Is that clear?"

The man, who was seriously frightened, seemed to have lost the power of speech, but he nodded furiously. Snowden signalled to Rubert to let him go.

"Be on your way, Enrico, but remember, not a word," said Rubert, with an accompanying shove.

\*\*\*

"Camí Ral", said Rubert, "the Royal Road." They turned right, away from Palamós. Snowden thought they were probably three miles or so from where they had landed, when he saw their destination, a house set back from the road, on a slight rise – a substantial building, rendered, and with terraced gardens. There were lights in the windows.

"Here we are," said Rubert.

Snowden, who had anticipated this moment every day, perhaps every hour, since he had met Wright in London, suddenly, in an uncharacteristic moment of self-doubt, almost asked aloud *'How did I get myself talked into this?'*, but checked himself in time and instead said softly, "Well, Rubert, there seem to be no guards."

"I will go around the side and perhaps I will find a kitchen door."

"Very well, Rubert, best of luck," said Snowden, and slapped the boatswain gently on the back.

He saw the dim outline of Rubert making his way around the side of the house, quiet on his espadrilles, and then – nothing. For long tense minutes he waited, pressed into the undergrowth, every sense alert, his pistol pointing towards the house, until he heard a soft scrape and Rubert reappeared. Snowden could see the boatswain's smile in the darkness and relaxed slightly.

"Well?" he asked, instantly regretting his impatience, though it made no difference to the smile.

"He is not here, Senyor. A man who says he is the butler came to the kitchen and told me the Conde had moved away. The man asks that you enter the house by the kitchen door. I am not sure the man is a butler. A military officer of some kind perhaps, but not a servant."

The door opened to a dimly lit kitchen, where they were met by a tall man, who, as Rubert had said, did not seem to have the deference that servants usually exhibited. The man looked at them appraisingly for a minute or so and then, seemingly making up his mind, said in almost perfect English with a distinct Welsh accent, "Gentlemen, I am Pedro Vilar." He paused for a moment as though casting around for the correct words. "Secretary to His Excellency Jose Delgado y Sanchez, the Conde de Premià."

Snowden realised that there was no possibility of disguising their identities from this man and held out his hand.

"Lieutenant Percy Snowden, Commander of His Majesty's Ship *Oleander*, and the ship's Bosun, Rubert Pujol."

Vilar's handshake was strong.

"I am glad to meet you. Your bosun has said you have been sent by the English government. We have been expecting, or rather hoping, for some contact. The situation for my master is becoming, you understand, increasingly difficult."

"So I appreciate", said Snowden, "and I hope we may be of service, to the benefit of both our countries."

Vilar nodded an acknowledgement and Snowden said, "Your English is excellent, Senor Vilar. Did you perhaps learn it in Wales?"

"Thank you, in Wales, yes. I was an engineer in our army, what you call a Sapper. I will not say how I was captured, because it does not reflect well on our arms, but I was a prisoner in your country, on parole. I'm not a man for idleness and I found employment at the ironworks at Merthyr, an exciting place for an engineer."

"So I have heard, Vilar. They say the night sky is lit up with the furnaces."

"Yes, it is. But I realised there was an opportunity here, and I returned with certain ambitions. We have a great supply of minerals in this country and I had a scheme for their extraction and use, on a large scale. His Excellency became involved in funding my scheme, but then came the affair with the French, and his Excellency fell out of favour."

Vilar turned to Rubert and said in a tone that seemed slightly sarcastic to Snowden, "I think you are not a born Englishman, Senyor Puyol. A Catalan, undoubtedly, but your accent. I cannot place it. From the Islands, perhaps …"

"From Menorca, Sir."

"*Boatswain* Puyol?"

"Yes, Sir, I have been many years at sea."

"Puyol, from Menorca? A boatswain? I see."

Rubert gave the engineer a rather challenging look and said deliberately, "Yes, Sir, Puyol, bosun."

The conversation seemed to Snowden to be going in an entirely unexpected and undesirable direction, so he said, "Yes, he is Boatswain of my ship, HMS *Oleander*."

"Very well, Lieutenant Snowden and Bosun Puyol, I am sorry to say that His Excellency was here, but he has gone away."

"Away?" asked Snowden. "Where is he? We were told he'd be here."

"He has gone to his house near Girona, a larger establishment. He is rather elderly, you understand, and appreciates his comforts. The house there has been in his family for many generations."

"So we must return to our ship without him? That is a

pity."

"I hope not. My instructions are to take you to Girona."

Snowden pictured the map in his mind. Perhaps twenty miles, he thought. "Can His Excellency not come here?"

Vilar sighed, "He is an important man, for many years the King's first minister. He is not one to stand overmuch on ceremony, but he is elderly and, I am afraid, in rather low spirits."

"But my ship?"

"Will she come back if you are not there to meet here tonight?"

"Yes, she will be there until we return."

"Then she will have to do without her Commander and Boatswain for a little while."

"Girona, I believe it is perhaps twenty English miles?"

"Yes, about that. Can you ride, Commander?"

"Yes, Sir, but I do not know …"

"About Bosun Puyol? A Puyol unable to ride! I think not, Snowden!"

Snowden wondered – Rubert had been *Oleander*'s boatswain since the ship called at Gibraltar on her way back to England after her expedition to Corsica, but Snowden knew little of his background.

"We must leave immediately," said Vilar. "If you'll excuse me, I'll collect my things. Please help yourselves to the food," he indicated an assortment of food on the table, and left the room.

The seamen walked to the table and began to eat. Snowden looked at Rubert. "Bosun, I thought I knew you, but now I'm not so sure. Perhaps you could enlighten me."

"Sir, I hope I have done nothing to deceive you – well, almost nothing. My family is somewhat famous in this part of the world, in all Spain, actually. We are traditionally soldiers, Sir, soldiers for hire, and the Puyol Company has a certain fame attached to it. This man", he gestured to the door through which Vilar had left the room, "knows of my family's reputation. I am sorry I did not speak more of it when I was teaching you Catalan aboard the ship."

Snowden felt the situation was becoming complicated and realised he had missed an important clue when he had been speaking to Captain Wright, who had mentioned in passing that he had known Rubert for a long time.

"Your relationship with Captain Wright?"

"I know him well. We were children together, and I have assisted him on several occasions."

In a moment of revelation, Snowden asked, "Assist, Rubert, or advise?"

The Boatswain looked at him, unblinking. "Sir, I am the Boatswain of your ship and have always done my duty."

At that moment Vilar entered the room, dressed for travel.

# CHAPTER 16 - GIRONA

The road was white in the moonlight, at first straight and then winding, rising through wooded hills. Vilar led the way, and Rubert and Snowden rode side by side behind him. The countryside was peaceful and completely silent when they halted periodically to listen for other travellers. This was the second time Snowden had travelled through enemy territory. Enemy? he thought. Was that the right expression? His first journey had been at the head of a party of men returning from the raid on Napoleon's invasion barges, and that had been in Brittany, in France, so there was no doubt that they were on enemy territory, and any French troops they encountered would immediately attack. But the attitude of the Bretons themselves was nuanced, often by no means enamoured of the French and their revolution, and frequently friendly to the English. And here? His mission was clearly based on an ambivalence in the Spanish attitude to the French and their war against England. He was even less sure about the attitude of the Catalans to the Spanish, or to the French for that matter.

They passed uneventfully through sleeping villages, occasionally provoking a dog to bark, and the eastern sky was beginning to lighten when Vilar led them through an imposing gateway and up a long winding drive to a substantial country house. They went around the side and a servant emerged to take their horses.

A more senior servant approached them, rather ruffled with sleep and clearly just roused from his bed. He bowed to the engineer.

"Welcome, Senyor Vilar", he said, but did not enquire anything of Snowden or Puyol, merely nodding in their direction and saying "welcome gentlemen."

They were soon sitting in a small dining room, and servants bustled to lay out breakfast on the sideboard. After half an hour or so, the senior servant came into the room.

"I have informed His Excellency of your arrival and he asks that you attend upon him this afternoon. If you will follow me, I will show you to your …"

"This afternoon?" interrupted Snowden, incredulously. "I have risked my ship and …" He noticed that Vilar was shaking his head and stopped himself, finishing rather lamely "we would be delighted to meet His Excellency this afternoon."

Snowden's room was comfortable, shuttered and dark, and he was immediately asleep, to be awakened after what seemed to him to be only a few minutes by someone gently shaking his shoulder. He looked up and in the dim light saw the outline of a woman above him, dressed in white, her hair cascading over her shoulders.

"Teniente, Teniente, wake yourself."

Snowden, astonished, sat up and reached for the candle on the table. The woman took his hand with considerable strength and held onto it.

"No, Teniente, no light, no sound."

She released his hand and pressed a finger against Snowden's lips, suppressing Snowden's "Who…?"

"I am the Condesa Premià, wife of the man you are to rescue."

The Condesa sat on the bed and leaned her head close to Snowden's, her hair brushing across his arm. He looked at her wonderingly.

"You are his wife?"

"His second wife, yes."

"What do you want from me, Condesa?"

"You are here to take my husband back to England?"

Snowden hesitated.

"Vilar told me."

"Yes, I am."

"I want you to take me with you when you return to your ship."

"Will you not accompany your husband when he leaves?"

"I will accompany him if he leaves, but I am not sure that he will leave. He can be a fool, foolish enough to stay if he sees that as his duty. He is a good and able man, but he is an enemy of Godoy, and if he stays he will be thrown into prison or killed, and all he has worked for will be lost. His work must continue."

"And you?"

"They know that I support my husband, and I will be in danger, perhaps forced to take the veil. I have been in England and I know that I could do much more for Spain from there than from a Spanish convent. Spain should not be an ally of France."

She leaned forward, so that her lips were so close to his ear that he could feel her breath, and whispered, "I rely on you, Teniente."

She stood and left the room, leaving Snowden wondering.

*\*\**

Snowden was woken again from a deep sleep by a servant, and saw that a bath had been prepared. He had just finished dressing when there was a knock on the door and Vilar entered, accompanied by Rubert.

"Good afternoon, gentlemen," said Snowden.

"Good afternoon. I trust you slept well?" replied Vilar.

"Er, I …Thank you, yes."

Vilar continued, "As you have probably realised, His Excellency is a very proud man. He was formerly at the heart of affairs, the King's minister, but the French party is in the ascendency, and he is too favourable to the English and, I must say, too much in tune with the national mood to be part of the government. He is a clever man, popular and with many good works to his credit, but he dwells very much on his fall. It will be a grave step for him to travel to England. It is imperative that you persuade him that he will have the backing of the English government."

"I understand", said Snowden, "I will proceed with as much tact as I can muster."

They were shown into the dining room, where food was laid out on a sideboard.

"Better than *Oleander*," remarked Rubert.

"Mutinous talk, Bosun, you get your whack aboard," replied Snowden good-naturedly. Vilar smiled.

They were led into a large, well-decorated room where an elderly man in a green fur-trimmed robe and white shirt sat at a table.

He rose to meet them, and Vilar made the introductions, in Catalan: "His Excellency, the Conde de Premià" and "The Honourable Percy Snowden, Commander of His Britannic Majesty's Ship *Oleander*".

Premià bowed.

"And Rubert Puyol of Menorca, also of the *Oleander*."

The Conde bowed again.

"I knew a Puyol, a captain of infantry, in the Netherlands."

"My father, Sir."

"A brave man, and the Puyol Company is a fine body of

infantry."

"Thank you, Sir."

Snowden felt in his jacket and brought out a sealed packet.

"I have been asked to deliver this on behalf of His Britannic Majesty."

He handed it to Premià, who looked at the packet and its seal, opened it, scanned its contents, and rang a bell. The butler appeared.

"Gentlemen, I ask you to leave me while I read this with Senyor Vilar."

The butler led them back to the dining room, brought wine and biscuits, and departed.

Snowden was coming to realise that the Boatswain of his ship had an uncommonly good knowledge of Spanish politics and asked, "I presume you know that Premià is invited to accompany us to England? What do you think he will do? He has no option but to go with us, surely?"

"Captain Wright kept me informed of our mission, Sir, so I know of the invitation."

Snowden considered this extraordinary statement as Rubert continued. "It will be a hard decision for him. If he stays, he will be arrested, and even be in danger of his life. He will be unable to help Spain free herself of the French. Logic says that he should go, but he is Spanish, a proud man, and he will not want to be seen to be deserting his country or doing anything dishonourable. This is of great importance to him."

Snowden thought that speculation was probably unprofitable and asked, "How did you come to join the Navy, Rubert?"

"I had always disliked the notion of following in the family trade of soldiering, and as my two elder brothers had joined my father, my mother, bless her, thought that was enough. In Mahon there were many Royal Navy ships. I did not exactly run away to sea, because my mother helped me, but I volunteered."

"Why not as a Middy?"

"I thought that would be difficult without my father's approval, but I knew that few questions would be asked of a volunteer for the lower deck. As I became more involved with Wright's schemes, it seemed to us that – well, I don't really know how to put it – a disguise perhaps, as a sailor, would be effective. Nobody takes much notice of a sailorman in a tarry jumper."

"But the pay?"

"A Boatswain's pay is not too bad, and of course there is the prize money. And Wright gives me …"

There was a knock on the door and Vilar entered.

"Gentlemen, His Excellency asks that you join him."

They returned to the large room. The Conde was standing by his chair, holding the letter in his hand. He nodded towards them.

"Commander Snowden, Senor Puyol … The name of your ship, Commander, *Oleander*. What does her name mean? I have not heard the word before."

"*Baladre*, Your Honour," said Rubert. "There are a great many of these flowers in Bermuda, where the ship was built."

"Thank you, Puyol."

Premià nodded to the letter. "I suppose, Commander, that you know of the contents of this letter?"

"I do, Sir", said Snowden, and added carefully, "it is an invitation to you from His Britannic Majesty to travel to England, to discuss …", he searched for the right phrase, "matters of state, Sir, matters of great importance."

"I understand that, Commander Snowden, and I believe that perhaps it is something I might consider. The French party, you understand, at Court, is becoming very dominant." He looked at Vilar. "I may say, frankly, that I am here because of them."

Snowden realised that he must be very careful in what he said.

"Your Excellency is perhaps in some danger from them?"

Premià stood, pulling back his shoulders.

"That is nothing to me, Commander. My personal danger is of no importance, but the country must not be under the heel of the Corsican. Like many of my countrymen, in all stations of life, I cannot bear that. We are at war with you English because you took our treasure ships. Of course we could not tolerate that, but I think the English would not have taken them if they had not believed that the money was destined for France."

That may have been true, thought Snowden, but perhaps Premià had underestimated the incentive of prize money to the Royal Navy.

"Already our fleet is under the control of the French. Ships that we have paid for. And men of our country are used by them to fight in their cause. Why, even now, the French are marching our sailors east to join ships in Toulon."

Though Premià looked slightly ludicrous in his green robe, his voice was sombre, and his sincerity was obvious.

Snowden spoke in a quiet voice, "His Majesty's government knows of your patriotism, and ...", he struggled for the right Catalan words and looked at Rubert, who continued, "if you were to come to England, Your Excellency, for consultations, it would be the basis for a return to Spain when you have built support, and it is time to drive out the Bonapartists. We understand, especially myself, a Puyol, that honour is everything, but honour is not always served by useless sacrifice."

"But in England I have few connections and little …"

Snowden began to reply, "His Majesty's government will …", but could not find the right words, and nodded towards Rubert, who continued, "will ensure that you and your family will be well looked after."

Snowden looked at The Conde appraisingly and realised that they were very close to having their man.

"Of course, Your Excellency, His Majesty's government has authorised me to state that an allowance of" – he named a figure that seemed ludicrously high – "will be paid to you during your stay in England."

Snowden knew that, honour or not, this would be important to Premià.

"It is difficult for me, Commander, but I believe I have no option but to accept. If I stay here, it is quite possible that I will die uselessly in prison. If I go to England, there is hope for the cause of Spain. I require some time, a few days, you understand, to …"

Vilar interrupted, "Excellency, we do not have a few days. The Bonapartists are agitating for your arrest, and they could move against you at any time."

The Conde looked at him shrewdly. "Very well, we shall depart on the day after tomorrow."

Snowden said. "We must leave at night, Excellency. I should like to leave today, as soon as it is dark."

"No, Commander, we will not leave tonight. It is impossible for me to put my affairs in order by then."

Snowden began to object, but Premià rose and said, as one used to obedience, "My final word, gentlemen – leave if you please, but dine with me this evening."

# CHAPTER 17 - ARREST

Snowden was in his room, asleep on a chair with his feet on a stool, when he was wakened by a knock on the door, which opened to admit the Condesa de Premià and a girl of about six years old, who was holding her hand. The Condesa was simply dressed, but to Snowden's eyes she seemed very beautiful.

Snowden started to rise, but the Condesa said, "Stay where you are, please, but remove your feet from the stool so that we can sit down. I am sorry to have woken you twice in a few hours."

As the Condesa and the girl arranged themselves on the stool, Snowden said, "A pleasant experience, if I may say so, Condesa. And this is?" he nodded towards the girl who was regarding him shyly.

"This is my daughter, Lucia. Lucia, this is Teniente Snowden. He is English, the captain of a ship."

"I am pleased to meet you, Senor."

"And I you, Lucia. How old are you?"

"Six, Senor."

Snowden looked at her mother. "Is this merely a social visit, Condesa?"

The Condesa grimaced. "I am afraid not. I have come to warn you. The servants say that there is a commotion in Girona, a body of men has arrived from Madrid, with Senor Cabral at their head. They have come to arrest my husband, and probably me too."

"Does your husband know?"

"He knows, but his pride …"

"And Vilar?"

"He is fully aware of the situation and tries to persuade my husband to leave immediately. Teniente, I do not want my daughter to be frightened of you if we have to leave. Could you perhaps speak to her for a few minutes?"

"Of course. What should I say?"

"Perhaps you could tell her a little of your home and childhood?"

Snowden was slightly taken aback, but did as he was asked.

"I'm Percy Snowden, Lucia. By the way, I have a cousin called Lucy. She is grown up now, but I used to play with her when we were children."

"What is your home like, Senor?"

"It is a large house, made from grey stone. I left home when I was twelve and joined the Navy."

"Have you been to many places?"

"Very many, Lucia, I have been travelling since I was twelve, most of my life."

As Snowden talked to the child, he noticed that her mother was paying rapt attention, and the following half hour was delightful for Snowden, the spell eventually broken by a knock on the door. He looked quizzically at the Condesa, who nodded.

"Please enter."

Rubert came into the room and, in a gesture more gracious than expected from a boatswain of a naval ship, bowed to the visitors, his face expressing no surprise at their presence.

Snowden stood. "Condesa de Premià, this is Rubert Puyol,

the boatswain of my ship."

"I am pleased to make your acquaintance. The boatswain of a ship? I thought you Puyols were soldiers."

"Most of us are, Condesa, but I am a seaman, and, as the English say, the black sheep of the family."

The Condesa smiled, and rose to leave.

When she had gone, Snowden said, "She is worried, Rubert. The servants have told her that there are men from Madrid in the town. They are led by a man called Cabral and have been sent to arrest the Conde."

"She is right to be worried, Sir. Cabral is a very bad man. We must be ready to leave quickly."

The dinner was as convivial as could be expected under the circumstances. The Conde and Rubert were deep in conversation, the Conde regaling Rubert with stories of campaigns in the Low Countries in which he had fought with the boatswain's father. As far as Snowden could make out, it seemed that the Puyol Company was a considerable fighting force, much admired by the Conde. Vilar was preoccupied and taciturn, which Snowden did not mind as it left him free to converse with the Condesa.

Snowden stood as the Condesa rose from the table. She gestured for him to accompany her, and they left the room. Rubert and the Count hardly noticed, but Vilar's eyes followed them.

Once outside the dining room, she stopped and spoke softly to him.

"I will be in the room next to yours tonight. There is a connecting door."

Snowden must have looked surprised, for she smiled and added quickly, "With my daughter. In case we have to leave quickly."

"I wish your husband would agree to leave tonight."

"He will not."

"Goodnight, Condesa."

"Goodnight, Percy."

Snowden went back to the dining room and, seeing that Puyol and the Count were still in conversation, indicated to Vilar that he wished to speak to him.

In the hall, Snowden said, "Vilar, it seems to me that we should be ready to leave at very short notice."

"Indeed we should, Snowden, but the Conde will not be diverted from his plan to leave tomorrow. I believe he is wrong, quite wrong to delay, but I can do nothing to change his mind."

"What if they come early? There is the question of the Condesa and her daughter. It will go hard with her if the Count is arrested."

Vilar looked at him, smiling. "Ah, the power behind the throne!"

Snowden raised his eyebrows quizzically.

"Yes, Snowden, rather like her namesake of old, the Condesa Isabella is a very clever woman, with decided views on the future of Spain, views that I agree with, as it happens. Her husband is a good man, well intentioned and effective, especially when he was younger, but compared to his wife …" He let the sentence trail off. "She has been unable to persuade her husband to leave earlier, but in everything else she has great influence on him."

"She is apparently in the room next to mine, with her daughter and baggage. I think that we should at least get the baggage out of the house."

"You are right, Snowden, of course. I think we should picket some horses in the woods, saddled, away from the road. If anything should happen, we can leave quickly down the back stairs. Come with me and I will show you the way, and then I will ready the horses."

Vilar led Snowden upstairs and showed him the way through several corridors to narrow stairs which led to a door in the outside wall of the house. It was not far from there to the wood where Vilar would picket the horses. If the time came, Snowden thought it should be possible to get away.

When Snowden returned to the dining room, the Count and the boatswain were taking leave of each other, with shaking of hands and slaps on the back.

"Until tomorrow, Puyol," said the Count, as Rubert walked out of the room, pretty steadily, thought Snowden, after a long after-dinner session with the decanter.

"Boatswain," said Snowden quietly. Rubert looked round and walked over to him.

"Sir, before you ask", he said, "I have not been able to persuade His Excellency to leave tonight. He knows the danger very well, but it is a matter of honour for him not to be rushed out of his home. I think perhaps it is more than that and he feels that he cannot face the journey to England and the task of organising a party there, with all the lobbying and scheming that would be required."

Vilar returned, dishevelled, with his clothes full of burrs. "The horses are saddled and picketed in the wood with a groom in charge."

He looked questioningly at Rubert, who shook his head. "Sorry, he will not go."

Snowden and Rubert went upstairs to Snowden's room and knocked on the interconnecting door. The door was opened by the Condesa, and the two men went into the room. Snowden noted with misgivings the quantity of baggage and a young woman, presumably a maid, quietly sleeping on the bed.

The Condesa caught Snowden's look and kicked at a bag

on the floor. "Do not worry, Teniente, we only have to take this bag. The rest are unimportant and can be left."

Rubert picked it up and said, "I will take this and load it onto the horses, Sir." He left the room, carrying the bag.

"Condesa", said Snowden, "we have horses ready in the woods. If anything happens, we will go down the back stairs and out of that door. It may be dangerous – are you sure you would not rather stay?"

"There will be nothing for us here," she replied. "We will come with you for better or worse."

Later, Snowden sat in his room, fully dressed, with his cutlass and pistols to hand on the table beside him. The bosun, also dressed, lay on the bed, snoring.

By Snowden's watch it was eleven o'clock when there was a violent hammering at the front door of the house, followed after some time by the complaining tones of a servant. "No need to break the door down, I'm coming."

Rubert woke violently, got off the bed and stood beside it, sticking his pistols into his belt.

"Go through to the Condesa," said Snowden. "I am going to take a look."

He unlocked the door and went softly along the corridor. The front door was visible from the top of the wide marble stairs and he crouched behind the banisters to observe the scene below. The servant opened the door and a party of soldiers, with a civilian at its head, rushed through, roughly pushing the servant aside. The civilian went over to the servant and grabbed his coat.

"Where is your master?"

"In bed, Senor Cabral," said the servant, who seemed to know the visitor.

"Fetch him," said the civilian. "These men will

accompany you."

"I cannot awake the Count at this time of night, Senor."

"Wake him, or we will drag him downstairs in his sleep."

The servant turned to go, but Cabral grabbed his arm.

"Is anybody else in the house? Visitors?"

"No, Sir, we have no visitors anymore."

"And the Condesa?"

"In her room, Sir."

Snowden, fascinated, was torn between the desire to get himself and the Condesa away and the necessity of seeing what would happen to the Count, which he knew would be important to Wright.

He did not have to wait long before the Count appeared, fully dressed, with Vilar at his side, and flanked by soldiers.

"Good evening, Senor Cabral," he said.

Cabral opened a document. "Conde, I have here a letter authorising the arrest of you and your wife."

"On what charges, Cabral?"

"There is no charge, Count, I am merely instructed to arrest you. The letter is signed by Godoy."

"That does not surprise me," the Conde raised his voice to a shout, "but my wife has nothing to do with this."

Snowden waited no longer but walked softly back along the corridor, breaking into a run as he neared his room.

"They are arresting the Conde", he said, "and, Condesa, they wish to arrest you as well. Do you intend to submit to them or to take your chances with us?"

"Who came to arrest us?"

"Cabral!"

In the dim light, he saw the Condesa pale. "There is no choice for us, Percy, we will come with you. We are ready."

"We should leave the maid."

"We cannot."

Snowden was about to argue, but decided this would waste valuable time and gave it up. They went into the corridor, hurrying, Rubert leading, followed by the Condesa, who half led and half dragged the child, and the maid, who, given the circumstances, was surprisingly calm.

As they went through the doorway onto the stairs, there was a great commotion behind them, the clatter of boots on the wooden floor, the raised voices of men and the sound of splintering wood as a door was knocked down. There were shouts of frustration as the soldiers realised their prey had escaped, and then the sound of men running along the corridor. Snowden knew that soon the soldiers would be on them, and a great excitement, the exhilaration he always felt before battle, settled on him.

As the party ran down the stairs Snowden stopped and shouted, careless that his voice would be heard by the pursuers: "Rubert! To the horses, I'll hold them off." Rubert turned and acknowledged his order with a wave, scooping the child up into the crook of his arm as he reached the bottom of the stairs.

Snowden went back a few steps to the top of the stairs, which were at right angles to the corridor, so that his body was behind the wall, out of view of the pursuing soldiers, though he could tell by the noise that they were almost on him.

Briefly wishing that he had his Baker rifle, Snowden, a pistol in each hand, stepped out into the corridor, which was almost dark, to see several men rushing along it, he couldn't tell how many, the nearest no more than fifteen feet away. The man saw Snowden and, surprised, checked his progress, the men behind bumping into him, pushing him forward.

Snowden fired his first pistol, saw the man drop and heard him scream, and then discharged the second into the mass of men, so tightly bunched in the narrow corridor that he could not miss, and saw a second man fall. The soldiers hesitated, and Snowden, allowing his pistols to drop on their lanyards, drew his sword and launched himself forward into them, slashing wildly, kicking, shouting, until he realised that the soldiers were running away, and he was running with them.

Collecting himself, he stopped and turned, running back to the stairs, stumbling over men who were lying on the floor, groaning. He threw himself down the stairs, but stopped at the door. Ahead of him he could see the dark wood, but to the right a great fire was burning. The stables, he thought, and only just in time stepped back into the doorway as a group of riderless horses galloped past. Shots rang out from the direction of the stables as Snowden ran towards the woods.

He reached the clearing where the party was already mounted, Rubert and the Condesa's horses close together, stirrup to stirrup, the horses' heads towards the house, intermittently illuminated by the firelight filtering through the woods. As he reached them, he saw that the maid was seated behind Rubert, her arms round his waist, and the child was in front of the Condesa.

"Time to leave!" said Snowden.

"What is happening?" asked the Condesa.

"They have taken the Conde. I had a fight at the top of the stairs, and some of the soldiers ran away. I don't know about the fire – it seems to be in the stables, and the horses are loose – but it will distract them, and thank God for it. We must go now."

"I know the way", said the Condesa, calmly, "I often ride here. Follow me."

Snowden looked at Rubert, who nodded and handed Snowden the reins to another horse. Snowden swung himself into the saddle and they followed the Condesa, who set a fast, but not reckless pace through the woods, over scrubby fields and eventually onto a rough track that wound over the hills.

# CHAPTER 18 - ESCAPE

*Rosa* returned at dawn, bumping alongside the hove to *Oleander*, and Pascoe climbed aboard.

There were quiet orders, the slatting of sails and the creak of spars as the ship was got underway and headed offshore.

"No sign of the Old Man then?" said Kennedy.

"No, Ken, nothing."

"I don't like this, Pascoe. Skipper's place is in his ship."

"Our skipper's place is as close to the action as he can get, as you well know, Ken. *Oleander*'s just a way of getting him to it. He'll be back before long, he has the devil's own luck."

"You're right, I suppose." Kennedy turned away from Pascoe. "Come on, you at the wheel, the mainsail luff's flapping like your mother's washing on the line."

\*\*\*

Snowden, at the rear, urged his horse on and overtook the Condesa, who was in the lead. When Rubert joined them, Snowden said, "It is about to get light. I think we must stop and wait for darkness again."

"I agree", said Rubert. "Some of the time we will be on the Camí Ral, which will be busy during the day."

"I remember there is a wood ahead on the left side of the road," said the Condesa. "It may be suitable."

They continued for about half an hour, the light growing stronger, until the Condesa stopped and pointed to a grove of oak trees a hundred yards or so from the track.

"What do you think?"

They made camp as best they could, eating the bread and cheese that the Condesa had packed, washed down with wine. Rubert and Snowden decided to split the watch between them, but the Condesa would not agree.

"You look exhausted, Percy, and you, Rubert, seem little better. I am sure that Bianca" – this was the maid's name – "and I are perfectly capable of keeping watch. Please sleep at least until noon. In that way you will be ready when the time comes."

Snowden could find no logical argument against this, and, after looking to the horses as best they could, he and Rubert settled down to sleep.

When Snowden awoke, bright sunshine was dappling the forest floor and he could see blue sky through the branches overhead. Apart from the cicadas, it was quiet. He looked at his watch, shocked that it was one o'clock, and then glanced around the clearing. He heard voices and saw that Rubert and Bianca were playing with Lucia, laughing together.

He rose and went over to them. Lucia saw him coming.

"Hello, Captain. I am playing with Bianca and Rubert."

"So I see. Where is your mother?"

"She is watching."

"Have you seen anything?" Snowden asked Rubert.

"Nothing at all, Sir, not a single person has gone along the track."

"That's good. I will go and see the Condesa. Do you know where she is?"

"On the rise," he pointed to an elevated part of the wood behind them. "There is a good view of the track from there."

Snowden made his way uphill, and after a hundred yards

or so saw the Condesa sitting on the ground, her back against a raised rock, looking out over the track.

"Good afternoon, Condesa," he said.

She turned her head. "Good afternoon, Commander."

He could see that she had been crying, and said, "Condesa …"

She interrupted him, "My God, Percy, what has happened? My husband arrested, the house burning, fighting, fleeing to God knows what future." Her body shook with sobs, and Snowden, hardly knowing what he was doing, sat beside her and put his arm around her shoulders.

"I am sorry, Condesa, I really don't know what to say. I can offer little comfort except to say that I can take you away on my ship. You and Lucia will at least be safe."

She leaned her head against his shoulder. "Perhaps so, but I am not sure that you are a comforting man, Percy. How many men did you fight last night?"

Snowden thought back to the ruckus in the corridor. "I am not sure, perhaps six or ten. It was dark."

"And what happened to them?"

"I cannot say with certainty, but it went hard with some of them."

"Hard? You mean you killed them! It is a great shame that in the struggle against Bonaparte, Spaniards die."

Snowden had not thought of this – he considered Frenchmen and Spaniards alike to be enemies.

"I suppose so," he said.

"Well", she said, pulling closer to him, "at least I am free to continue the struggle against our enemy."

\*\*\*

In the gathering gloom, they saddled the horses and moved

away from their camp. Before long they reached the Camí Ral, and they worked the horses into a trot along the white carriageway. Snowden was almost beside himself with worry that they might meet a party of soldiers and rode in advance of the party, but there was hardly any traffic on the road in the dark, and no military presence whatever.

Long before it was light, they dismounted, leaving the horses to take care of themselves, and made their way through the scrub to the shore, this time meeting no poachers. As they reached the top of the low cliff, Snowden thought he heard pistol shots in the distance and, in a great hurry, they scrambled and slid down the cliff to the rocks below. To Snowden's immense relief, he saw the glint of reflection from oar splashes, as *Rosa* idled just off the shore.

With his heart beating, Snowden struck a light, and the signal was returned from the boat. Within minutes he heard Pascoe's voice: "Ready there at the bow, backwater together, oars." And then there was a splash as a man jumped onto the rocks and a grating sound as the boat grounded.

"Good morning," drawled the man, in a strong Bermudian accent.

"Good morning, what, Iris?" replied Snowden.

"Sorry, Your Honour Sir," replied Iris.

Snowden laughed, "You have no idea how good it is to be back."

"Good to see you safe and sound, Sir."

They hurriedly boarded the boat, Snowden greeting Pascoe like the old friend he was.

"We thought we heard shots inland, Sir", said Pascoe, "sounded like pistols."

"I thought so as well", replied Snowden, "but perhaps it was only poachers."

The boat scraped off the rocks and turned her head towards the sea. They had gone perhaps a quarter of a mile when there was a commotion ashore, shouting, and then small arms fire. Above the noise they heard a shout "Please take me!"

"That's Vilar", said the Condesa, "you can't leave him."

"Lie down on the bottom boards," said Snowden. "We will see what we can do … Turn her round, Mr Pascoe, there's a man ashore we must try and pick up."

"Very well, Sir."

Before long the boat was moving swiftly towards the shore.

"He'll be on the beach, Pascoe. Give the cliffs above a bit of grape."

The swivel in the bow of the boat fired, the noise deafening in the silence, the muzzle flash briefly lighting the scene with stark orange light. They were close to the low cliff now and the swivel fired again. Snowden was aware of flashes ashore and a lucky musket ball thudded into the gunwale near him. As the swivel fired for the third time, he heard behind him the sound of *Oleander*'s broadside. He turned his head and saw the ship's outline, wreathed in smoke, against the lightening sky.

Iris's voice came from the bow of the boat: "Man swimming in the water just ahead!"

"Pick him up, Pascoe", said Snowden, "that'll be Vilar."

# CHAPTER 19 - A PLAN

Snowden was breakfasting in the cabin with Kennedy, Pascoe and Watton, a cabin much reduced by the partition that had been installed to make accommodation for their passengers. Snowden had told them of his time ashore, leaving out only the details of Spanish politics and the background of the ship's bosun which he thought might be better kept secret.

The ship was headed west, towards Gibraltar, but progress was slow as there was little wind.

They had nearly finished their meal when there was a knock on the door. The marine sentry put his head inside the cabin and said, "Mr Vilar is here, Your Honour."

"Send him in."

Vilar, rather bruised looking, made his way into the cabin, and, at Snowden's insistence, sat heavily in a chair.

"How are you, Vilar?"

"Reasonably well, Snowden, your surgeon, Butterfield, has patched me up, rather painfully, I might add." He pointed to a sewed-up cut on his head and Snowden winced.

"However, I am very relieved to be on your ship. I thought briefly that I had missed you."

"You nearly did."

Snowden introduced the officers, and Kennedy asked the obvious question: "You are Spanish, Mr Vilar, but, and I speak as someone who has been involved in the coal trade, you speak English like a Welshman. Have you been in Wales?"

"Mr Kennedy, you're very perceptive. I have been in Wales, in Merthyr, and I picked up the accent there."

"Can you tell me the story of your escape, Vilar?" asked Snowden.

"Briefly. I was with the Conde when he was arrested."

"I watched the arrest from the top of the stairway."

"Did you? You saw Cabral then?"

"I did, and the Condesa has told me of his evil history."

Vilar nodded, "He is evil, beyond doubt. I don't know how much you saw, but the Conde began to shout a warning to his wife. Cabral and the soldiers tried to silence him, and he struggled. They were so focused on the Conde that I was able to slip away."

"The fire in the stables? The shooting?"

Vilar smiled, "That was me. I thought that you would benefit from a diversion, so I got the horses out and fired my pistol a few times, and then threw my lamp into a pile of straw. Very dry it was and the stable went up beautifully. And then I set out for the coast."

"Did you have a horse?"

"No, I should have kept one from the stables, but I didn't, and so I set out at a run."

"I kept going through the night, and most of the day. I was able to keep off the roads nearly all of the way – I know the area very well as I have prospected some of it for minerals. I was making my way to the landing place when I saw your party and, at the same time, a group of mounted soldiers, obviously pursuing you but unsure where you had gone. I thought another diversion was in order."

"My word, Vilar, you have stuck your neck out for us, thank you."

"For Spain, Snowden."

***

After the officers had left, Vilar looked closely at Snowden and said, "I have an idea, Snowden."

"You do? Concerning what?"

"You know of the Spanish sailors who are making their way to Toulon."

"I do, Senor."

"I think that there is a way we can strike at the enemy, that is the French, and strike very hard."

"When you say 'we' Vilar, who do you mean?"

"Us, Snowden, and this ship."

Snowden felt the stirring of excitement.

"Please tell me."

"Well, Captain, the sailors cannot travel to Toulon by sea, as it is likely that they would be intercepted by English ships. it is difficult for the French to march the Spanish sailors, who have no desire to fight your Royal Navy on behalf of the French and who do not like walking. There is considerable desertion."

"Go on."

"You have heard, I'm sure, of the Royal Canal, now called the Canal du Midi. Excuse me, do you have a map or chart of the French coast?"

"I do, Vilar." Snowden fetched the map, laid it on the table and Vilar continued.

"Thank you. The Canal du Midi runs from Toulouse, here, to the coast at Sète."

As he spoke, Vilar identified the places he mentioned on the chart with the points of a pair of dividers.

"Sète is a port that was built especially for the canal, but, as you know, the Gulf of Lions is a bad place, and to avoid it they have now built the Canal du Rhône à Sète which runs inland along the coast, joining the Rhône here, at Beaucaire. It enables barges to get almost to Marseille without going to sea."

"I have been reliably told that the Spanish sailors will walk as far as Narbonne, and then embark on barges to travel up the old canal from there to the Canal du Midi. They will then be taken to Marseille by barge, all without walking a step. On the barges they will have less opportunity to desert, and progress will be faster than walking. They do not march like soldiers!"

"So you are proposing to attack in some way, Vilar?"

"I am, Sir. I believe it can be done so that a great blow is struck against the French, and for Spain. A Spanish warship without a crew is of no use to them."

Snowden gripped his chair arms in excitement.

"Tell me more, Vilar."

***

Snowden sat, deep in thought, for over an hour, from time to time measuring distances on the chart, and poring over a detailed map of southern France. Eventually, he rose and knocked on the slightly ramshackle door of the partition.

"Condesa, are you there? Can I speak to you?"

The Condesa emerged from her part of the cabin.

"Good morning, Captain, how is our progress?"

Snowden gestured outside. "There is not much wind, and what there is, is against us, so we have not made much progress towards Gibraltar."

"I would like to say that that is a shame, but I think that being here on your ship is like a holiday for me."

"I have not often heard that *Oleander* is regarded as a holiday ship, Condesa, but I know what you mean."

"Condesa, something has come up, of great importance."

"I know, Percy, I am ashamed of myself for eavesdropping, but I heard Vilar."

Snowden realised that until the Condesa moved ashore, he might have to conduct sensitive interviews elsewhere.

"As I was not able to fulfil my instructions to bring your husband to Gibraltar, I believe it is my duty to attempt to interfere with the transfer of the Spanish sailors to Toulon. This will mean that *Oleander* will head east, away from Gibraltar. I intend to send *Rosa* to Gibraltar with despatches, but it is about 600 miles, a long journey for a small boat. I believe it is better if you stay aboard *Oleander*, although there is the possibility that she may be in action and may suffer damage. If you do wish to go in *Rosa* I will seek to accommodate your wishes."

The Condesa thought for a moment.

"I think we should stay on your ship, Percy. I believe it is the less dangerous of the two options for Bianca and Lucia, assuming, of course, that you have no objection to sharing your cabin with us."

Snowden smiled. "None whatsoever."

***

Snowden sat at his table, his despatch nearly finished.

"… I send this despatch with Mr Pascoe, who has rendered such valuable service during his time in *Oleander*, in the tartan *Rosa* …"

He placed the despatch in a weighted bag, tied it up carefully and, with it in his hand, rose from his chair and went on deck. *Oleander* was hove to, out of sight of land, in a light south-westerly breeze. *Rosa* lay alongside, bumping gently. Pascoe was leaning against the rail, looking down at her.

He turned when he noticed his commander's presence, and looked at Snowden, his eyes alight with excitement.

"Sir!"

"A good command, Mr Pascoe, perhaps not large, but I have no doubt she will serve to get you to Gibraltar."

"I'm sure she will, Sir."

"Here are the despatches. You must be sure, at the first sign of serious trouble, to put them over the wall. It should be no matter if they are lost, as you know the content of my report and can relay it verbally."

"I have it by heart, Sir."

Snowden looked at him appraisingly. "I have no doubt about that, Pascoe."

They were joined by Kennedy, and Snowden said, "Mr Pascoe, are you sure you'll be able to find Gib?"

Kennedy smiled, but Pascoe, who, despite his youth, was rapidly turning into one of the finest navigators in the Navy, bristled, relaxing when he saw Kennedy's grin and realised that Snowden was joking.

"It's that big, Sir, I don't think we can miss it."

Snowden smiled at the riposte.

Rubert arrived and stood at a respectful distance. *He's slipped into his boatswain's role*, thought Snowden as the Catalan touched his cap and said, "The boat's ready, Sir", and then "Chippy knows what to do with the longboat."

He seemed to reflect and added, "Sir, it has been a privilege to work under you."

Snowden, surprised, replied, "The feeling is mutual, Rubert. Good luck, boatswain."

"Bona sort, Capità!" said Rubert, turning and climbing down into the boat.

"Mr Pascoe, you may start immediately."

"Aye, Sir."

Snowden kept *Oleander* idling until the boat was a dot on the western horizon.

# CHAPTER 20 - FONTAINEBLEAU

The journey from Agen had seemed interminable to Odile Morlaix, worried as she was about her husband, but she was pleased to be back in Paris. The house had been in a rather disappointing state when they had arrived, but it was now open and aired, even if it took a great deal of effort to imagine the glittering soirées that she had held there – she thought of the time that had elapsed – not very long ago. She had begun to renew her acquaintances, and there was a gratifying readiness on the part of the political class to accept her invitations to small gatherings, driven, she knew, by news of her husband's recall by the Emperor.

And now, as she helped her husband climb into the carriage that had met them at the jetty on the Seine, her emotions were mixed: pleased, elated almost, to be accompanying her husband to meet the Emperor at Fontainebleau, but concerned for Morlaix' health, although he seemed for the moment to be cheerful and energised in a way she had not seen for a long time.

After a short wait inside the Palace, a beautifully uniformed army officer arrived and saluted Morlaix.

"I am instructed to take Admiral Morlaix immediately to the Emperor."

Morlaix, who was not yet fully used to his wooden leg, struggled to stand, dropping his crutch in the process, to the obvious embarrassment of the soldier.

Odile picked it up quickly and said, "I think it best if I accompany my husband as far as the meeting room."

The officer, relieved, agreed, and Morlaix, with his wife's occasional support, stumped determinedly along the seemingly endless corridors until they reached a waiting room, not very large, but richly decorated.

As they waited, Odile said, "They have bought some more furniture!" They knew that the Palace had been stripped bare during the Revolution.

"Vive l'Empereur," said Morlaix, with an edge of sarcasm. As they laughed together, the door to the audience room opened and Napoleon himself came into the room, smiling.

Morlaix again dropped his crutch as he rose, but Napoleon gestured for him to remain seated and pulled up a chair of his own opposite them.

*I know exactly what he is doing*, thought Morlaix, *but I can't help myself falling for it.*

Napoleon grasped both of Odile's hands and exclaimed, "Odile, it has been too long. You look more beautiful than ever. I trust you have been looking after my Breton. France has need of his services again."

Odile, the seasoned political operator who had helped drag a cannon to Versailles, blushed.

*And he's doing it to my wife as well*, thought Morlaix.

Napoleon went with Morlaix into the audience room. A large chair stood on a raised dais, the Emperor's throne. The Minister of Marine, Decrès, was already at the table beneath the dais, surrounded by aides. Decrès rose, smiling, when he saw Morlaix approach, and embraced him.

"Morlaix, how good to see you. Not since the old *Richmond* I think!"

He turned to the Emperor. "Morlaix and I are old shipmates. We both bear scars from the Saintes."

"Not only shipmates", said Morlaix, "we were once, as the English say, 'in the same boat'."

During the Battle of the Saintes, off Dominica in the West Indies, the frigate *Richmond* had attempted, under fire, to tow a damaged French 74 to safety. Morlaix, then a young boatswain's mate, had been bow oar of the boat commanded by Decrès that had attempted to take a line to the stricken vessel.

"Indeed we were." Decrès shuddered as he returned to his seat.

Morlaix had a great deal of respect for Decrès as a man of action, but was less sure about his ministerial ability.

The Emperor seated himself, not on his throne but at a chair at the head of the table. He spoke to an aide, who took a huge map of Europe from the cabinet and laid it on the table.

Napoleon pulled a document from his coat and passed it to Morlaix, who scanned it quickly.

"I see", he said, "Snowden again."

"You may think this is beneath the notice of an Emperor, gentlemen, but we will be ridiculed by the English papers, which always seem to find their way across the Channel somehow."

He looked pointedly at Decrès.

"He did not get away with Premià but he came damned close to it, and it seems he has the wife. He is in league with that damned Sidney Smith, beyond doubt."

Napoleon had what almost amounted to an obsession with Smith, the unconventional Royal Navy captain who, by lifting the siege of Acre, had put paid to Napoleon's adventure in the Middle East, and who had prophesied that Bonaparte would end his days in the Temple prison, a prophesy which the superstitious Corsican took seriously.

"Breton, we must anticipate where he will strike."

Morlaix thought. "I do not know if that is possible to predict. He captured a frigate in Lézardrieux", he pointed to the river in Brittany and then traced the coastline around to the Mediterranean, "and then turned up in Palamós, here. That is a great deal of coastline to cover, and there must be a vast number of potential targets. The best course of action may be to identify these targets and strengthen their defences."

"That", said Napoleon, looking at Decrès, "will be a huge drain on France's resources. Can we not be more clever?"

"I don't know if we can, Sir. Additionally, if Snowden continues as he is, before long he will undoubtedly overreach."

"Or", retorted Napoleon, "the enemy will realise his success and he will be reinforced and his actions become grander and more damaging."

"That is true, Sir, but success in small-scale raiding does not necessarily translate into success in larger-scale warfare."

Napoleon waved his arguments away.

"Nevertheless, Admiral Morlaix, I want you to try. Please dine with me tonight, and bring Odile."

# CHAPTER 21 - ROSA

Though they had seen no land whatsoever except for the smudge of mountains on the horizon as they passed between Ibiza and the mainland, the weather had been clear and Pascoe had been active with his meridian passages and lunars, not having been able to bring himself to take his precious Berthoud chronometer in the boat. He had just taken a noon sight and, with Rubert sitting beside him in the boat's well, worked it up and, with a slightly self-important air, marked the line on the chart and announced, "Here, Rubert." He worked with the dividers. "In Gib this evening, if the wind holds."

Rubert looked at the sky. "It will hold, but the current will become stronger as we near the Strait."

One of the sailors, a Corsican, shouted above the noise of *Rosa*'s progress through the waves, "Sail", and pointed to the starboard quarter.

Rubert climbed onto the weather gunwale, holding the shroud, shading his eyes as he looked to where the man was pointing.

"I don't like the look of her, Sir. A Moor without doubt."

There was a shout from forward. "Gib, I can see Gib." Pascoe looked over the bow and saw the Rock in the distance ahead, wearing its customary Levanter cloud.

The stranger grew nearer and they could see the white wave at her bow, the straining canvas of her lateen sails bellowing in the easterly wind. By late afternoon Gibraltar was close enough to make out details of the mountain, but the corsair was very close.

Rubert looked at the corsair, which was a fairly large vessel, with three lateen rigged masts and a number of guns already run out.

"What you English call a 'Sally Rover', I think", he said to Pascoe, and then in explanation, "from Salé, on the Atlantic coast of Morocco, a hundred or so miles south of Gib. There are not many of them now."

They saw men on the corsair's bow working at a gun, and then a puff of smoke and a splash as the ball hit the sea.

"Not much of a shot," said Pascoe to Rubert. "Let's have that big ensign up."

They hoisted a British ensign from the yardarm. It flapped in the breeze, seemingly almost as big as *Rosa*'s lateen sail. Britain had a truce with the Barbary states, but the corsair seemed disinclined to honour the agreement, as almost at once the pursuer fired another shot, which came a little closer, though the shooting was still wild. Undeterred by the violence, dolphins played around *Rosa*'s bow as she sped through the water.

The corsair was nearly on them when the Corsican seaman Bernadetto said to Snowden, "Sir, I am a good shot with the Baker, Captain Burney showed me when we were on Corsica, and I used one at Macinhagiu. Please allow me to try to hit the Moor. Castello here knows how to load."

Pascoe knew that the swivel on *Rosa*'s bow would be useless unless the pirate made an attempt to board, and so the rifles, of which there were three on the boat, were the only means they had of retaliating. "Very well, Bernadetto, please try."

With Castello and another seaman loading, Bernadetto fired as rapidly as he could at the men on the rover, carefully aiming each shot, timing them so that both vessels were on the top of a wave. The men cheered as one of the men at the gun on the pirate's bow fell, and again as another standing on her deck near the mast was hit.

"Good shooting, Bernadetto," shouted Pascoe.

The pursuers dropped back slightly, safely out of musket range, but the Bakers could still hit the pirate, and Bernadetto continued to fire. The rover, apparently discouraged, dropped further back.

There was a shout from forward: "Sail ahead, coming out from Gib I reckon."

Pascoe tore his gaze away from the pirate and looked ahead. He passed his glass forward and the lookout put it to his eye. "Frigate, Sir", and then, minutes later, "one of ours."

Thank God, thought Pascoe. "Fire the swivel", he ordered, "and keep firing .The frigate will hear it soon enough."

The sight of the frigate was clearly too much for the corsair, who hauled his wind and headed north, towards Spain, shots from the Baker rifles chasing him along.

"Saved, by God," said Pascoe, and he heartily joined in with the men as they broke out into cheers.

# CHAPTER 22 - THE GULF OF LIONS

Snowden, accompanied by Ensign Watton, looked at the longboat in her chocks on *Oleander*'s deck.

"What do you think, Sir?" asked the Carpenter, who had been working feverishly to change the British-looking boat into something with a Mediterranean appearance.

Snowden took in the lateen rig, the prominent, lewdly carved stempost and the carefully created air of decrepitude. A new name, *Liberté*, had been painted on her stern.

"Looks convincing to me, Chips. Well done."

"Thank you, Sir. She's just about finished. I'll start on the other boats directly."

\*\*\*

Kennedy may not have had Pascoe's talent for mathematics, but he was an experienced and competent navigator. He came into the cabin, slate in hand, where Snowden, Vilar and Watton were waiting. A chart was laid out on the table. Kennedy murmured under his breath, "Declination …," as he wrote on the slate. Completing his calculation, he leaned forward over the table, took up the parallel ruler and drew a line on the chart. He muttered to himself as he worked, "Pretty well stopped since the morning sight, bit of west-going current probably, so …" He worked with the parallel rulers again.

"Just about here, Sir", he used the dividers to measure,

"perhaps fifteen miles off the coast."

"Thanks, Ken," said Snowden. "Let's take her in until we can see the land, and …"

He was about to say "keep an eye on the soundings", but knew that such an injunction was unnecessary and might even irritate Kennedy, first-class seaman that he was.

\*\*\*

As the afternoon wore on, the ship crept into the coast. Luciani, who was familiar with the Provençal coast from trading there in his father's ship, was at the masthead. There were no sails in sight, the efforts of the Royal Navy combined with the opening of the canal having reduced the trade almost to nothing.

About five in the afternoon there was a shout from Luciani, "Deck there. I see the land ahead, the high ground behind Montpellier."

Kennedy nodded. "That's about right."

Later, there was another shout, "Land on the port bow, four points. High ground behind Sète."

The ship was in the Gulf of Lions, bounded to the east by the Camargue swamp and with a low, sandy coast, bleak, windswept and almost uninhabited stretching away to the west

At the next shout, "Constance tower, starboard bow, four points", they looked again. The Constance tower guarded the approaches to Aigues-Mortes, an inland walled town, and dominated the surrounding marshes. Kennedy, careless of preserving his dignity, scrambled up the foremast rigging, sextant in hand.

He returned, disappeared into the cabin, and then announced, "On the right track, Sir, should see …"

There was another shout, "Cathedral dead ahead."

Kennedy smiled in satisfaction. "To quote Mr Pascoe, 'just about where I thought we were'."

From the masthead they could see the saltwater lagoons behind the beach, with the Canal du Rhône à Sète running through them between rocky banks. The canal was busy with barges, but there was no coherent convoy in sight, something the French Navy might be expected to organise for the unwilling Spanish sailors.

In the dusk, they took the ship inshore until the abandoned Maguelone Cathedral, on its lonely mound just inland from the sea, was easily visible from the deck. Kennedy took the newly named *Liberté* inshore nearly to the beach, taking careful soundings as he went. From the foretop they could see the canal, cut almost straight through the lagoons.

They repeated the exercise on the following day, but on the third day the sky was a glittering metallic blue, the Mistral blew hard off the land and the ship made difficult progress inshore, arriving only when it was nearly dark. They could hardly see the canal from the masthead.

"This is no good", said Vilar to Snowden, "we will miss the convoy, if we haven't already done so."

"I don't see what else we can do."

"I'll go ashore and keep watch."

"That's very dangerous, Vilar."

Vilar smiled. "I can always swim away. Give me an hour, and I'll be ready."

Vilar left, and Snowden thought carefully about what he was about to do. There was a knock on the door and the Condesa, Luca and Bianca came into the cabin, dishevelled from the windy deck.

The child and maid greeted Snowden cheerfully and went into their part of the cabin, but the Condesa paused. He glanced up at her, thinking how enchanting she looked.

"You look worried, Captain," she said in a low voice.

"I am, Condesa. Sometimes command is rather lonely."

"I'm sure that it is. You can tell me of it if you wish, it will go no further."

"It's Vilar. He wants to be put ashore so that he can warn us when the convoy with the Spanish sailors is coming along the canal, a dangerous thing to do. He showed at Palamós that he is a brave man, but he will be entirely by himself, in a hostile land for several days, and if he is caught …"

"That is true, but I know Vilar well. He had big plans for minerals with my husband, and now that is gone. This scheme is his idea. I imagine he sees it as a big chance. It's true that it is very hard to be alone, but perhaps there is someone you could send with him."

Snowden's mood lightened somewhat. "Perhaps I could ask Luciani, though it is very far from his normal duties."

"I have noticed Luciani – the Corsican."

Snowden looked at her and continued, "He has spent a lot of time in Provence, as the master of his father's ship. He can speak the language, so he says, and in Corsica he was very valuable. He could help Vilar."

"At least poor Vilar would not be alone," she said, and, to Snowden's surprise, leaned over and kissed him lightly before turning and going through the door to her part of the cabin.

Snowden, rather astonished at this turn of events, called out to the marine sentry, "Have Mr Luciani come to the cabin, if you please."

Snowden suspected, based on the speed of his acceptance, that Luciani was slightly bored with *Oleander*'s routine and relished the chance for something different and, probably, as a Corsican, against the French as well.

That evening, Luciani and Vilar sat in the cabin, both dressed nondescriptly.

"So that is it", said Snowden, "a task for volunteers. It is not in my power to order Senor Vilar to undertake this work, and I am not even sure that the Articles allow me to order you, Luciani, to participate. If you do this, it will be as volunteers, accepting the risk attendant on it. Is that understood?"

They both nodded agreement.

"It is very important that at the first sign of trouble, you leave. The longboat", he corrected himself, "that is, *Liberté*, will be as close as possible to the shore, and you will have the dinghy. The wind is offshore presently, so you have a good chance."

"We know the plan, Sir," said Luciani. "There will be no trouble."

Snowden smiled. "Very well, gentlemen, please proceed."

Snowden had intended to take the men ashore himself, but Kennedy insisted that he should go.

"I haven't stretched my legs on land for a very long time," he said, and Snowden, though he knew that the real reason was that Kennedy did not want to be left out of the action, realised that to overrule him would breed resentment.

He watched the boats depart, *Liberté* towing the dinghy, but he did not see them land, though the shore was visible as a line of white breakers in the night, and then waited anxiously until the longboat returned.

"Vilar and Luciani are ashore, Sir," said Kennedy. "They didn't even get wet, though I'm at a loss to explain how these waves build up with the wind offshore as it is."

"And the dinghy?"

"Buried, Sir, four posts knocked in as markers, in the dunes, pretty discreet."

"Good work, Ken, turn in, I have the ship."

Before dawn, *Oleander* drew away from the coast, leaving *Liberté* anchored, they hoped unobtrusively, in her place.

\*\*\*

On the beach, blown sand stinging his face, Luciani watched as the dim shapes of *Oleander*'s men, outlined against the white surf, boarded the longboat and rowed out into the night, back to the order and security of the ship.

"Best get off the beach," said Vilar, in Catalan, breaking the Corsican's reverie.

"You are right," replied Luciani in Provençal. They had found that they could communicate satisfactorily in this way, Vilar speaking Catalan and Luciani Provençal, rather than using English, which they felt could betray them if they were overheard.

They walked up to the top of the dune, which had a flat top several hundred yards wide, covered in rough vegetation, and stopped in a small stand of scrubby trees which they hoped would give a good view of the lagoons and canal on the landward side of the dunes.

# CHAPTER 23 - WATCHING

Vilar and Luciani took it in turns to sleep. It was rather cold, and the trees provided little shelter from the wind. With the dawn's light, they realised that they had picked their lookout place well. Spread out in front of them they could see the lagoons, with the Canal du Rhône à Sète running through them, perhaps half a mile from their hiding place. Close to them, to the north-east, the ruined Maguelone Cathedral dominated a dry route across the lagoon between the beach and the canal. They could see quite a long way along the canal to the west, but to the east the view was restricted by the higher ground on which the cathedral stood.

There was a small fishing village, Palavas, about three miles away, but it was hidden from their view by the cathedral mound. According to the chart, which they had so closely studied aboard *Oleander*, the village was on the estuary of a river, the Lez, and had a small fort. This fort had caused considerable concern, and they had studied it closely by telescope from *Oleander*'s masthead. As far as they could see, the fort was very old, appeared deserted and flew no flag. Inland, beyond the lagoons, the white walls and red roofs of the town of Villeneuve were visible, and further inland, the city of Montpellier. In the distance, the blue hills of Provence stretched into infinity.

As the sun rose, barges, some of which had spent the night moored to the bank near the cathedral, began to make their way along the canal. They were quite large, propelled by small sails, and moved slowly. Most were freighters, a few carried passengers, but there were no organised convoys, and no barges carrying large numbers of sailors. They spent the day in the thicket, bored but simultaneously worried that they would be discovered, but the dune was entirely deserted, and there were no fishing boats at sea, probably because the Mistral still blew strongly.

"Do you think anyone will notice *Liberté*?" asked Vilar, pointing out to sea where the longboat was just about visible in the distance, riding to her anchor.

"The fishermen will, without a doubt", replied Luciani, "but I believe they will think she's on passage and has stopped to shelter from the Mistral", he paused and considered, "though she is anchored further out than she might be if she was just seeking shelter."

"Could she be taken for a smuggler?"

"That's probably the most likely explanation they'll come up with – there's a good deal of contraband coming in, especially to Marseille. If they take her for a smuggler, they'll leave her alone. They won't be going out anyway with the Mistral blowing, and they're not likely to report her to the authorities, even if there were any in the village."

Reassured, Vilar continued his surveillance of the canal. At midnight they carefully lit a blue lamp and shone it briefly towards *Oleander*, or at least to where *Oleander* would be if she had, as arranged, anchored in the same place as *Liberté*. To their great relief, they saw an answering blue light from the ship almost immediately.

They settled back down, but after a while Luciani, who was on watch, heard a sound not far away. Footsteps! He shook Vilar awake and picked up his cutlass. Crouching in the sand with their swords ready, they waited, hardly breathing, listening as the steps came closer. The footsteps were very close and Luciani was sure that they were about to be discovered when they heard a quiet voice, distinctly English, "Hello, Mr Vilar, Luciani, are you there?"

Astonished, Luciani called out, "We are over here, Watton. We didn't hear the boat landing."

"Not surprised in this wind," said Watton as he and another man stood over them. "I'm very pleased to see you."

"I'm staying ashore with you, but Iris here will return to the ship. Tell Iris what has been going on so can relate it to the Old Man. Best do it quickly as he'll want to get the ship well away before first light."

Iris listened intently as Vilar relayed what they had seen. When he had finished, Watton said, "Iris, are you sure you have all that?"

Iris touched his head. "Aye, Lieutenant, all in here."

Vilar passed a sketch he had made to Iris. "Give him this as well."

"Go on Iris, back to the boat. Good luck."

"And good luck to all a' you," said Iris, as he started back down the dune.

"I didn't expect to see you here," said Vilar to Watton.

"No, I didn't expect to come, but I persuaded the Old Man that I should have sight of the ground before we do anything ashore. In the end he agreed, and here I am."

Luciani chortled to himself, imagining the badgering that Snowden must have endured from the enthusiastic Marine.

\*\*\*

In the morning, as they waited for the sun to warm them, Vilar said to Watton, "The causeway past the cathedral is the only dry way to the canal, so we'll have to take the men along it."

"You're right, Vilar. I've been thinking that we should familiarise ourselves with it before the attack. If you're willing, perhaps we could walk along it to the canal tonight. Then, if the convoy comes – when the convoy comes – at least we will know the way."

*\*\**

On the following night, after they had seen *Oleander's* signal, Watton and Vilar slipped quietly away. There was a sliver of moon, giving sufficient illumination for them to avoid the occasional clump of bushes as they crossed the ridge and descended to the base of the dune, to where it met the muddy lagoon. Occasionally, they disturbed some night creature, but they saw nobody as they worked their way round the dune and came to the causeway. They walked for a mile or so along the path leading round the cathedral mound, Vilar counting steps, consulting his compass and making notes as they went.

The path ended at an ornate gateway which looked as though it should have been part of a wall, but there was no wall and they skirted round the gate and came out onto the canal bank. The canal was sheltered from the worst of the wind, but there were still occasional gusts which ruffled the water. The canal was wide near the gate, almost a lake, but it narrowed back to its normal width after a hundred yards or so.

A substantial flat-bottomed boat was made fast to the bank, which they realised must be a ferry to take passengers and livestock across from the north side of the canal to the causeway. There was a narrow path along the side of the canal, and barges were made fast to the banks in both directions.

"Let's have a look up there", whispered Vilar, pointing along the canal to the east, "we can't see that way from our lookout."

They walked along the path in the dark, without seeing a soul. Occasionally a dim light shone from a barge and once or twice a dog barked. Afterwards, Watton could never quite believe they had strolled so freely along a path in enemy France, but that is what they did, until, after half an hour or so, they came to a junction in the canal. Vilar looked at his compass, made a note in his book, and then knelt at the bank, scooping up a handful of water and tasting it.

"I think this is the junction with the River Lez, which goes to Palavas. It seems to have been canalised, or at least this bit has."

"Looks like it, Vilar."

Vilar said thoughtfully, "Do you think we could get a boat up here?"

"I know what you're thinking," said Watton with an edge of excitement in his voice. "Why don't we walk down it a distance and see."

They turned right along the river, and almost bumped into a man who was walking, slightly unsteadily, in the opposite direction.

"Bonsoir," said Vilar, affably, and the man made a slurred reply and continued on his way, presumably to one of the barges in the canal. Slightly shaken, they continued along the canalised river, which seemed to have little current in it. Before long they saw buildings ahead, and Vilar made more notes.

"Palavas", he whispered, "we're not far from the sea. I think we should return now."

They returned to the lookout without incident just as dawn was breaking, and described their findings to Luciani.

"I know of this Palavas", he said, "but I've never been there. I think it is not much of a port."

"Could we get a boat up the river?" Watton asked him.

"If they have turned the river into a canal, it must be possible. I expect it is shallow, but we saw fishing boats there from the masthead, so at least the entrance has some water."

\*\*\*

That night, as soon as it was dark, they shone their red light towards *Oleander*, and soon Vilar and Watton were aboard, working at the cabin table.

Watton went on deck and saw Snowden and Kennedy talking. He approached.

"Excuse me, Sir, we have completed the drawing."

The four men gathered round the table, looking at the sketch map Vilar had produced.

"It has all been done by pacing, Sir, but I believe it to be reasonably accurate."

"It looks like good work to me, Vilar," said Kennedy, and Snowden nodded his agreement.

"So what do you propose, Ensign Watton?" asked Snowden.

"Well, Sir, it seems to me …"

# CHAPTER 24 - CONVOY!

They had been waiting so long that Vilar, back on the beach again, had almost lost faith in the existence of the convoy. He reassured himself from time to time that it could not have passed unobserved, and that it was the logical way of transporting unwilling, almost mutinous sailors. Thankfully, Snowden had kept faith, and now in the late afternoon at the lookout, he could hardly stop himself from running onto the beach and shouting for *Liberté* to pick him up.

"What do you think?" he asked Luciani, whose elation showed through the exhaustion on his face.

"I think we will soon be able to get off this damned beach. At least the Mistral has stopped, but I never want to see any sand again in my life. It must be the prisoners, though." He lifted the glass again to look at the convoy, which consisted of four barges, three flying Spanish flags.

He looked again and said, "Vilar, what do you make of the leading barge? There are no sailors in it as far as I can see, but there are quite a few soldiers aboard. Guards for the sailors perhaps, but I'm not sure."

Vilar picked up the telescope. "I see what you mean. It's as though they're guarding someone special, or something valuable. It could be a Spanish admiral or government man."

Vilar considered. "Perhaps. It's late in the day and they'll have to stop for the night soon. It seems too good to be true, but

I think they may stop just after the cathedral."

In the event, the barges did not make it quite as far as the cathedral causeway, making fast to the narrow embankment separating the canal from the lagoon to seaward. As it grew darker, they saw fires lit on the canal bank and large numbers of men began to gather around them. The barge with what they supposed to be its important passenger was moored at the front of the convoy, slightly separate from it.

\*\*\*

Back in *Oleander*'s cabin, Vilar reported what he had seen, inking in the position of the barges on the plan he had drawn.

"The barges have moored here", he pointed to the plan. "As you can see, I have labelled them. The one at the head of the convoy, the one carrying the guards and perhaps the important person, is *Barge A*, and behind that we have *Barges B* and *C*, with *Barge D* at the rear of the convoy."

"Thank you, Senor Vilar", said Snowden, "I will summarise our scheme."

He looked around the table, at the men who relied on him and his judgement. *You're good men*, he thought, *I hope this scheme isn't the undoing of you.*

"We will be divided into three parties: the 'Lagoon Party' led by Sergeant Riley, the 'River Party' led by Mr Kennedy and the 'Causeway Party' with myself and Mr Watton."

The men nodded and he continued, "The Lagoon Party's purpose is to create a diversion and block the canal and path to the west. It will cross the lagoon by raft with a gun and powder and set up behind the convoy on the bank." He paused. "Thank you, Riley, you are quite right, here, behind Barge D. At about one o'clock it will cause a large explosion and fire the gun, and reload and continue to fire, blank fire, because of the risk of hitting our own men."

"The River Party's purpose is to block the canal and path

to the east. *Liberté* will enter the canal by the river Lez and moor at the head of the convoy, near Barge A. Immediately following the explosion it will fire its guns as quickly as possible, again, blank fire."

"The main attack will be by the Causeway Party. We will take the path along the cathedral mound and halt just short of the canal. When we hear the explosion, we will attack and take possession of the barges. We hope the Spanish seamen will not put up much of a fight, and that the resistance of the French will be reduced by the element of surprise."

"However, in the event of unexpected resistance, the Causeway Party will make a fighting retreat to the beach along the path, covering other parties as necessary. Are there any questions?"

When the questions subsided, Snowden looked round the men at the table. "Well, gentlemen, we all have our tasks. Let us be about our work."

\*\*\*

On deck, *Oleander* was surrounded by every boat she possessed, except the dinghy buried on the beach, and the deck was crowded with sailors and marines. Under the able supervision of Kennedy, the boats were manned in excellent order, with hardly a word spoken, and shortly the Lagoon Party set off, followed by the River Party in *Liberté*.

When they had gone, Snowden returned to the cabin and was buckling on his sword and checking his pistols when he heard the partition door open, and the Condesa walked towards him. Without preliminaries, she embraced him warmly.

"Good luck, Percy," she breathed, and kissed him.

After what seemed like a long time, she let him go.

Smiling, he said, "That's the best send-off I've ever had, thank you", and walked onto the deck.

***

From the lookout on the dune, Luciani saw the faint outline of *Oleander* in the moonlight and then the occasional glint from the oars as the boats rowed ashore. Before long, two boats were on the beach and a large number of men disembarked. He walked down to the beach, to be met by Vilar, Gunner Trott and Sergeant Riley. Riley's reputation and his imperturbability were infinitely reassuring.

"Hello, Giotto", said Riley, "how are things looking ashore?"

"No activity as far as I can see, fires are still burning on the bank and some of the men are singing. They have guitars."

"You know what we intend?"

"I do. I will return to my lookout and keep watch."

Trott turned to the men. "Come on, byes, there's work to be done. We know what to do, the gig first."

With some men lifting at the oars they had lashed across the boat as improvised handles, and some tailing on ropes, they made pretty fast, but, to Luciani's ears, rather noisy progress over the dune and to the lagoon, where they launched the boat into the shallow water. They returned for the other boat and handled it in the same way. Vilar stood in the lagoon up to his knees, directing operations. The gun was next, dragged on an improvised sledge made from sizable timbers. Vilar had been concerned that a single boat would sink too deep under the load of the cannon, and so they had made holes in the boats' gunwales, through which they now passed the timbers, lashing them so that they effectively had a double-hulled raft with a platform for the gun. With much exertion, they lifted the gun aboard.

Vilar and Trott inspected their work. "She'll do", said Trott to the boatswain's mate who was in charge of the rigging, and then, after consulting his watch, "push her out, lads."

The trip across the lagoon was something none of them would ever forget – sometimes pulling the raft through the mud, sometimes up to their waists in slimy water, and on one or two occasions swimming out of their depths in the warm lagoon, all the time watching the reflections of the Spanish sailors' fires and hearing their songs, accompanied by guitars.

\*\*\*

Kennedy, in the sternsheets of *Liberté*, briefly worried about leaving the ship in the charge of Master's Mate Soares, but he rapidly became absorbed in alternately watching his compass and the shoreline as he steered the boat towards the mouth of the River Lez. Before long, a gap appeared in the white breakers and he altered course slightly towards it.

Iris, in the bow, said softly, "There be a beacon."

Kennedy saw it and turned the boat to port, into the river entrance, the muffled oars making no sound as the boat made her way through some disturbed water and entered the river. As the river began to narrow, he saw fishing boats made fast to a rough quay, and he realised that the current, what there was of it, was with them, flowing into the canal. *Something to do with the Mistral*, he thought, *must have pushed the water out of the canal, and now it's flowing back in.*

"Easy oars," he said, and the bow wave subsided so that the boat seemed to glide soundlessly over the water. They were in the river itself now, passing through the village, which was almost dark with only one or two dim lights in the houses.

"Quiet now," he said unnecessarily.

After a few minutes they were through the village, and Kennedy was reasonably sure that they had not been seen.

A few minutes more and Iris called out softly, "The junction's ahead", and then they were in the canal itself, wider than Kennedy had expected, with barges moored at its bank.

\*\*\*

Snowden, sitting in the stern of the gig as she made her second trip ashore, packed tightly with marines and sailors, had the same thought as Kennedy – *Will she be all right with Soares in command? If she isn't, I can probably say goodbye to my career.*

Like Kennedy, he banished such thoughts from his mind and concentrated on the job ahead. The boat's keel grated on the beach and the men disembarked in good order, in commendable silence, and the boat backed off to await their return.

He found Ensign Watton, who whispered in his ear, "I believe we are ready, Sir, shall we move?"

"Very well, Watton, let us start. You've reconnoitred the ground, so I suggest you lead."

"Aye, Sir."

Snowden took up station at the rear of the party, which was in double file. They made their way cautiously along the path round the cathedral mound towards the canal, the path illuminated by the weak moon and the flickering fires of the Spanish sailors, the tension increased because from time to time they could hear the sounds of the improvised raft traversing the lagoon, a few hundred yards to their left. There was no reaction from the barges on the canal, and Snowden hoped that the raft's progress might be inaudible over the sound of the sailors singing.

The huge gateway at the end of the path was clearly visible when Watton stopped the party, the men lying down in the rough grass beside the track. Snowden made his way to the front of the column and crouched beside the Ensign. He saw, ahead of them, perhaps a hundred yards away, the leading barge, *Barge A*, moored to the bank, which was quite wide at that point. Several tents were pitched on the flat ground, and people who looked like soldiers were sitting round a fire. He saw movement and realised there were sentries picketed around the encampment, their outlines silhouetted against the camp fire.

He nudged Watton and pointed. "I've seen them", whispered Watton, "but I'd say they look pretty slack, if there's really an admiral aboard."

They stayed where they were for what seemed like a long time, and then Snowden asked, "What time have you got?"

"Coming up to one," replied Watton. "Soon be time. Best get the men into position."

\*\*\*

"Here we are, lads", said the Gunner, as they reached the bank of the canal, "make sure the boat's anchored, and we'll get this this bastard up onto the path."

Some of the men, filthy with mud from the lagoon, climbed to the top of the bank and let down ropes. With remarkable quietness, if not complete silence, the gun was dragged and pushed up the slope, its canvas cover, carefully sewed by *Oleander*'s sailmaker, was unceremoniously slit with a knife, and the cannon reunited with its carriage. Under Trott's careful supervision, the gun crew loaded the piece and then lay down at its side, their ears stuffed with oakum. Riley took the remaining men and they also laid down on the path with their ears blocked.

"If you're set, Riley, we'll move the raft out into the lagoon now."

Riley lay on the ground, interminably, it seemed. The singing round the fires showed no sign of slackening, and he remembered his visits to Spanish ports and the locals' preference for late nights.

Suddenly, the Gunner was at his side. "About five minutes, I reckon, before …"

The men waited, their arms covering their heads.

\*\*\*

Kennedy turned *Liberté* into the wide canal, and they rowed briskly along it, passing barges moored to the bank. After half an hour, Iris in the bow said "Bend ahead", and Kennedy thought of Vilar's map.

"Very good, easy oars."

They crept to the bend, the muffled oars almost silent, and as they rounded it Iris said, "Barges, and campfires, couple of cables' length away."

They went on until the leading barge, *Barge A*, the one with the guards and the supposed valuable passenger, was quite close, and then Kennedy, by judicious use of the oars, brought *Liberté* round so she was at right angles to the bank and moored her fore and aft.

"Right, lads", he said, "get the swivels up."

\*\*\*

With whispered commands, and a little bit of shoving, Snowden and Watton got the men into position, some kneeling, with the butts of their rifles on the ground, and some lying, sighting along their weapons.

"Any minute …," began Snowden, but he did not finish as the night was illuminated by a huge orange flash, followed almost immediately by the roar of an explosion.

"My word!", said Watton in the silence that followed, "Gunner's done us proud", and then "Up and at 'em, lads."

The men lying down fired their rifles, Snowden saw sentries fall, and then he was running, cutlass in hand, along the path at the front of the men, shouting. A cannon fired behind him and then three smaller guns from ahead. *Good old Ken*, he thought. He saw the men around the fire next to *Barge A*, Frenchmen he realised, look up in horror, as other men tumbled out from the tents, trying to pull on their clothes, and yet others, officers, appeared at *A*'s bulwarks.

The men around the fire, and their comrades from the

tents, put up their hands and some of them knelt. *Sensible fellows*, thought Snowden, but he saw that the officers aboard *Barge A* were made of sterner stuff and had drawn their swords. Snowden, careless of whether anyone was following, threw himself over the bulwark of the barge, tripped on a rope, fell heavily, and looked up to see a French officer standing over him, sword in hand.

The man struck and Snowden rolled desperately, but felt a sickening blow on his head. He struggled to rise and was on his knees when the man clutched at his chest and, with a surprised look on his face, collapsed onto the deck. Snowden glanced behind and saw a marine with a Baker at his hip, smoke curling from its barrel. He touched his hat to the man, picked himself up unsteadily and, with intense pain in his left ankle as well as his head, limped forward towards the bow where a group of French officers, swords in hand, had gathered around the barge's raised bowsprit. He was roughly pushed aside by marines who, with Watton at their head, stopped and levelled their Bakers at the Frenchmen.

"Rendez", shouted Watton, "rendez", and the officers, faced with such overwhelming odds, dropped their swords to their sides.

Watton nudged him, and Snowden walked unsteadily towards what was evidently the senior officer, who was holding out his sword, hilt first. Snowden, rather dazed, took the weapon without saying anything when the man said, in English, but with a strong accent, "I am Lieutenant Schnieder of the Imperial Navy. To whom do I have the honour?"

Snowden found himself unable to find the right words, but Watton said, loudly, "You have surrendered to Commander Snowden of the Royal Navy."

"Ah", said the Frenchman, "Snowden. It is no dishonour", and added, seemingly as an afterthought "the money is yours."

"What do you mean by that?" asked Watton.

The Frenchman, as far as they could see in the darkness, looked surprised. "You did not know? I will say no more."

Watton turned to a marine corporal. "Simms, if you please, take two men and search this barge."

\*\*\*

The explosion to the east set by Trott was huge, bigger than Kennedy had anticipated, but he quickly gave the order, "Fire, lads."

The three swivels fired one after the other, were reloaded and fired again. They got the boat underway, and as they started, they heard the sound of rifles and saw an ill-defined mass of men run along the bank. They heard shouting, followed by silence. Kennedy steered the boat into the bank and leapt ashore.

"Come with me, Iris. Cox'n, take the boat back into the middle of the canal", he said, "and stop anyone from coming this way. I'm going to see what's happening."

He ran along the bank to where the fires were still burning, and saw a dejected group of Frenchmen sitting on the ground next to *Barge A*, guarded by marines with rifles pointed at them. He went onto the barge and saw Watton supervising marines moving a group of French officers to a shelter in the vessel's stern.

"Ensign", he said "what news?"

"Everything has gone well, Ken, they've all surrendered. This barge had Frenchies on it and no Spaniards, but there were only Spaniards on the other three. We're putting the Spaniards aboard *B*, *C* and *D*."

"Any casualties?"

"The Old Man's had another bang on the head. He's wobbling a bit presently, but lying down over there."

Kennedy ran over to where Snowden was lying.

"How are you, Perce?" he said, urgently.

"You should see the other fellow," replied Snowden. "Right as rain in a minute. Get on with it, Ken."

*\*\*\**

Sergeant Riley stood and shouted, "With me, *Oleander*s," and ran along the bank towards the nearest campfire, next to *Barge D* at the rear of the convoy. Vilar was with him, and as they reached the barge he shouted in Spanish, "Get aboard the barge" to the Spanish sailors who were mostly lying on the ground, arms over their heads, worried that there would be another explosion.

The Spaniards, seeing the heavily armed British party, showed no sign of resistance, but got up and filed meekly along the gangplank onto the barge. The British moved to *Barge C* with the same result, but at Barge B, the third one they came to, though the sailors boarded the barge, a Spanish officer, the only one they had seen, stood his ground, despite the menace of the rifles pointed at him.

"Who are you?" the Spanish officer asked Vilar, with considerable courage.

"Pedro Vilar, secretary to the Conde de Premià. I am attached to the English Navy, and you are Lieutenant …?"

"Eduardo Pizzaro, Senor Vilar. Attached to the English Navy? Perhaps you have not heard that we are at war with England."

"I have heard, Lieutenant, and have to say that I am ashamed that my country's government is entirely subordinate to the Bonapartists, men who do not have the interests of Spain at heart."

"It happens that I agree with you", replied the Lieutenant, "but I am an officer of the Navy, and my orders are to take these men to Toulon". He thought and added, "Those that are left."

"Are there any more officers?"

"There were three others, Vilar, but I am the only one

remaining. The others left at Narbonne. I cannot say I blame them, but I have given my oath."

"Come with me, Lieutenant."

Vilar, accompanied by the Spanish Lieutenant and two marines, left Riley to the task of shepherding the Spanish seamen aboard the barges and walked along the path to *Barge A*. He saw Kennedy, who was talking to Watton. They looked up and Watton said, with enthusiasm, "Splendid explosion, Vilar. Boney probably heard it in Paris!"

"Do you know where Snowden is?"

"He's over there, on the barge. He had a nasty crack on the head", Kennedy said, "another one, but not so bad this time. We should see what he intends now."

They boarded *Barge A* and went over to where Snowden was sitting on a bollard, his head in his hands, his hair soaked in blood.

"How are you, Sir?" asked Kennedy. "You don't want too many bangs on your head."

"Not too bad this time," replied Snowden, his voice no longer slurred. "I didn't pass out. It would have been much worse if it wasn't for O'Rorke's quick work. Please pass my compliments to him, Watton."

"I will, Sir."

Kennedy said, urgently, "The Spanish have surrendered, Sir, if that's the right word. We've put them on the other three barges. There was only one officer, and we have him. The officer says a lot of men have deserted, but there's still perhaps five or six hundred sailors left."

"That'll keep a 74 in port, but too many for us to take prisoner," said Snowden. "Keep the French prisoners together on this barge. Make sure they're disarmed."

## CHAPTER 25 - COBS!

At that moment, Corporal Simms came up, his excitement evident even in the darkness. "Cobs", he said, "cobs, gold, I can't …"

"Calm yourself, Corporal", said Watton, "tell us what you've found."

"There's chests down there, Sir, I don't know how many. We broke one open", he looked concerned, "you told us to search, Sir, and that's what we were doing. We weren't …"

"You did right, Corporal", Watton reassured him, "please continue."

"Well, Sir, it's full, full of gold pieces. There must be …", he searched for the right phrase, "hundreds of them, no, thousands."

"Show me," said Watton, and, followed by Vilar, he made his way to the hold of the barge, which was entered through a companionway near the vessel's tiller. Minutes later they emerged, and strode over to where the French officers were standing.

"Lieutenant Schnieder", said Watton, "can you explain the gold this barge is carrying?"

"I can," said the Spanish Lieutenant, Pizzaro, stepping forward. "It is our gold, Spanish gold. It is given in tribute to France by our abject government."

"Quite right", said Vilar, "well said."

"Yes, it's Spanish gold", said Schnieder, "we were to take it to Toulon, to finance the Navy." He paused, "But now I suppose it will fund the English Navy."

Stunned, they walked over to Snowden and told him what they had found.

"Get your men aboard, Ken, and take *Barge A* to sea. You may have to tow her, so take the longboat as well. Transfer the cargo into *Oleander* as soon as you can – and keep a record of what there is."

He turned to Watton. "We'll keep the French officers on *Barge A* and take them with us in *Oleander*. We can't take the French rank and file, and the head money's pretty small compared with the gold, so we'll let them go just before we leave."

Kennedy left, and Snowden turned to Vilar, beckoning him over, and said, quietly, "Before Kennedy goes off, please go down below and bring up some of that money. I want to use it to …"

\*\*\*

Snowden sat at the capstan in the bow of *Barge B*, flanked by armed marines, as Vilar explained to the Spanish sailors what was to happen.

"I am Pedro Vilar, and I speak for Commander Snowden of the English Navy. You will come forward, one man at a time, and we will give you each a piece of gold." He held one up to show them, provoking an outbreak of noise from the prisoners.

"When you have your gold, you must go ashore, as we intend to burn the barges. The gold is a present from those that represent the true spirit of Spain. When you are ashore, you are free, and undoubtedly will want to return to your homes."

The distribution of money went smoothly, the men went ashore, and they repeated the process on *Barge C*, but after Vilar had made his speech aboard *Barge D*, an elderly seaman, probably a warrant officer, shouted, "Do not burn this barge, we can take it back to Spain."

"Can you?" said Vilar.

"We can try", retorted the seaman, "at my age, drowning is better than walking."

As the sun rose, Snowden, sitting shivering on the beach, could see *Oleander* anchored offshore, with *Barge A* alongside. They had heard firing from the east, presumably associated with the escape of *Barge D* piloted by the elderly seaman.

He saw the ship's sails raised, and as she headed in towards the beach, the longboat, *Liberté*, detached herself and men rowed her quickly ashore. The bowman jumped down, and soon Snowden, shaking with either cold or relief, was being helped up the ship's side, then into the cabin, where he felt a woman's hands exploring the wound on his head and then carefully bathing it.

***

Ashore, on the beach, Watton had heard the gunfire with great concern. "Coming from that fort, I reckon, Riley, perhaps not quite as abandoned as we thought."

"Perhaps not, Sir, but in my experience the Frogs react to something like this pretty quickly, so it may be men from a distance away who heard the goings on in the night. And those ..." He pointed inshore to where the burning barges were sending up impressive columns of smoke, and then to *Barge A*, which was slowly drifting along the shore, burning fiercely. "Those will attract attention as well. Anyway, we're pretty well set", he gestured to the marines who had dug into the sand, lying behind banks of sand they had made, "and I think Mr Kennedy will provide a bit of cover."

There was a shout from the lookout, "Frenchies – here they come."

Riley looked inshore and saw French soldiers, in skirmish order, making their way along the top of the dune to the east.

As he spoke, *Oleander's* Carrons fired. Though their range was short, they were impressively noisy, and the French threw themselves flat on the ground and started to fire their muskets at the marines on the beach.

*Oleander* turned so that she was broadside to the beach, moored fore and aft.

"Wait, lads", shouted Riley, and, as *Liberté* grounded on the beach, "Corporal Simms' men to the boat." Half of the men stood up and ran over to the longboat, which was being held in the surf by her crew.

"In you get, lads."

The boat, heavily laden, was pushed off by marines and sailors and set off for the ship.

"When you have a good target, lads", shouted Riley, and, one by one, the rifles fired.

The French did not seem to have a great deal of enthusiasm for the work, thought Riley, as he saw several of them scrabble back to less exposed positions, one of them dropping as a rifle found its mark.

The longboat was now alongside *Oleander*, and Riley could see men climbing up her sides. *Oleander* fired her broadside, one gun at a time, and Riley imagined the Gunner, safely back aboard after his night ashore, carefully aiming each gun before it fired. He heard the shot whistle overhead and the balls kick up sand and skitter along the beach near the French positions.

The longboat left the ship and was soon back on the shore. Riley called out names, and one by one the marines made their way to *Liberté* as the sailors held her in the surf. Grapeshot whistled overhead, and Riley ducked involuntarily before he jumped aboard.

The French were foolishly rushing towards the boat. "Go on then," he shouted to the gunner at the swivel, who fired. The

French, very sensibly, turned and ran.

Snowden followed what was happening by the sounds filtering into *Oleander*'s cabin: men running on deck, anchors dropped and weighed, sails lowered and raised, guns firing. Eventually the tumult ceased and the ship heeled.

"Under way, thank God," said Snowden quietly to the woman attending him. "Be in Gib in no time."

# CHAPTER 26 - WESTWARD!

"What's that?" asked Kennedy to Luciani as they looked towards Palavas, which was rapidly receding as the ship gathered way.

The Corsican took a glass and made his way up the weather mainmast shrouds, inspected the river entrance carefully, and slid rapidly back down.

"It's that barge, Sir, *Barge D*, the one we left them. Coming out of the river. It has some sails set."

Kennedy walked over to Vilar. "Did you hear that?"

"I did, Kennedy."

"Is there anything we can do?"

"I don't think so, they will have to make their minds up about where they are heading. That barge is hardly seaworthy, so I expect they will take her as far west as they can while the wind holds, and then ground her and make their way home. To make your way home after an attack is one thing, but to do so under the protection of a British warship is something else, and could be taken as treason. No, we must leave them to their own devices."

*\*\*\**

Kennedy and Luciani sat at the table in the cabin. A chart of the Mediterranean was laid out on the table, with parallel ruler and dividers resting on it and several almanacs and tables to one side.

"It has been from one bit of land to another for me in my father's ships so far, Kennedy, nothing scientific", said Luciani, "not scientific, though some skippers in our trade know how to get a latitude, but my father never taught me. When I went to America it was only as an ordinary seaman, so I was not involved in the navigation. I believe we were never quite sure of our position, and there was a good deal of argument when we thought we were near Bermuda."

"A lot of skippers in the coasting trade round England just use their eyes and the lead, but if you want to advance in the Navy, to get your ticket, you have to know your navigation", replied Kennedy, and continued, "Bermuda's a nasty place for the seaman, or at least it is when he's at sea. Very low, completely invisible. The first thing you see are the waves piling up on the North Rock Shoal." He paused, recollecting, "Very nice when you get in though. Let's run through this once more."

Luciani nodded, and Kennedy continued, "It's best to get the form filled in before you get your sight, so let's do that now. The first thing's the correction for height of eye. Now, we've kept up our reckoning since we left Maguelone, so we know our position fairly well. Here it is ..." He pointed at the chart. "Measure off the latitude – roughly will do."

Luciani used the parallel rules and inspected the chart's latitude scale. "About 40 N, I think."

Kennedy thought aloud, "Sun will be pretty high at noon, say about 70 degrees."

"How do you know it will be 70 degrees?"

"Because it always is at noon in the Mediterranean at this time of year. Look up the correction. We're 18 feet above the sea."

Luciani ran his finger over the table. "The correction's 12 minutes". He entered it on the slate.

"Now", said Kennedy, "declination."

He handed the almanac to Luciani, who looked at the

Berthoud chronometer and then at the figures in the table, eyes screwed up in concentration. "Looks like 22 degrees, 42 minutes."

"Write that down on the slate," said Kennedy. "Now, it's nearly noon, let's get our sights."

As they went on deck, *Oleander* was running steadily south-west over the glittering blue sea, a gentle easterly wind on her port quarter. Snowden, his head bandaged, sat in a chair on the starboard side of the deck with the Condesa beside him, watching Lucia playing hide and seek, a game supervised by the maid Bianca, but which closely involved Ensign Watton, seemingly much of the on-watch crew, almost unemployed in the 'soldiers breeze', and one of the five French officers who had been captured at Maguelone.

"Very domestic," said Kennedy to Luciani as they walked over to the port bulwark. They braced themselves against the rail and looked through their sextants.

"There he goes, Mister", said Kennedy, "still going up, but nearly there. Wait, there it is, he's hovering now, see?"

"I see it", said Luciani, and then, "got it", and, after a pause, "definitely descending now."

The men stepped back from the rail and inspected the scales of their sextants and locked them. As they walked back across the deck, Snowden said, "Get it, Luciani?"

"Yes, Sir," replied the Corsican. He looked closely at the scale of his instrument. "70 degrees, 53 minutes."

"Same as me," said Kennedy. "We'll go and work it up."

In the cabin they worked through the calculation. "Sextant plus height correction gives the altitude," said Kennedy. "Subtract from 90 to get the zenith distance." He watched as Luciani worked on the slate. "Now, add your declination, and you're there."

Luciani looked up. "41 degrees and 35 minutes North, Mr Kennedy."

He drew a horizontal line on the chart and then circled a point "Here. I think it's time to alter course."

"We should not go too far off the land", Luciani said, "there is a favourable current if you stay inshore."

They went on deck and Kennedy watched as Luciani gave directions to bring the ship round on her new course.

In the night, the wind backed to the north-west and increased dramatically in force.

"The Tramontane," said Luciani.

The ship heeled, the decks were wet with spray, and the occasional wave top came aboard, but she sailed fast, and they were soon through the strait between Ibiza and the mainland, and after three days they arrived at Gibraltar.

# CHAPTER 27 - THE ADMIRAL

*Oleander* had been alongside in Gibraltar dockyard for a long time, routine dockyard work was complete, and she was revictualled and rearmed. Snowden, for once in his life, was in no hurry to get his ship away, he was recovering well, and, in fact, for most of the time, he was hugely enjoying himself, the only blot being his difficulty with Jameson, the Admiral of the squadron that was blockading Cadiz and the Strait. Jameson had insisted that *Oleander*, her mission as complete as it could be, was under his command. Snowden knew that, strictly speaking, Jameson was right, but he had become used to independence, and fretted under the unbending command of the Admiral, who, seemingly alone of all the sea officers in Gibraltar, acted with great coldness towards him.

Still, thought Snowden, *if I have to kick my heels here, I may as well enjoy myself*, and that the reason for that enjoyment was another man's wife only occasionally troubled his conscience. He met the Condesa often, as their fame meant that there was a steady stream of invitations to the many social events organised on the Rock for officers and diplomats. Their liaisons outside these occasions were always, he prided himself, discreet, as he moved his arm over her as she slept.

***

Pascoe, reunited with his ship, climbed aboard *Oleander*. "Old Man around?" he asked Luciani.

"Ashore with his lady friend, in her boudoir no doubt," retorted the Corsican.

"Again? I wanted to speak to him about the landing boats."

"I cannot blame him", said Luciani, "I would do the same in his circumstances."

"I hear you *are* doing it," retorted Pascoe.

Luciani raised his arms "Perhaps," he said.

*Oleander*'s return had been a triumph. As soon as they had docked, Snowden had requested – insisted on – an immediate meeting with the Governor and the Admiral. To ensure secrecy, the gold, carefully counted by Kennedy and Pascoe aboard the ship, had been carried ashore by *Oleander*'s marines under cover of darkness, and counted again once there in the presence of *Oleander*'s officers, the Admiral and the Governor. The secrecy was a sensible precaution, though entirely futile, as Gibraltar's entire population knew about the gold by the following morning.

Snowden was careful not only to engage a local prize agent, but also to write two copies of an account of his actions, and the sums involved, to his lawyers in Plymouth. He personally gave them to the captains of ships about to depart to England as escort for a convoy. He had no doubt that the gold was a legitimate spoil of war – England was at war with Spain, and the treasure was seized as part of a naval operation on enemy territory.

What he did not reckon with was opposition from Isabella. He was sure, well almost certain, that their relationship was based on mutual attraction, but he realised that she was an astute political operator, and considered that the gold belonged to Spain and, by extension, that as Spain had an illegitimate government subordinate to the French, she, as her husband's representative, should have control of it. This led to some lively domestic debates, but Snowden insisted, correctly, that any decision on the ownership of the gold would be decided at a much higher level.

"Do you want me to steal it again?" he asked, and was rather discomfited when she looked at him appraisingly.

\*\*\*

They had been in Gibraltar for nearly a month when he was summoned to meet the Admiral, who was not aboard his flagship but rather in an office. An aide showed him into a room where the Admiral, alone, was seated behind a large desk. Jameson's coldness towards Snowden had been explained when he realised that the Admiral was married to the sister of Commodore Parkinson, who had taken his own life aboard his ship in the Basque Roads following a meeting with Snowden. He did not appear friendly now.

"Lieutenant Snowden, I am considering another raid on the French coast," he said. "I am informing you of this as you will be required to play a part in it, though your role will be one of support. You have some experience of this work, though your previous activities have been on a rather small scale, and we are planning something of larger import."

Snowden thought, *my work may be small in scale, but the results are big*, and then, *I don't want to be part of anything dreamed up by this pompous fool.*

"It might be best to wait until the excitement over the last one has died down, Sir."

"Nonsense, Snowden, strike while the iron is hot, I always say."

Snowden struggled to conceal his contempt.

"Yes, Sir. Has any plan been decided upon?"

"Yes, Snowden, it has."

"And what is the target?"

"The one you mentioned in your despatch, the canal. We had been thinking along those lines already, and perhaps your report clarified our ideas somewhat. However, Snowden, before I speak of this there is another matter, a serious irregularity, which has been brought to my attention."

"And what is that, Sir?"

"It concerns the Spanish gold, Snowden. The Spanish gold that you took from the barge on the canal. As I said, there is an irregularity ..."

Snowden's experience had been that money had the potential to turn even good friends into rivals. He knew that it would not have a beneficial effect on the attitude of this man to him.

"An irregularity, Sir? The gold has all been accounted for and is in the possession of the agents of His Majesty's government."

"Not all of it, Snowden."

"What do you mean?"

"Did you not disburse some of it to Spanish sailors? It seems to me to have been an entirely unnecessary act, giving money to enemy combatants who should have been taken prisoner."

Snowden felt a tide of icy rage rising in him and said, "If you, instead of sleeping in your warm bed that night, had been on the canal bank with thirty men, would you have tried to take six hundred Spaniards prisoner? Six hundred men, odds of twenty to one. Would you have done it for the head money? Or would you, like I did, have found a way of keeping them as happy as possible, enabling them to return to their homes in Spain, allowing us to make an orderly retirement, without a man lost, and depriving Boney of the crew of a 74?"

Jameson made no reply, angering Snowden still further. He felt an almost irresistible urge to strike the man, perhaps to kill him, but forced himself to stop, to collect himself.

There must have been something in his manner that transmitted itself to the Admiral. He looked at Snowden with fear, deep fear, in his eyes. He tried to speak, but no words came out, and instead he reached for the bell on his desk which summoned the secretary. Before he could reach it, Snowden, with great deliberation, moved it across the top of the desk, away from the Admiral.

Snowden stood, placed both hands on the desk, and leaned forward. The man looked petrified as Snowden spoke.

"Listen to me, Jameson, I'm not a man for playing politics, but I know what you are doing, and I advise you to stop. I'm too successful now to be brought down by a time-serving bastard like you. I hope I make myself clear."

The Admiral said nothing, but looked transfixed at Snowden.

"Do you understand?"

Jameson nodded.

"I'll leave now, but before I go, I will tell you that you are entirely mistaken about Parkinson. I know that because he wrote me a letter to be opened after his death. If you wish to see the letter, please let me know."

Snowden walked to the door, past the aide at his desk, and out of the building.

The aide watched him leave and then went into his chief's room. The Admiral had collected himself somewhat, but he still looked white and strained.

"Are you well, Sir?" said the aide. "Has something happened?"

"No, Johnson, I'm a little tired, that's all. I think I shall go home now."

\*\*\*

Snowden knocked on the front door of the Condesa's small house, which was opened by Bianca, who let him in and announced, "She is in the salon, Capitaine."

Snowden opened the salon door. Isabella was sitting at a table, writing. She turned as he entered, looked at his face and threw herself into his arms.

"Percy, whatever has happened? You look terrible."

"Isabella, I have done a stupid thing."

"Tell me, Percy."

"I have had a row with the Admiral, Jameson. I called him a 'time-serving bastard'. But what is more, I came within an ace of killing him, there in his office, and he knew it. If he had spoken to me in the wrong way I would have ... I would have run him through. I shall face a court martial."

"Calm yourself. Tell me what happened."

"It's complicated. We were hard pressed in battle, on the land, in Corsica. Just offshore there was a British squadron, but its Commodore refused to come to our assistance. He was to be court martialled but had powerful friends. A few months ago, when *Oleander* was in the Basque Roads, I went aboard his ship. He sore provoked me and I was sarcastic to him. My words were justified, but they upset him, and in the night he committed suicide."

"That is horrible, but you could not have known he would do that. What does this have to do with Jameson?"

"He is married to Parkinson's sister. When I was in his room – there was nobody else present – he criticised me because I had let the Spanish prisoners go and asserted that giving them some of the gold had been 'irregular'. I'm not sure what he was working up to, it was clearly a threat, but I reacted badly, and now", he drew a deep breath, "now I am in desperate trouble. I have been insubordinate at the very least. Sometimes I cannot help myself – something comes over me and I lose all fear."

"Percy, did you draw your sword, or put your hands on him?"

"No, I suppose I did not, but he knew …"

"My Love, do not fear the worst …"

At that moment there was a loud knocking on the front door. Snowden stood frozen.

"Isabella, they've come to arrest me!"

She put her arms around him and whispered, "He will make a fool of himself if he has you arrested."

They heard the front door open, hurried footsteps cross the hall, and then, to their astonishment, Rubert burst into the room.

"What is it, Senor Puyol?" asked Isabella.

"Your husband, Condesa, your husband is alive. He has been taken by the corsairs."

"By the corsairs? What do you mean?"

"The Moors have him. He is in Salé."

"Salé?"

"It is a city on the Atlantic coast of Morocco."

"And there are corsairs there? I thought we had a treaty with them."

"There are corsairs in Salé, probably not many, but it used to be a separate republic and is still rather independent. Relations between Europe and Morocco are strained in any case."

Snowden, who was slowly rousing himself from his depression, thought of the report Pascoe had written about his voyage from Maguelone to Gibraltar.

"You were with Pascoe, Rubert, when you had that run-in with the Moors just off Gib. Pascoe said you thought they were the Sally Rovers."

"I think they were, Sir, I've seen a few pirates in my time, Algerians, Tunisians, but I think these ones were flying the flag of Salé. When they broke off from us, they turned north, towards Spain."

"They sent word from Salé that they had him?" asked Isabella.

"They did. A man has turned up in Gib, we're not sure how he arrived, a renegado, a Christian turned Musselman. He looks like an Arab but speaks like an Englishman. One of the men, Wright's men you understand, went to talk to him, and he said he was from Salé, he had news about the Conde, and he wanted to speak to the Governor."

"Has he spoken to the Governor?" asked Isabella.

"No", said Rubert, "not yet. I went down to meet him at the quay, and now he is here, in the hall."

"Here?" said Isabella.

"Yes", replied Rubert, with a certain air of showmanship, "shall I show him in?"

# CHAPTER 28 - STOP HIM!

While his office in the Ministry was being prepared, something which he was assured would only take 'a day or so', Morlaix had turned his home into the centre of his nascent command. The irony that the room had previously been used by Jack Stone of the Royal Navy was not lost on Morlaix.

His aide, Captain Badeau, who seemed to Morlaix to be a very capable though bookish man, walked over to him, carrying a despatch in his right hand. His left arm, which had been badly injured in an action with a British frigate, was permanently supported in a sling. Morlaix and Badeau had an instant rapport, referring to their operation as the 'Cripple Command'.

Badeau put the despatch in front of Morlaix.

"Your demeanour, Badeau, is even more sombre than usual – I'm guessing this is not good news. Perhaps you could summarise it for me."

"You're right, Admiral, it is not good news. It seems that our friend, Snowden has been up to his tricks again."

"Where, Badeau, and what has he done?"

"Near Montpellier, Sir. He has attacked barges on the Canal du Rhône à Sète."

"No!" said Morlaix. "Barges and canals again, just like in Brittany!"

"Not exactly the same, Sir. You'll remember he was ashore

in Spain, at Girona, trying to abduct the Conde de Premià ..."

"And getting away with the Condesa! Remember, Badeau? The Emperor himself told me of it. In very forceful terms as well! It's not something I'm likely to forget."

Badeau, nonplussed, continued, "No, Sir. Well, we don't know what he found out when he was ashore – remember that Vilar, The Conde's secretary, has disappeared – but there was a large body of Spanish sailors in the area, on their way to Toulon. It seems to me probable that Snowden found out about this and that they were to be transported by canal barge along the canal du Rhône à Sète as far as Beaucaire. As you know, the canal runs through lagoons, only a few yards from the sea."

"Can we get a map?"

"Sir, they are at the Ministry."

"There are some here." He raised his voice: "Odile, can you come here?"

Odile was clearly not far away as she came into the room almost immediately. She looked at Morlaix and at the despatch. "Bad news?"

"It's that damned Snowden again. In Provence this time. Could you fetch that map?"

Odile laid the map on the table. "Snowden", she said, "Jacque's friend. The man who burnt your barges in Brittany. And he was here, in this house, he came to the soirée when we had both Fouché and Talleyrand."

"He has the devil's own luck," said Morlaix.

"Indeed he does," agreed Badeau. "There's more. He got away with a huge consignment of gold."

"Gold?" asked Odile.

"Gold?" repeated Morlaix.

"Yes, gold from Spain. It was on its way to Toulon. It went

with the barges carrying the Spanish sailors. Administrative convenience, I suppose."

Morlaix took up the despatch and read rapidly through it.

"It seems he anchored that damned ship just offshore for several days and nobody did anything about it. He probably had men ashore as well, watching."

"And then the barges showed up and moored exactly where he must have wished them to. In the night, they strolled ashore and captured the barges, and the gold as well."

"The Spanish sailors?"

"He lined them up, cool as you like, and gave them each a bit of gold and sent them on their way. Some of them took a barge to sea, but others just started walking back to Spain. There have been reports of robberies attributed to them, and there was some fighting between them and French sailors who Snowden released at the same time."

"How much money did he get? No, don't tell me, I'll look it up in the despatch."

Morlaix paused. "The sooner we can set up in the Ministry, the better."

\*\*\*

This time, the meeting was at the Tuileries.

As they sat in the waiting room, Morlaix asked, "Have you met him before, Badeau?"

"No, Sir, I saw him in the distance once, at Boulogne, that is all. I don't really understand, Sir. These raids are really no more than an annoyance, I don't really understand why the Emperor is so interested in them."

Morlaix started to say, "Sidney Smith ...," but they were called in before Morlaix could finish. Napoleon and the Minister, Decrès, were already seated at the table, with their aides and officials.

"Admiral Morlaix and Captain Badeau," announced the aide.

"My Breton, please be seated. Captain Badeau, I have heard the story of your arm, I congratulate you on your heroism."

Badeau, flattered, smiled.

*His for life*, thought Morlaix.

"This latest raid, Morlaix, what do you make of it?"

"I think the English, that is Snowden, was very lucky. All of the pieces fell exactly right for him."

"I believe that consistent luck is indistinguishable from genius."

Morlaix realised the Emperor had a point and said, "We make our own luck, Sir, to a large extent."

"We do, but we made it easier for him to become lucky." He pointed to the map. "We, the modern, efficient, enlightened government abandoned the fort, here", Bonaparte stabbed at the map with his finger at Palavas, "the fort which, as far as I can tell, the *Ancien Régime* built and manned continuously for hundreds of years. If the *ci-devants* could do it, then why couldn't we?"

Morlaix suspected that *ci-devants* had built the fort mostly to suppress the salt smuggling trade, rather than as a defence against the English, but he knew anything he said would sound like an excuse and kept silent.

"What are we to do, Breton? I sense the hand of Sidney Smith in this work."

Morlaix glanced at Badeau and slightly inclined his head.

"He laughs at me, Smith, but an Emperor cannot be laughed at."

"Sir", said Morlaix, "careful work is required. We must assess the risk for each stretch of coast, and strengthen defences accordingly. I do not know if the hand of Sidney Smith is behind this, I suspect not, this has all the aspects of a daring man – Snowden – acting independently and taking such chances as he comes across. I am sure that Snowden will not last long – he undoubtedly makes his own luck, but eventually his luck will run out, he'll make a mistake, or overreach, and we will have him."

"I did not appoint you, Breton, to do routine work strengthening defences and training men, and to wait for this Englishman's luck to run out. Do you know why I appointed you?"

"Please enlighten me, Sir," Morlaix replied, with a slight edge of sarcasm, more, probably, than Napoleon was used to.

"For your flair, Morlaix. You came close, very close to capturing the English king. You alone realised that the barges in Brittany were vulnerable, and warned me. I regret that I did not heed the warning. Have you thought about the English's next target?"

"Yes, Sir, I have thought of little else since I was appointed."

"And your conclusions?" asked the Emperor.

"France badly needs her canals. The economy has remarkably improved since they opened, and now that the English disrupt our coasting trade, they are vital. Snowden has twice attacked canal barges. He, and perhaps Smith, and possibly the Admiralty, may have realised that damaging the canals themselves would cause more harm to France, much more harm, than destroying any number of barges."

"Go on," said the Emperor.

"Before long, I believe, we can expect a determined attempt to damage the fabric of canals." He gestured to Badeau, who laid a map on the table. "We have identified some potential targets for English aggression, here ..."

Napoleon listened with great attention. "I think you may

be right, Breton. If Decrès agrees, I believe you should move your command down there, perhaps to Béziers. I leave it to you to choose the location, but south you should go."

# CHAPTER 29 - RENEGADO

The man who entered Isabella's salon with Rubert certainly had a thoroughly Arab appearance, dressed in an immaculate, beautifully made robe. He looked at Snowden and Isabella and then turned to Rubert and said in perfect English, "Who are these people, Senor Puyol?"

"This is the Condesa de Premià, and Commander Snowden of the Royal Navy, HMS *Oleander*."

The man nodded. "Pleased to make your acquaintance."

"And who are you, Sir?" asked Snowden.

"I am an emissary, from Salé."

"And do you have a name?"

The man looked at Snowden. "Yes, Sir, I do. I am Ahmed el-Inglizi."

"You have news of my husband?" asked Isabella, urgently.

"It is possible that I do, Condesa, but I was instructed to carry my message to the Governor."

El-Inglizi looked at Rubert. "I am not sure what the position of this man is. He is a Spaniard I think, and I would rather put my trust in you, Commander, an Englishman."

"You may trust me, Sir. Rubert is the boatswain of my ship, well, at least sometimes he is."

"An unusual boatswain, but we'll let that pass. As I said,

my instructions were to speak to the Governor, but the presence of the Condesa has perhaps made things more interesting."

"You have my husband?" asked Isabella. "And he is well?"

"We have your husband, and when I left Salé he was well."

"When did you leave?"

"On Monday, Condesa, three days ago."

"Can you prove that you have him?"

Ahmed el-Inglizi reached into his robe and drew out a piece of cloth with a button on it.

"I expect, Condesa, you will recognise this."

"I do, Senor, it is the cuff of my husband's dressing gown."

"I also have a note from him, but it is addressed to the Governor, and I do not believe I can deliver it to anyone except him."

"I suppose", said Snowden, "that you intend to ransom the Conde, but why did you come to us, rather than the Spanish?"

"My masters do intend to ask for a ... gratuity, Sir. As for the second part of your question, the Conde himself was insistent that we should approach the English first. I understand that he is in dispute with the government of Spain and does not wish to return there."

Snowden thought quickly. "If you will take a seat, Mr el-Inglizi, we would like to leave you alone for a moment while we discuss this amongst ourselves."

"Very well, but I must insist on an interview with the Governor directly."

Snowden joined Rubert and Isabella in the hall, speaking in low voices. There was another knock on the door to the street. Isabella opened it herself. Vilar stood there, his eyes widening when he saw the two men in the hall.

"Snowden, Puyol, good evening."

Snowden and Rubert nodded, and there followed a rapid exchange of Spanish or Catalan between Vilar, Isabella and Rubert.

Vilar, looking shocked, said, "I understand", and then, "What is your view on this, Puyol?"

"I think that there is double dealing. I am not sure how the Conde fell into the hands of these people. I cannot believe the Spanish would send him by sea at all, and especially in a vessel so small it could be taken by the corsairs. It is my view that the Spanish have given him to the Moors, but the Moors have realised he is valuable to the English and have double-crossed the Spanish."

Vilar nodded his assent.

"I agree", said Isabella, "I also cannot see why my husband would have been transported by sea, especially in a ship that could not fight off the corsairs. The Spanish government, or rather Cabral, has used this as a fiction. My husband is popular, and they probably feel they can't kill him. If they imprisoned him in Spain, there would always be a danger that he might escape or that he would be freed by his supporters. If he is a prisoner of the Moors, though, they can absolve themselves of all responsibility. The Moors have without doubt been paid well by Cabral, but now they have spoken to the Conde and have realised that the English want him, so much in fact that the Royal Navy was sent to take him to England."

"So, what can we do?" asked Snowden. "We must take him to the Governor."

"We must", said Isabella, "but before we do, we should have a plan. He is my husband, and I want him back, quickly."

Snowden thought, fleetingly, that the Condesa seemed to be able to enjoy herself very adequately in the absence of her husband, but he gallantly suppressed the idea. Instead he said,

"I have orders to take the Conde out of Spain, something I was unable to do previously. However, if I am now presented with the opportunity to complete the task, it is something I believe I should do."

"Speaking as your boatswain, Sir", said Rubert, "this is a perfectly sensible interpretation of your orders, and one that I am sure would meet with approval in high places."

"Thank you, boatswain, I will always be sure to consult you if any matters of high policy arise in future."

"Will you take *Oleander* to Salé, Percy? That would be for the best, I'm sure."

"I don't know if I will be allowed to, Condesa. I think I can make a good argument for going, but it may be taken out of my hands by Admiral Jameson."

"You have the funds, Percy!" said the Condesa forcefully.

Snowden, surprised, said "What do you mean?"

"She means, Sir", said Rubert, reflectively, "that Captain Wright gave you funds specifically to facilitate the Conde's escape. Paying a ransom from that fund would be easily justifiable, but payment from some other fund would be a protracted business. That is a powerful lever for you to control."

***

The hastily called meeting at government house did not last long. The Condesa was not in the room, but Snowden thought that the participants were acutely aware of her presence in the lobby. El-Inglizi was shown into the room and was gracefully received by the Governor.

"I understand your master is holding the Conde de Premià, Mr el-Inglizi."

"No, Sir, the Sultan of Morocco, Mawlay Sulayman bin Mohammed, is my master, and he would not engage in such activities. He would, however, like to see that this difficult situation is resolved."

He handed the letter to the Governor, who read it. It did not take him long, and when he had finished, he beckoned to Snowden who got up and went over to him. The Governor gave Snowden the letter.

"You know the Conde, Snowden. Skim through this quickly and tell me if you think it authentic."

Snowden read the brief note, signed by the Conde, which stated he was well treated and expressed the hope that the British government would intervene on his behalf.

"Authentic as far as I can tell, Sir. Should I take it into the lobby and show the Condesa? She is bound to be familiar with her husband's hand."

While they waited for Snowden to return, the Governor, obviously very curious about el-Inglizi, pressed him to reveal his origin.

"You are English, are you not, Mr el-Inglizi?"

"I am a Musselman, Governor."

"But you were born in England, went to school there?"

"Sir, I do not wish to be rude, but I am here only as a messenger, and my personal background is not germane to that task."

El-Inglizi folded his arms and remained silent.

Acting Governor Trigge was a successful veteran general, an imposing man, and was not used to being snubbed in that way. However, he was politician enough to give in gracefully, and he smiled and said, "Very well, Mr el-Inglizi, I apologise for any intrusion – curiosity only, you understand."

The renegado was nodding in acknowledgement as Snowden returned to the room.

"The Condesa confirms that the letter was written by her

husband, Sir."

"Thank you, Snowden. Mr el-Inglizi, would you be so good as to wait in the lobby while we discuss the matter amongst ourselves?"

The Governor waited until the renegado had left the room.

"Now, Snowden, I understand that His Majesty's government wishes to bring the Conde de Premià to England, and that you were previously ordered to", he searched for the right phrase, "facilitate the move."

"Yes, Sir."

"And you still have the funds that were allocated for that purpose?"

"Yes, Sir, I have the funds."

"And are you willing to take your ship to Salé and negotiate the release of the Conde? It seems to me our government considers that his presence in England is important, and that such a course of action would be within the remit of your original orders. That is, of course, if Admiral Jameson is in agreement."

"Yes, Sir, I would certainly be willing."

Snowden had the impression that the Governor felt that the less he had to do with spies, corsairs and Spanish ministers, the better. He was responsible for Gibraltar, with its immense strategic value. He had played a major part in its capture, and he was determined that after the instability of the preceding years, order and discipline would be imposed. It was to be a naval operation, and there were orders from Sidney Smith. It didn't concern the running of the Rock, or require any funds, so it was really nothing to do with him.

Admiral Jameson, uncharacteristically subdued, seemed likewise disinclined to interfere, saying, "Snowden here has orders to take possession, as it were, of the Conde. It seems that there is now an unexpected opportunity for him to carry out at least the spirit of these orders, so I am perfectly willing for him to detach *Oleander* temporarily from my command. Your ship is fully victualled, I believe, Snowden, and as time seems to be of the essence, I suggest you depart at your earliest convenience."

*Can't wait to get rid of me*, thought Snowden, but said, "Thank you, Sir. I believe we can leave almost immediately."

"I will have your orders sent down directly."

In the anteroom, Snowden went up to the Admiral who was in conversation with his aide.

"May I have a word, Sir?"

They moved to the side of the room and Snowden said, "Sir, it concerns what went on between us earlier. I would like to explain what I know of Commodore Parkinson's death. I wondered, Sir, if I might speak to you and your wife together."

Jameson looked surprised as Snowden continued, "Sir, I could show you and your wife the note Parkinson wrote to me. If your wife reads it, I think it may lessen her animosity towards me. I don't know if it will ease her distress, but at least if she knows the facts ..."

***

Snowden stood in the drawing room of the Admiral's residence. Jameson and his wife, Adelaide, sat at the table. Snowden looked at the woman.

"I am very sorry for the death of your brother, Madam. I have thought long and hard about it. Your husband, I am sure, knows how difficult command can be."

Jameson nodded. "Very hard, sometimes."

"Your brother, Madam, had a good record in the Navy, but off Corsica, he made a mistake, and did not have the courage to admit his error. He lost the confidence of his command, and hi commander, and he should have retired. In the Basque Roads his squadron, and indeed his own ship, was almost mutinous. One mistake, not admitted to."

Snowden paused and then continued, "It was not I that made the formal complaint against him, but he knew that I could be a key witness against him, and in the cabin of his ship he attempted to blackmail me. I was sarcastic and dismissed his attempt, and that night, well, you know what happened."

"In the morning, his clerk gave me this note." Snowden handed it to the woman:

*… I treated you very ill this evening. I did not know at the time that you had cut a frigate out of Lézardrieux, but even so I should not have spoken as I did. To be known as a coward, to be in command of a squadron in which every man holds me in contempt, is more than I can bear …*

She drew a deep breath and sobbed

# CHAPTER 30 - ISABELLA

From the first time she had seen him, in the house at Girona, Isabella had been attracted to Snowden. She could not deny that, but she could also not deny her affair with him had been influenced by a colder calculation.

Her husband was very much older than her. He was a learned, kind man who she admired, a man of affairs, important. She came from a political family, was deeply interested in politics and her views broadly aligned with those of her husband. It was not that she deliberately set out to influence him, but they discussed matters of state almost incessantly, and the Conde often came round to her view. She admitted to herself that she enjoyed the power she wielded through him.

She had no doubt that her husband loved her dearly, and she loved him in return – after all, he was the father of her child – but it was not a passionate love, such as she might feel for a younger man.

During the rescue, she realised there was much to admire in Snowden. He was clever, brave and resourceful, although she was disquieted by the way that violence took him over when he was confronted by an enemy. She had not minded nursing him on *Oleander*, not at all. His men clearly admired him greatly, as did the whole of Gibraltar society, even, she thought, the ones that envied him.

In Gibraltar, with her child, she felt alone and insecure,

her power gone, one mishap away from destitution. Her husband had certainly been arrested by the hideous Cabral and might well be dead. She would have to go to England, where her existence would still be precarious, and there would be endless intrigues by Spanish expatriates. Snowden was English, he was heir to an estate and the possessor of some wealth, and he was clearly able and willing to be her protector. She did not have to try very hard to subdue her conscience.

And now, she knew her husband was alive and Snowden was to be the agent of his release. She felt the irony of the situation deeply. If the Count was rescued, she believed she had no choice, at the earliest opportunity, to tell him what she had done and why she had done it. He would undoubtedly feel let down, by Snowden as well as herself, but he was a man of the world and she thought he would understand.

She hoped, very much hoped, that Snowden was successful.

# CHAPTER 31 - THE STRAIT

Dawn revealed an unpleasant scene. The sky was dark and the visibility poor, with occasional heavy showers, and the African coast, a few miles away, was not visible. The wind blew, hard, from the west.

"Well, Ken", said Snowden, "it doesn't look very good, does it?"

It was difficult, probably impossible, to get a ship through the Strait and into the Atlantic with a westerly wind, the Poniente, blowing. The Navy never tried, but the Poniente could blow for days.

"Probably couldn't even get her off the berth", he continued gloomily, "wind's blowing us right on, but it's vital we get away quickly."

"I hear what you say, Percy, but we've been talking about this."

"Who has been talking?"

"Me, Rubert, Pascoe and Ahmed."

"Ah", said Snowden, "Ahmed is an *Oleander* now, is he?"

"No, not exactly. He's an engineer, Percy, was in the British Army, he's been in Morocco for about fifteen years I think. He helps build castles and that sort of thing for them – well, for the King it seems. Anyway, we were talking, and Rubert was saying, he's from these parts you know, that he thought that *Olly* could get through the Strait against the westerly if we got the tides right and tucked ourselves into the African coast. Ahmed piped up and said that one or two of the Salé ships had done it, and he would help plot the course if we wanted him to. He's pretty keen to get home."

Snowden's gloom lifted slightly.

"Very well, Ken, bring them in."

Pascoe laid the chart on the table, and Snowden could see that a tracery of lines, points and circles had been marked on it.

"Explain yourself, Pascoe, if you please."

"Very well, Sir. Usually, ships don't try getting out of the Med when the, Poniente is blowing, against both the wind and the current flowing into the Med. *Oleander* is a different type of ship, though, the best in the Navy to windward. And, Sir, if we're careful and have a bit of luck, we can get a boost from the tidal stream – it's just coming up to springs. We'll have to keep close to the African shore, but there's a favourable current in there for a few hours, and there's a good chance we can get through."

"That sounds interesting. Go on."

"Well, Sir, we get the ship over to the African coast, just west of Ceuta, here …"

"We have to get her off the berth, first!"

"Yes, Sir, but if we get her over there, a couple of hours before high water …"

***

With the aid of the dockyard, they pulled the ship off the berth in the teeth of the wind and headed south towards the African coast. Gibraltar disappeared in a rain shower after about fifteen minutes and did not reappear. The weather was nasty, a strong westerly wind, and the seas large, their breaking crests occasionally striking the ship and sending spray and sometimes solid water over her deck.

Pascoe and Kennedy moved anxiously between the log and the charts on the cabin table.

Luciani stood near the helm, outwardly calm but ready to bring the ship about at the first sign of trouble.

"Any minute now," said Pascoe, returning from inspecting the log to look anxiously ahead and then up to the foremast, where two lookouts were perched on the crosstrees.

"Deck there", came the call, "land on the port bow, one point, high cliffs."

"There it is", said Luciani, pointing, "Ceuta without doubt."

Pascoe, crouched over the binnacle, noted the bearing of the forbidding looking headland and went into the cabin.

When he came out Kennedy said, "I suppose, Mr Pascoe, that we're *just about where you thought we would be*."

Pascoe started to agree. "Yes, just a …", but looked round, saw the laughter on the faces of the men round him, and grinned.

"I recommend, Sir, that we put her on the wind, and go about when we're close under the cliffs." He looked at his slate. "Tide should be with us in an hour."

For the next six hours, *Oleander* was worked as she had never been worked before. In the gale, under heavily reefed mainsail, foresail and staysails, she fought her way to windward, heeling, moving fast, the noise of the sea and the wind like a living thing. She crashed into the waves, dipping her bowsprit, pounding so that they feared she would start her seams. Spray flew, driven by the wind, stinging the eyes and faces of the men on deck. In the tide races, and there were races off every headland, breaking waves swept the deck from bow to stern, forcing such crew members who were caught, exposed, to leap for the lifelines that had been rigged. She was steered, in alternating one-hour tricks, by Kennedy and Luciani, generally acknowledged to be the best helmsmen in the ship, with the assistance of two seamen. They stood at the wheel, their eyes, reddened with salt spray, moving between the luff of the mainsail and the pattern of the waves.

Snowden and Pascoe navigated, Pascoe continuously taking bearings, horizontal and vertical sextant angles, and log readings. They tacked inshore, until either Snowden could bear to go no closer to the surf-fringed cliffs of the African coast or Pascoe shouted "Tack her now, Sir". Occasionally, el-Inglizi would point out a cape or landmark, and once shouted a warning that the headland they were aiming for had an offlying reef.

And tack her they did, perhaps fifteen times in six hours, never more than a league from the coast, seeking the favourable inshore tidal stream. On each occasion she went round beautifully, Kennedy or Luciani running her off slightly to gain speed, and then, judging the moment to perfection, putting the helm down so that she rounded up into the wind. She never missed stays, which was just as well given the proximity of the land, once or twice hanging momentarily in irons, but always, infallibly, falling off on the other tack, heeling hard until she got going.

By six o'clock, Tangier was in sight on the port bow, and they held the port tack a little longer than usual, out into the grey Atlantic, until Pascoe said to Snowden, "We'll fetch Spartel now, Sir," and they went about, passing the blurred outline of the Cape, the north-west corner of Africa as it was getting dark.

The wind gradually became favourable until it was a light north-westerly. The galley stove was relit, and the men fed.

# CHAPTER 32 - THE ENGLISH ENGINEER

Snowden had invited Ahmed el-Inglizi to dine with him, and now they were sitting opposite each other in *Oleander*'s cabin.

As Cox the steward placed food before them, el-Inglizi said, "I congratulate you on your ship and crew, Snowden."

"Thank you."

"To go like that through the Strait, against the west wind, some of our corsairs have done it, but I've never heard of a Western ship doing it before."

"No, she's a unique ship, built in Bermuda from cedar, very strong and light," said Snowden thoughtfully. "Apparently you're an engineer, el-Inglizi. You might like to see this … excuse me for a moment." He stood and opened a drawer, and carried a notebook back to the table.

"See this", he handed the book across the table, "I think it will appeal to you. We spent several weeks sailing the ship on trials and noting her speed, leeway and so on for every wind speed and direction. We didn't need to guess anything, we had instruments to measure the force of the wind, the speed of the ship and the angle she was heeling at. The result is that little book you have. We know exactly how to sail the ship because it's written down in those tables. We also sailed her against other ships of the Navy and she beat all of them, except for when we were sailing directly well off the wind, when the larger ships had an advantage."

El-Inglizi looked at the book with considerable respect. "That is tremendous work, Snowden, I am very impressed. And your crew is excellent. I was especially impressed by that young man, Pascoe. He clearly has an excellent grasp of mathematics. He navigated the ship with considerable precision. I do not wish to be rude, but I think he may be wasted in the Navy."

Snowden smiled. "Perhaps he is. I think he would like to be off to University, if he could, and I think now he will have sufficient money to do it."

"Indeed, Snowden, I have heard that you have been extraordinarily lucky in the matter of prize money. Well, I suppose you have made your own luck."

"We have been very lucky, very lucky indeed. Do you consider yourself to be a lucky man?"

"Reasonably so, Snowden. I can see that you are curious, so I will tell you something of my background. It is probably better to build some trust between us before we arrive in Salé."

He folded his hands under his chin and thought for a moment.

"I come, as no doubt you have realised, from England, from Hampshire in fact. My father was a merchant in Southampton, a reasonably well-to-do man. I joined the Army, the 67th Regiment of Foot. I had a bent for engineering, and had a reasonable career, but I didn't really feel I was suited to the Army. I went home on leave, and when I walked down to the docks with my father, I saw there was a strange ship alongside, lateen rigged. My father explained that the wars against the French meant he could no longer export tea to Europe, and he was trying to find alternative markets. The ship was a Moorish trader which was loading what they call 'gunpowder tea' for the Moroccan market."

"To cut a long story short, I became friendly with the master of the Moorish ship, my father asked me to go with them as supercargo, and I resigned my commission. I went to China twice on English ships – we traded directly with Morocco by then, and I found my engineering skills were valued by the Moroccans. I have been working on the fortifications of Salé and other projects there for many years. I have become a Musselman and have a family there."

"The Sally Rovers are not so active as they used to be, very much reduced. I'm sure you know that in their heyday they ranged far and wide, slaving, and during the English Civil War even took Lundy and used it as their base for several years. Brother Oliver put an end to that when he had a moment, but they were much feared. And now, as I said, they are much reduced."

"We had a run-in, not so long ago, with some corsairs. Pretty small ships."

"They attacked *Oleander*? A British ship?"

"They did, I think they believed we were American. It was a pretty amateurish affair, really."

"They can't have been from Salé, or I'd have heard about it. Or indeed from anywhere in Morocco – there's been a treaty with the United States of America for several years. I suppose it ended badly for them."

"It was very one sided, yes. I was completely at a loss to understand why they didn't haul off when we fought back. I put a shot across their bows and did everything I could to discourage them, but they took no heed."

"I've lived there for a long time, and often I feel I don't understand them myself!"

"And there was the matter of *Rosa*, our Spanish tartan. Pascoe took her independently to Gibraltar and he was attacked by a pirate. Rubert the boatswain, who has some experience in these matters, was in the boat, and he thought the pirate was from Salé."

"Ah, Senor Puyol, who knows so much more than most boatswains."

Snowden remembered Rubert's suspicion about the Conde's abduction. "Pascoe said that the pirate made off towards Spain. Was that …?"

"I cannot say, Snowden, and perhaps if I did, I would not. You must remember there is a complex relationship between Spain and Salé. There are many there who still consider themselves to be Moriscos, and there are Jews who speak a sort of Spanish among themselves. We even have an Andalusian Wall. However, at present, officially, our relationship with Spain is not good. The Sultan has decreed that there will be no trade at all with Europe, but this does not mean there are not still personal relationships."

Snowden was now all but certain that the Conde's kidnapping had not been a random event, and that *Rosa*, which was a Spanish lateener, had been attacked because the corsairs thought she was the boat carrying the Conde. In order to be credibly portrayed as a kidnapping, some fighting had to take place, but the corsairs had not expected serious return fire. He decided he would discuss it with Rubert later.

"And now the Conde is in Salé. Is this a result of official policy?"

"No, Snowden", said el-Inglizi, "my master Sulayman bin Mohammed is a careful statesman and he would not countenance any involvement in something like this which could affect our international relations. He has all but stamped out the corsairs in Salé. The affair has come to his notice, and that is where you come in, with your English money."

The rest of the meal passed in the discussion of uncontentious issues. El-Inglizi was very much interested in hearing of the progress England was making, and comparing it with what he saw as the stagnation of his adopted country.

"The Arabs used to be the repository of learning. The mathematics and science that were developed were ahead of anything in the world. Even a hundred years ago, ships from Salé travelled to the New World. Then everything slipped away. I am not sure of the reason, but Europe, and especially England, have embraced science and progress with much more enthusiasm than the Moors."

# CHAPTER 33 - SALÉ

Cape Spartel fell astern, and the wind steadied into a light breeze blowing from the north. *Oleander* made her way slowly down the African coast, very green to start with, but drying out as they went further south.

The noon sight on the following day placed them on the latitude of Salé, and they sailed east until they saw, on the horizon, the Kasbah of the Udayas, the huge citadel guarding the entrance to the estuary of the Bouregreg River, which flowed through Salé. They turned the ship and headed out to sea, spending the night tacking backwards and forwards out of sight of the land. Snowden turned in immediately after dinner and slept soundly, only woken by the sounds of the ship coming to quarters as the dawn broke.

When he went on deck, the land was close, the kasbah, with its reddish walls fringed at the bottom by white surf, and further inland he could make out the high square Hassan Tower. Kennedy and Pascoe approached him.

"El-Inglizi says it is best to cross the bar a couple of hours before high water," said Pascoe.

Snowden knew that this made sense. The entrance to the river faced west, open to the Atlantic swell that was an unceasing feature of the Atlantic coast of Morocco. The entrance was shallow, and the swell might break there, especially if the tidal stream was flowing out of the river. Two hours before high water would give almost maximum depth and a flooding tidal stream running into the entrance.

"High water is at eleven, Sir, so we should be off the bar at nine."

"Is there enough water for *Oleander*?"

"I don't think there is", Kennedy said, "according to el-Inglizi, not reliably, anyway, and it'll be going off springs tomorrow, so there's the matter of getting back out again. We don't want to get neaped somewhere like that."

If *Oleander* scraped over the bar at high tide at the top of springs, she would not have the opportunity to depart until the next spring tide in two weeks, and even that delayed departure would be dependent on favourable conditions – no onshore wind and no heavy swell breaking at the entrance.

*Oleander* approached the river entrance, with a huge white flag flying at her maintop. *Rosa* and the longboat were towing behind.

"Twenty fathom," called out the seaman supervising the sounding machine.

"Fire the salute and then bring her to and anchor, if you please, Mr Kennedy."

When the ship was anchored, rolling quite heavily in the swell which, despite the considerable depth, was piling up in rather steep waves, Snowden and Pascoe climbed the mainmast to inspect the entrance.

"Certainly better over there", said Snowden, pointing, "on the kasbah side."

"Yes, Sir, I agree. Not the sort of place you'd want to try if there was much swell."

"It appears to be quite manageable now," said Snowden, and climbed down to the deck.

He walked over to el-Inglizi. "I presume we should now await their response."

"We should. They will respond to your flag from that

platform there, on the kasbah, the semaphore."

A minute or so later, a gun was fired from the rampart of the kasbah and a white flag unfurled from the pole on the semaphore.

"Seems they've noticed us."

"They have", said el-Inglizi, "they will send a boat."

A boat appeared, smartly turned out, rowed by men in colourful uniforms.

"They are taking this seriously", el-Inglizi said, "that is the sultan's barge. The governor is in it."

The boat tried to come alongside *Oleander*, but was defeated by the swell and the rolling of the ship.

Snowden handed the speaking trumpet to el-Inglizi. "Tell them the ship is too deep for the bar and we will take our boat into the port."

El-Inglizi shouted in Arabic through the speaking trumpet. Discussions took place on the barge and there was a further conversation between el-Inglizi and the people on the barge, which turned round and went back into the port entrance.

"The governor is seasick," said el-Inglizi, with a smile.

"I'm not surprised", said Snowden, "this place is lumpy enough to upset the most hardened sailor."

***

"We must be very careful with these people, Percy," said Kennedy, as they sat in the cabin. "I know we're here at their invitation, but it would be very easy for things to go wrong. We can't take the ship in, so you'll be very vulnerable when you're ashore."

"I intend to take Pascoe with me."

"That will be some help. What about taking Watton as well?"

"I think that's an excellent suggestion. I was thinking the boat that takes me in could stay while I was ashore, perhaps anchored in the river rather than alongside."

Kennedy said thoughtfully, "Yes, we'll get the swivels mounted, and perhaps we could put a small party of marines in the boat as well as the seamen. Riley could go. We can fight the ship adequately without him. Do you expect to be away for more than a day?"

"It's difficult to say, but I think it's highly likely that the process of extracting the Conde will be quite protracted."

"We have two sizeable boats, the longboat and *Rosa*. If we send you in *Rosa*, she could wait until the next daylight high water, and the longboat could relieve her."

"We can put Puyol in charge of one boat and Luciani in charge of the other. They are both pretty resourceful. Let's get Pascoe and Watton in – there's a few things to discuss with them."

In the cabin, Snowden addressed Pascoe and Watton. After outlining the plan he and Kennedy had decided on, Snowden said, "We may be ashore for several days. It is very important that we do nothing to upset our hosts or the local population. I expect no trouble, but we will be as well armed as we can be – dirks as well as swords, and a pair of pistols each, and we will have some coin sewn into our coats."

\*\*\*

"Well, Ken", said Snowden, as they stood on *Oleander*'s deck waiting to board *Rosa* for the trip ashore, "you have the ship. As we discussed, keep her just off – I suggest you get out to sea a bit or she'll roll herself to death – and keep her hove to or sailing slowly. Make sure you can see the flags on the kasbah at all times."

"Yes, Sir."

"And, I don't think it will happen, but be ready for any

attempt to board!"

"We'll be ready."

Snowden, Pascoe and Watton boarded *Rosa* with el-Inglizi, and the boat was soon heading towards the entrance, the men pulling hard at the oars. *Rosa* was flying her large ensign, with an equally large white flag below it.

Rubert Puyol stood at the tiller, alternately looking forwards at the entrance and astern at the waves behind, alert for any breakers.

"Looks fine to me, Sir, no surf across the bar," he said to Snowden.

Before long, the boat was over the bar, the sandy bottom clearly visible beneath them, and was running alongside the pink wall of the kasbah, which was, Snowden thought, rather grim looking, despite the bright sunlight. The wall seemed to merge seamlessly with the living rock of the low headland upon which it was built. He could see men on the ramparts looking down, long guns on their backs.

El-Inglizi, who was sitting opposite Snowden, pointed to a round tower with gun ports, high above the water. "Do you admire my tower, Snowden?" he smiled, "I think it is one of my better efforts – I could sit and admire it all day. Took five years from the time I started the design until it was finished."

Suddenly, they were in the river itself, and simultaneously the town. The Atlantic had given way, in a few yards, to a sheltered waterway running through a busy city. Boats, crowded with passengers and rowed by men standing over their oars, crossed the river, and small fishing boats were moored in the stream. Boys, shouting to each other, dived into the river from the bank. The place had a general air of activity and bustle.

El-Inglizi pointed to a group of men waiting on a quay on the left bank of the river.

"Our welcoming committee," he said, and Luciani ported the helm and steered *Rosa* towards them. Behind the group, moored to the quay, were several lateen rigged ships, not large, probably about sixty feet long. Snowden looked at them appraisingly – *xebecs, useful looking*, he thought. He was jolted from his reverie by an animated conversation between Pascoe and Puyol.

"That's the one, bose, I'm sure of it," said Pascoe.

Puyol nodded. "It certainly looks like her, definitely a corsair ..."

"What are you talking about?" asked Snowden.

"That xebec there, Sir", responded Pascoe, "that was the one that was after us."

Snowden looked at it again. "You fought that thing off? With *Rosa*? You did very well."

Puyol said, thoughtfully, "Perhaps they were not trying very hard."

"Perhaps they were not," agreed Pascoe.

The high spring tide meant the boat was almost level with the quay, and the bowman stepped ashore without difficulty and helped el-Inglizi, followed by Snowden and Pascoe, onto the quay.

As they walked towards the group of waiting officials, Snowden looked behind to see *Rosa* pushing off from the quay. He knew Puyol would anchor her on the other side of the river, to await orders until relieved the next morning by the longboat.

El-Inglizi made introductions. There were four men and a small guard of soldiers, some mounted on horses, with long lances held vertically. As each man was introduced by el-Inglizi, the English officers saluted. Snowden made no attempt to remember the names, he knew he would forget immediately and that if anybody could remember them, Pascoe could, so he concentrated on trying to size them up, as he would with gambling opponents.

The most important man in the group was the Governor, the man who had been in the boat, a short, well-fed man with an intelligent face. Another man, tall, brown and lean, with a formidable curved dagger in his belt, was introduced as the owner ("Also the reis, the captain," murmured el-Inglizi) of the ship that had captured the Conde. The man fitted Snowden's mental picture of what a corsair captain should look like so well that he could hardly look away from him.

When the introductions were complete, they boarded small carriages and were taken a short distance uphill towards the kasbah. They went through an enormous gate, distinctly Islamic in design, set in a huge rose-coloured wall which opened, to Snowden's astonishment, onto a beautiful, shaded garden, with running streams and gardeners working patiently.

They walked through the garden, up some steps and into a house, where they were shown into a room, decorated in a way that was entirely new to Snowden, painted in blue and white, with perfectly proportioned arches and intricately patterned tiles. A low table, surrounded by cushions, was set with ornate silver tableware and glasses.

They sat on the cushions and tea was served, sweet and flavoured with mint. The corsair spoke, and el-Inglizi translated for Snowden.

"He says he has seen your boat before, the small one that entered the port."

"I believe he has. I was not in her, but Mr Pascoe here was."

"He says he did not intend to spill blood."

Snowden answered, "I am sorry that blood was spilt, but Mr Pascoe was acting in accordance with his duty."

The corsair spoke to el-Inglizi who translated. "What muskets were you firing at us?"

Pascoe answered immediately, "Not muskets, rifles – Baker rifles, very fine weapons."

"I have not heard of these weapons."

The meeting concluded, without any discussions of substance.

"You will stay at my house," said el-Inglizi.

"Can we see the Conde? Where is he being held?" asked Snowden

"At my house", el-Inglizi replied, with a smile, adding, "please accompany me. It is only a short walk."

Accompanied only by el-Inglizi, they strolled through the gardens and into the medina, a warren of narrow streets, shaded and cool, but busy with markets and shops where craftsmen could be seen working. They went through an unassuming doorway, which led into a garden surrounded by a low balconied house.

"My house," said el-Inglizi. "It is a traditional design, a riad, though I built this one myself. Would you like to meet the prisoner?" He pointed. "He is just over there."

Snowden saw the Conde in a sunny corner, stretched out on a chair with his feet up on a cushion and his hat tipped over his eyes. They walked over to him, el-Inglizi coughed politely and the Conde woke, looking in confusion at Snowden and Pascoe. He struggled to rise, straightening his clothing as he did so, recognition dawning in his eyes.

"Commander", he paused and thought, "Commander Snowden."

"Yes, Your Excellency, and this is Midshipman Pascoe, and Ensign Watton. My ship is at anchor off the port."

"You escaped, then? Is there any news …?"

"I did, Sir, and you will pleased to know that your wife and daughter are safe in Gibraltar."

"Thank God for that," said the Conde, and Snowden felt a slight pang of guilt.

"And Vilar? Puyol?"

"Both safe. Vilar is in Gibraltar, and Puyol is not a mile from here, in one of the ship's boats!"

Snowden looked at el-Inglizi. "Is there somewhere I can talk to the Conde privately?"

# CHAPTER 34 - BÉZIERS

In his headquarters in Béziers, Morlaix was kept busy with the usual minutia of command, including a flood of correspondence, reports, requests and complaints generated, in large part, by his recent inspections of coastal defences. He dictated orders to his secretary, studied maps and charts with his aides, and pored over the designs of the small boats they were building.

At about six o'clock he threw his pen down rather violently and said in an irritated voice

"Our great leader once said to me that '*if an order can be misinterpreted, it will be*', but I don't see how even Lebas could have confused what I wanted to that extreme!"

Badeau, imperturbably, looked up but continued to write.

"I've had just about enough of this. I am going home."

"Do you want me to call your chair, Sir?"

"No", said Morlaix, shortly, "thank you, I'll hop."

It was only a few yards to the house Morlaix had rented, but when he arrived, his leg was quite painful.

"Come into the garden", said Odile, as she met him at the door, "we can have some lemonade."

In the garden, Morlaix started to recover his equilibrium.

"It seems that I do nothing but canals. First Brittany and

now this. I am supposed to be a naval officer!"

"I know", said Odile, allowing her revolutionary fever to shine through momentarily, "but we must be prepared to defend France wherever she is threatened. And you cannot go to sea", she saw the displeasure on his face and added, "yet."

"The canals are vulnerable from Narbonne almost to the Rhone. That's nearly a hundred miles of shoreline. The English are dominant at sea, so we can't patrol in the normal way. The only thing we can do is try to anticipate where they might strike, and be ready for them."

"I know, but ..."

"And I am not even sure, not half sure, that the English will try to hit the canals. They are very busy blockading, keeping us bottled up in port, perhaps they have no interest in anything else. I could be entirely wasting my time and, I might add, considerable resources."

"That is true, but they've had great success, at little cost, so they will be very tempted to try again. You may be wasting your time, but to try to intercept them is entirely rational, and we are supposed to be a society based on rationality."

Morlaix smiled. "Perhaps you are right."

# CHAPTER 35 - SEALED AND DELIVERED

Snowden and the Conde sat around a small table in a room just off the courtyard, speaking in Spanish.

"Are you well treated, Conde?" asked Snowden.

"Yes, thank you. These Moors have more humanity than we commonly give them credit for, and I cannot complain of the hospitality of Ahmed el-Inglizi." He gestured to the courtyard. "So, Commodore, you have come to rescue me, again. I regret, in hindsight, that I did not accept your offer more quickly last time."

"That's in the past", said Snowden, "I am glad to see you well. My ship is in the offing, and I have orders to take you to Gibraltar."

"There is the small matter of payment."

"We have not addressed that point yet with your hosts, but I have some funds which I can use for that purpose"

"I have no doubt my capture was a ruse by Cabral to get rid of me. The Spanish will never ransom me, they would rather I died quietly."

"We know that, Excellency."

"Until a few weeks ago, I had no knowledge of Moroccan politics, and though my understanding is still rather shallow, I will outline what I believe the situation to be."

Snowden nodded. "Please continue."

"I have heard before that Cabral has links with the Moors, and I believe there was an agreement between Cabral and Idrissi, that corsair reis, to capture me."

*That was the corsair's name*, thought Snowden, *Idrissi*.

"I think Idrissi made a mistake by conspiring with Cabral. As you know, the Sultan's relationship with Spain and the rest of Europe is not good, and there is supposed to be no trade. It is seriously embarrassing for one of his subjects to hold a prominent Spaniard prisoner. Additionally, the Sultan is not well disposed towards the corsairs, precisely because of incidents like this."

"Can he not just order your release?" asked Snowden.

"No, as I understand it, he cannot as the corsairs are popular here. Instead he sent his most trusted adviser, el-Inglizi, to Gibraltar, and now Idrissi must negotiate a settlement with you, with the Governor and el-Inglizi overseeing negotiations."

Snowden felt, as a gambling man, that he had been dealt a very strong hand.

***

Four miles away, in the darkness, *Oleander*, hove to on the starboard tack, forereached gently in the light north-westerly breeze. From his position on the starboard rail, Kennedy watched the lights of the city visible astern, and lanterns from a few boats fishing nearby.

"Not much company," he said to Luciani, who had the watch.

"No, Sir, the boarding nets were perhaps a precaution we did not need."

"Perhaps they were, but this is or was a notorious pirate port," said Kennedy.

"What do you think the chances of the Skipper getting

the Conde back are?" asked Luciani.

"Pretty good, I think," Kennedy said thoughtfully. "He's got a good hand, and if anyone knows how to play a good hand, it's the Old Man. He seems to achieve more or less whatever he sets his mind to."

"Shall I put her about? We could creep in and be just about off the bar by first light."

"Yes, Luciani, put her about."

\*\*\*

El-Inglizi's house was comfortable, almost to the point of luxury, and the English officers spent a restful night.

They enjoyed a lavish breakfast, with a dazzling array of fruits, bread and honey, washed down with orange juice and sweet tea, with el-Inglizi relating stories of his engineering efforts in Morocco.

"So, you have no intention of returning to England, Mr el-Inglizi?" asked Pascoe.

"I don't think so. I am very well settled here, as you can see. Even if the work from the government dried up, I have enough put by to keep me in clover for life. And the weather. It is a different story inland, where it gets very hot, but here, it is just about perfect, cooled by the ocean. I don't think I could stand a return to the English winter."

"And the religion?"

"I have never been a very devout man, and one religion suits me as well as another. It's all the same God apparently. Even though the Sultan is in favour of a rather puritanical form of Islam, the majority of the people here are very much more relaxed. When you are ready, gentlemen, we will make our way towards the kasbah."

Accompanied by el-Inglizi they walked back through the medina, already bustling and noisy with its inhabitants working and shopping. People stared at the British officers, but there seemed to be no hostility. They went through the huge gate, walked across the garden and into the house, and were soon seated on cushions round the low table.

After the formalities were complete, Snowden came to the point.

"His Majesty's government wishes to offer the Conde de Premià refuge in England. If this can be facilitated, I am sure some financial settlement would be bestowed on the man who rescued him from the Spanish." He inclined his head towards the corsair.

El-Inglizi translated this for the corsair reis, who laughed loudly and slapped his hand on the table. He spoke to el-Inglizi who translated.

"I am glad the English government values the Conde so highly that it has sent a warship to take him to safety – a warship commanded by the famous Snowden, a man who seems to be very young to have accomplished all that is said of him."

El-Inglizi interjected, "I hope you don't mind, Snowden, I gave him a condensed version of your service history."

Snowden, who had no objection at all to praise, said, "Not at all, el-Inglizi. Tell him we start young in our Navy, and work quickly."

This brought a further smile from the corsair, who spoke at length to the renegado.

"The gist of this is", said el-Inglizi, "the reis feels that the Conde is worth a good deal. In order to give him to you, he would have to break his agreement with the Spanish. He will have to claim he was acting under duress from the government here."

El-Inglizi added, "Which as it happens is true."

There was a further exchange between el-Inglizi and the corsair, with the Governor interjecting occasionally.

"He says now that if he crosses the Spanish, his trade will dry up and he will have to lay his ship up and pay off the crew. He says that will be expensive."

"Can he tell me how expensive it will be?"

El-Inglizi asked the corsair. "He says he would like some time to consider. He suggests a break in the meeting."

"Very well," said Snowden.

"Would you like to come and see my tower?" asked el-Inglizi.

They walked out of the house and up a hill, through the kasbah.

"The Kasbah of the Udayas", announced el-Inglizi, "an ancient fortification. Salé, as you probably know, really started when Moriscos arrived from Spain. There were several influxes, and for a while there was a republic, with the rovers venturing far and wide."

They walked through narrow streets, past a great mosque and onto the ramparts overlooking the harbour entrance. With a start, they saw *Oleander* half a mile or so offshore, in the act of manning the longboat.

"She looks glorious," said Pascoe, enthusiastically, and indeed she did, her sails white, her hull gleaming, and the huge ensign, with the white flag underneath it, flying from her main gaff.

"Doesn't she just," echoed Watton, and as he spoke, the longboat started to move towards the harbour entrance.

"Going to relieve *Rosa*," said Pascoe, and the Englishmen stood transfixed as the longboat, her rowers resplendent in their uniforms, pulled smartly into the river entrance, crossing the bar without incident.

The ship fired a gun and signal flags broke out on her mainmast.

El-Inglizi interrupted, "Gentlemen, my tower ...," indicating the way.

***

As the longboat got away, an easier process now that the ship was hove to, rather than anchored, there was a shout from the masthead, "Deck there, those figures on the ramparts."

Kennedy looked towards the kasbah and saw four figures watching the ship, three dressed in European clothes, one red and two blue.

"It be the Old Man and Mr Pascoe and Mr Watton," shouted Iris from the crosstrees.

Kennedy ran over to the flag locker, looked at the signal book and pulled flags from their pigeonholes.

"Run these up," he said to the sailor.

***

"Wait just a minute," said Snowden to el-Inglizi, and turned back to the ship.

'ALL WELL HERE'

translated Pascoe, who seemed to have memorised the signal book.

"Let's give them a wave," said Snowden, and the three officers took off their hats and waved them vigorously above their heads.

When they returned, after the inspection of el Inglizi's tower, they could hear heated discussions taking place in an adjoining room, and el-Inglizi excused himself and went through the connecting door. After a few minutes the discussions ceased and the Moroccans re-entered the main room and sat on the cushions at the table.

"Well, gentlemen", said Snowden for el-Inglizi to translate, "name your price."

The negotiations were not protracted. Both sides wanted the matter brought to a swift conclusion, and both sides knew that the British, that is Snowden, could not return without the Conde and that, for political reasons, the Moors could not keep him. The corsair, however, seemed remarkably resistant to pressure from the Governor and, though he had already been paid by the Spanish, held out for what Snowden thought was an excessive sum, justified, so he said, because he would have to lay his ship up for the foreseeable future.

The arguments went back and forth, without much convergence, until Pascoe spoke into Snowden's ear, "I have an idea, Sir. Could we speak privately?"

They stood and moved over to the corner of the room, well away from the table. Pascoe spoke softly, "Sir, this may be stupid, but if he has no use for his ship, why don't we buy it from him, include it in the ransom payment. She'd be very handy for work in the Med, and I could take her back to Gib, Sir, if you wanted me to."

Snowden thought *another independent command, Pascoe, you're getting a taste for it,* and then said, smiling, "That's an excellent idea, Pascoe. We came here to buy a Spanish Count, but perhaps we can buy a Moorish ship and get a Conde thrown in."

"Remember, Sir, if you're buying a ship, it's always 'subject to survey', and we haven't had a good look at her."

The proposed purchase of the ship was received with initial surprise by the Moors, but this was followed rapidly by smiles, and a meeting on the following day was arranged. Food was brought in and the meeting broke up.

The Englishmen, in the company of el-Inglizi, returned to his house through the medina. Snowden walked beside the renegade while the two young men walked behind. When Pascoe and Watton stopped at the shop of a leather worker, Snowden said to el-Inglizi, "It seems to me you have a difficult role here, Mr el-Inglizi. You are advising the Governor and the reis and at the same time speaking to me. On both sides of the negotiation, so to speak, and that is not to mention acting as jailer."

"That is true, Snowden, but things here are less clear cut than perhaps they are in England. All parties wish a successful outcome, and I believe it is in everybody's interest if I facilitate the negotiations, even if it could be said that I have apparently some conflict of interest."

"And, at the risk of increasing your conflict, could you tell me what you believe the state of negotiations currently is?"

"I believe we are well on our way, but, to quote an English proverb, 'there's many a slip twixt cup and lip'."

Snowden relayed the news to the Conde, who was grateful, but almost beside himself with anxiety.

"Thank you, Snowden, from the bottom of my heart," he said.

"I think it is Mr Pascoe you should particularly thank, Excellency," replied Snowden. "He has come up with a particularly clever stratagem."

"When do you think the negotiations will be complete?" asked the Conde.

Snowden looked questioningly at el-Inglizi.

"It will be soon, Conde, I think probably two days. There are some bureaucratic details to be taken care of. Mr Pascoe's strategy has made things much easier – the only document required will be for the sale of the ship – and of course Mr Snowden will have to produce the money. I suppose it is on *Oleander*?"

"Yes, the money is on *Oleander*. Mr Pascoe will return to the ship to fetch the funds when the documents are agreed," replied Snowden.

"I am sorry", the Conde said, "to be a drain on the

exchequer of England."

Snowden looked at Pascoe, who was trying to suppress a grin, and an equally amused el-Inglizi said to the Conde, "I think that after Commander Snowden's recent activity, the English exchequer is presently in funds."

\*\*\*

The atmosphere was relaxed as the three Englishmen walked to the quayside in the company of el-Inglizi, with the intention of looking over the Royal Navy's proposed acquisition.

"I have not much experience of the value of ships, Snowden, but I believe she is fairly new," said the renegado. "Ah, here is Idrissi."

At the edge of the quay, Snowden signalled *Oleander*'s longboat to come alongside. When it did, Luciani leapt ashore.

"Capitaine, it is good to see you." He looked at Idrissi with the Corsican's innate suspicion of the Moor and said softly, "Sir, I believe this man is a corsair."

"Indeed he is", said Snowden, "but he is about to retire, and he is our friend."

Luciani looked unimpressed.

Snowden said, "Luciani, we intend to buy that ship," he pointed to the vessel alongside the quay.

"That ship?", asked Luciani ,"the xebec? Why?"

"It's part of the negotiation", said Snowden, "and I think it may be useful to the Navy."

"If you say so, Sir," said Luciani, doubtfully.

"We must look her over," said Snowden. "You've bought ships with your father before now, surely, and you must know what to look for. Go with Mr Pascoe and have a good look at her."

"It will not be clean, Sir", said Luciani, "but I will do as you say. I will get a knife for Mr Pascoe from the boat, to probe the timbers."

"Very good, Luciani. When you go to the boat, please tell them to push off again and anchor. There's quite a crowd gathering round them on the quay."

# CHAPTER 36 - XEBEC

Luciani had surveyed the xebec with Pascoe, crawling into tight spaces to probe frames and seams, unfurling the sails with the assistance of *Oleander*'s longboat crew and Moorish sailors. He had an inherited dislike for the generality of Moors – after all, the Moor's Head emblem was the flag of Corsica – but he had found over the years that he was able to work with individual Moors, and even to like some of them. He conversed with them in a mixture of languages, with Spanish as the main component, and communication was reasonably good.

The corsair ship was about sixty feet long, her size, as Idrissi reis had explained, dictated by Salé's shallow harbour entrance, and her narrow waterline beam meant she was not burdensome. Not much of a trader, but she would probably be fast in light winds, and easy to row with the large sweeps which were stowed along her deck. She had long overhangs at bow and stern, and three short masts which carried the long booms for the lateen sails. She was armed with bronze cannons of various calibres and a bow swivel.

As far as they could ascertain, she was in good order – not like *Oleander*, which was almost new and kept up to a standard that was almost impossible to achieve without the backing of a well-funded and organised institution, but sound. The xebec was cleaner than Luciani had expected – not as clean as a ship of the Royal Navy, of course, where cleanliness was elevated to a cardinal virtue, but on a par with his father's ship.

\*\*\*

Pascoe arrived at el-Inglizi's house with a smile of satisfaction on his face and reported to Snowden.

"Sir, the xebec seems sound, and Mr Idrissi is a decent enough fellow, for a pirate that is. He seems to have no hard feelings about us shooting his men, even though he had to pay their families compensation."

"I hope you don't mind, Sir, but I've sent word out to the ship, and *Rosa* will be alongside soon with the cleaning stuff. If you've no objection, Sir, I'll get back down there directly. I'd like to take Luciani with me in *Daisy*, Sir, as master. He has a good deal of experience with the lateen rig and would be most useful."

Snowden smiled at Pascoe's enthusiasm for his new, though temporary command. "*Daisy*, Mr Pascoe?"

"Yes, Sir, the xebec. She's called *Zahrat Alluwlu* – pearl flower, or *Daisy* in English."

"*Oleander*, *Rosa* and now *Daisy*", said Snowden, laughing, "quite a bunch."

"Er, yes, Sir."

As he directed the British sailors, armed with mops and casks of vinegar, Luciani was aware of Pascoe's obvious pleasure in his command, remembering how he had felt when his father had, after a long apprenticeship, made him master of his smallest ship.

The Moors gave them a mixture of herbs, which, when burnt in the enclosed ship, were said to kill any insects aboard. The herbs released such a quantity of intense smelling smoke that Luciani was inclined to believe they might be effective. Taking advantage of a temporary lull in the wind, the British sailors, with the assistance of the Moors, practised raising and lowering the sails, and they even shipped the sweeps on the side of the ship away from the wharf, to make sure they would know how to use them when the time came.

The accommodation was makeshift, but the weather was

warm, there was no rain, and the men were used to hard lying. Marine sentries guarded the gangway, but there was no attempt at thieving, and the local population seemed well disposed towards them.

\*\*\*

Next day, while the men laboured aboard the xebec, Snowden and Watton sat with the Conde, who was extremely anxious, trying to reassure him. In the afternoon, two things happened almost simultaneously. A messenger arrived bearing a summons from el-Inglizi, requiring their presence at a meeting. Snowden was surprised by the curtness of the note and the insistence of the messenger that he immediately accompany him to the kasbah, but, as he was thinking, Pascoe came in, accompanied by one of *Oleander*'s marines, bearing a message from Kennedy which had been brought in by boat from *Oleander*. He read the note:

> *There has been an unfortunate development. When the longboat came out this forenoon in the charge of Soares, it was carrying four American sailors, the skipper and three men of a ship that was wrecked last year on the coast to the south. They have been held as slaves since then and have thrown themselves on our mercy. I would welcome your guidance as I do not believe the sentiment of the crew will allow the Americans to be returned ...*

Snowden's heart sank.

\*\*\*

Snowden, Pascoe and Watton sat on cushions across the table from the Governor and el-Inglizi. The mood was sour.

"Do you know why we have summoned you, Commander Snowden?"

Snowden sighed.

"Unfortunately, I believe I do, Mr el-Inglizi."

"It is the matter of the American seamen, who are the legitimate property of a merchant of this town."

"Legitimate …," snapped Pascoe, who stopped talking when Snowden held up his hand and glared at him.

"Yes, Mr Pascoe, legitimate, according to our laws."

Snowden started to speak, but silenced himself at a glance from el-Inglizi, who continued.

"For a man o' war belonging to a friendly power to facilitate the escape of such persons is entirely unacceptable, and we insist upon their return."

Snowden thought quickly. "It seems I have a choice – either to admit this was an official act, sanctioned by myself, or to state that my crew took the men without the knowledge of the ship's officers. A diplomatic incident or an admission of ill-discipline. That is a poor choice, and so I will tell the truth. My crew took these men on their own initiative."

"Will you order your crew to return them?" asked el-Inglizi.

"I will not, Mr el-Inglizi, for two reasons. Firstly, it would be repugnant to me, and secondly, I am not sure my crew would obey me. There are many Bermudians and Corsicans among them, both nationalities with strong views on this sort of thing. I am sorry, but we seem to be at an impasse."

Snowden began to stand, but said, "Unless, of course, we can come to some financial arrangement. If necessary, I will pay from my own private funds."

El-Inglizi smiled. "That will be possible, I have no doubt. I have had some experience of this, and had I known of their presence I would have begun to negotiate for their release. However, the Governor is not best pleased."

It was a rather gloomy party of Englishmen that relayed the news to the Conde, who nevertheless took it with reasonable calmness.

"It cannot be helped, Snowden," he said.

\*\*\*

Though the negotiations had become much more complicated by the presence of the Americans aboard *Oleander*, it was clear that the Governor was now very anxious to see the back of *Oleander* and the Conde, and discussions proceeded much more briskly. Snowden reminded the Moors that he was unable to use British public funds to pay the Americans' ransom and that his private funds were strictly limited.

After less than two hours, agreement was reached, tea was drunk, and Pascoe was despatched to the ship to bring the money ashore.

\*\*\*

Snowden was in the courtyard of el-Inglizi's house when Pascoe returned from *Oleander*. "The gold is in the longboat, Sir, with a strong marine escort, in case there was any trouble. Shall I fetch it?"

Snowden turned enquiringly to el-Inglizi, who nodded and said "Our meeting is in one hour. I suggest, Snowden, that we go to the wharf and pick up the money, rather than parading it through the medina with an escort of marines."

On the way to the wharf, Pascoe spoke to Snowden in a low voice. "Sir, the crew have had a whip round for a ransom for the Americans. They've raised quite a sum."

Snowden smiled. "Good for them, but I think it will be unnecessary."

\*\*\*

The transfer ceremony at the kasbah was a very low-key event. Tea was served, and Snowden, who was accompanied by Pascoe and Watton, signed the bill of sale for the ship. The money was handed over, but the Moors disdained to count it, and suddenly the Conde was a free man, the Royal Navy owned another ship, and the American seaman had gained their release.

Watton whispered to Pascoe, "What happens if the Navy won't take the ship?"

"I think the Old Man will buy her himself. He's not short of money."

Watton said thoughtfully, "He seems to own some Yankee slaves to man her if needs be!"

Afterwards, they walked to el-Inglizi's house, where the Conde was anxiously awaiting them.

"It has all gone smoothly", el-Inglizi told him, "you are free to go."

The Conde's face was a picture of relief, and he looked at Snowden.

"Thank you, Commander, for all you have done for me." He turned to el-Inglizi. "And thank you for your intervention. It was no light thing to travel to Gibraltar as you did."

Snowden pulled out his watch.

"We must be going – the tide waits for no man."

*Oleander* was hove to in her usual station, a mile off the entrance. They had found that the seas further out were smoother and the ship's rolling was decreased. Lounging on *Oleander*'s starboard rail, Kennedy heard the lookout's shout: "On deck – the longboat's coming out. Looks like the Old Man's returning." And then, "He's got somebody with him, could be the Conde."

Kennedy hoped the lookouts would remember not to call Snowden "the Old Man" when he was back aboard and refrain from speculation. He turned to the boatswain.

"Get the chair rigged and let's give them a welcome."

The welcoming party was as impressive as could be

arranged on such a small ship as *Oleander*. Snowden was first aboard, and as he stepped on deck and turned aft to salute, his face wore a broad grin. Pipes piped, marines and seamen stood in lines, and, once the Conde had been lowered to the deck in the sling, *Oleander*'s band, a rather grand title for a group of men who practised in their spare time under the supervision of the unexpectedly musical Watton, struck up *God Save the King*, *Heart of Oak*, followed rather incongruously by *Ça Ira*, which had been a favourite on board since Watton had heard it sung by French soldiers on Corsica. Snowden was not entirely sure that Watton was as innocent of its meaning as he pretended.

When the Count was safely installed in the cabin, Snowden took Kennedy aside.

"Ken, would you like to stretch your legs?"

"Very much, Sir."

"You heard about *Daisy*, the xebec?"

Kennedy nodded. "I knew about the xebec, but I didn't know she was called *Daisy*."

"Apparently that's her name translated from Arabic. I'll forbear from making the joke about now having a bunch of flowers."

"Thanks, Sir, I appreciate that," said Kennedy, smiling.

"Well, I need you aboard *Oleander* to make sure everything runs smoothly while we get the Conde safely to Gib, so Pascoe's going to take *Daisy* there. He'll have Luciani, so he'll be all right."

Kennedy nodded. Snowden had judged that Kennedy would not be disappointed that Pascoe was taking the xebec. Kennedy knew that his own reputation was secure, and that commanding a small ship for a hundred miles or so would not significantly enhance it.

Snowden continued, "But I'd like you to go ashore now,

and look the xebec over. I don't want to delay departure in case the weather gets worse. Pascoe and Luciani say she's quite ready, but I don't want anything to go wrong on that bar. You'll have to wait for tomorrow morning's tide now, about six I think, but if you miss the tide, don't chance it. I'll stay aboard *Oleander* and keep the Count happy."

When he saw *Daisy* for the first time as *Rosa* was pulled into the river, Kennedy felt a slight pang of regret that he was not taking her to Gibraltar, but this was quickly forgotten as he inspected her with Pascoe. She was stored with provisions either brought in from *Oleander* or purchased locally and was fully watered. The armament had been inspected by Gunner Trott, who had carefully sorted the balls into piles suitable for each piece.

In the evening, Kennedy and Pascoe dined at el-Inglizi's house, a generally cheerful occasion, though the renegado did express some regret that he would have no English people to converse with when they were gone.

As it became light on the following day, Kennedy and Pascoe were standing on the quayside with el-Inglizi and Idrissi as the river and town came to life. The xebec's crew were already aboard, and the four men closely watched the flow of the tide and felt the wind.

"Time?" asked Kennedy, pulling out his watch.

"I think so", said Pascoe, who had been carefully observing the time of high water over the last couple of days. "Two hours before high, so we should have a bit of slack in case of difficulties."

Kennedy turned and looked at Idrissi who nodded. "Go," he said.

Kennedy and Pascoe shook hands with el-Inglizi and Idrissi and boarded the ship.

"I think", said Kennedy as they watched the bowline

released and waited for the flooding tide to swing the xebec's head out into the stream, "I have never met anyone quite so strange as that corsair. Quite gives me the shivers."

"He does", agreed Pascoe, "but the Old Man probably has the same effect on him!"

They laughed, and Kennedy, judging the moment, called out, "Let go aft, give way together."

With the men straining at the huge sweeps, *Daisy* gradually pulled away from the quay, and when she had gathered way, Luciani moved the helm and turned her head towards the harbour entrance, *Rosa* following astern.

Kennedy said to Pascoe, "Let's get a bit of sail on her. It'll be slow going with just the oars against the tide."

Before long, *Daisy* was moving well under the influence of sails and oars, despite the foul tide. They went out of the river and were soon on the bar. Through the clear water, in the sunlight, they could see the yellow sand beneath the ship's keel.

Suddenly, Pascoe shouted a warning: "Breaker!"

Kennedy looked ahead and saw a wave approaching, larger than the rest, its crest tumbling down its face in a confusion of white foam.

"Come on, row," shouted Kennedy, and the men at the oars redoubled their efforts. He looked at Luciani at the helm, who was carefully watching the wave and making small adjustments to the helm so that the xebec met it exactly head on.

"Ready to lift the blades", shouted Kennedy to the rowers, "ready, NOW!"

As the wave hit, the men lifted their oar blades clear of the sea. The xebec's bow lifted and the water from the breaking crest sluiced over the bow and along the deck, but the ship was not pushed sideways, and before long she was across the bar, the oars were shipped and she was heading towards *Oleander*. *Rosa*, closely following the xebec, had been sheltered by the larger craft and had suffered no ill effects from the wave.

"No harm done", said Kennedy to Pascoe, "but it's a damned unpleasant entrance."

*\*\*\**

As the Conde was too exhausted to rise from his bed, on the first evening of their passage from Salé to Gibraltar Snowden dined with Nathanial Davies, the American skipper who had been redeemed.

"We've had a hellish eighteen months, Captain Snowden, and no mistake, since our shipwreck. The Moors, the ones from the desert, treated us abominably, though this improved when we were bought by the merchant in Salé, who was only interested in ransoming us and had an interest in keeping us healthy on that account."

Snowden nodded as Davies continued.

"I want to thank you, Snowden, and your crew as well, for rescuing us. I don't know what would have happened if you hadn't turned up. When I return to Boston I will make sure that you are reimbursed."

# CHAPTER 37 - READY

Admiral Morlaix sat at the head of the table in his headquarters in Béziers and looked at the expectant faces of his commanders at the sides of the table.

Morlaix stood. "Gentlemen, thank you for attending today. The Emperor has tasked me with defending France against further English raids from the sea on our canals, raids which so far have been highly successful. Now, it is true that these attacks have had a narrow focus – in the first case to destroy the invasion barges, barges for which I was responsible, and in the second case to intercept the convoy of Spanish sailors bound for Toulon …"

"But they got the money," said a man from near the end of the table.

"So they did, Leclerc, but I think the sailors were their objective, and they happened to stumble on the gold."

"I wish I could stumble on some gold occasionally," replied Leclerc, to general laughter.

"As I was saying", continued Morlaix, "so far the raids have concentrated on attacking and destroying traffic on the canals – barges. I believe, and so does the Emperor, that the enemy will realise before long that, in addition to interfering with traffic, he may be able to damage the canals themselves …"

There was a general nodding of heads as Morlaix continued, "And cause considerable economic damage to France. The English Navy has almost stopped our coasting trade, and we must ensure they do not do the same thing to our canal trade."

"Not to mention the embarrassment," said one of the men around the table.

"Embarrassment is not to be discounted, Major Berger," said Morlaix.

"This Snowden", asked Berger, "he seems to be extraordinarily lucky. He burnt the invasion barges in Brittany, your barges, Sir. In the last few months he has cut that privateer, a huge one, out of Lézardrieux, intercepted those Spanish seamen and taken vast amounts of our gold. All with one small ship and her crew."

"He has been lucky, but to some extent he makes his own luck by seizing opportunities, and", he paused for effect, "we gift him opportunities by our slackness. There is, however, one thing to remember: Snowden has worked at a small scale, with a nimble force. This does not mean his methods will not scale up to larger raids, especially as bigger attacks are likely to be led by more senior men."

Morlaix looked round the room. "So, gentlemen, no more slackness, no more gifts for the enemy to seize." He turned to Captain Badeau who was standing next to a huge map of southern France.

"Captain Badeau, please continue." Morlaix sat, glad to relieve the pressure on his leg.

"Very well, Admiral. The canal, or rather the two canals, the Midi and the Rhône à Sète, run from Toulouse to the Beaucaire lock on the Rhône. From a few miles west of Béziers, east to Aigues-Mortes, the canal runs close to the sea. Parts of the Rhône à Sète Canal, east of Sète, which was the subject of the most recent attack, are very vulnerable from the sea, but there is not much infrastructure to destroy, as the canal is more or less a banked ditch running through lagoons. I am not saying we should not guard against small-scale attacks on barges – we certainly should, and will – but we have identified three potential targets that are near the sea, and which, if destroyed, would put the canal out of use for months."

Badeau picked up his pointer. "All the targets are only a few miles from where we are in Béziers." He pointed to the map. "From west to east: firstly, the Malpas Tunnel, here. The canal runs under a tunnel in the hill. Damaging the tunnel would close the canal for a long time."

He moved the pointer. "Secondly, the Fonserannes Staircase, just outside Béziers itself, which brings the canal down to the level of the River Orb. Nine locks, gentlemen, a fine concentrated target."

The pointer moved again. "Thirdly, the Round Lock at Agde, which diverts traffic either towards the sea or to continue eastwards along the canal. There is a fourth possibility, the Ouvrages du Libron, where a special barge blocks the waters of the Libron from entering the canal in times of flood, but we consider this to be a less likely target."

He paused and looked round the room. "Gentlemen, our object is not only to defend these targets, but to destroy the attacking force to the extent that further adventures are discouraged. This is what we intend to do ..."

# CHAPTER 38 - GIBRALTAR

The meeting in Gibraltar was in many ways similar to the one that had taken place in Béziers, the Admiral at the head of the table, the officers sitting along its side. True, the uniforms were different, as was, perhaps, the ability of the presiding admiral, but in essence it was the same meeting.

"And that, Gentlemen, is the plan in outline," said Jameson. "You will each receive your written orders in a day or so, but I hope you have the broad outline of what we intend to do." The admiral looked round the room.

"Are there any questions?"

Snowden thought, *Are you out of your mind, Sir?* would be appropriate, but instead said, "Will the French not be expecting something of the sort, Sir?"

"I very much doubt it, Snowden. Frogs are often not very quick on the uptake. This operation is on a much larger scale than your previous efforts ashore in France."

At this, there was an audible intake of breath from the officers. Snowden's 'previous efforts' were legendary in the Navy, and indeed in the country more generally.

There was a murmur from the distant end of the table. "Pretty small-scale stuff, like taking on a regiment of chasseurs with a schooner" – a comment that resulted in general, though suppressed laughter.

Sensing that he might be losing his audience, Jameson continued.

"Commander Snowden's efforts are well known, but in this operation, he is providing a diversion away from the main attack."

The murmur came again. "We'd be pretty sure of a bit of prize money if he led it, I should think!"

As the laughter died down, an officer halfway down the table asked, "Sir, will we not weaken our squadron guarding the Strait and off Cadiz if we use a frigate for the raid?"

Scarcely bothering to conceal his anger, Jameson responded, "The French are in Toulon. One frigate will make no difference if they leave", and brought the meeting to a close.

The meeting continued, without the Admiral but with more uproar, in a tavern near the waterfront. Snowden, after the tension of the last few months, was unreasonably pleased to be amongst his own kind. A naval captain tapped him on the shoulder, and he turned.

"Clasby, by God. I haven't seen you since …"

"We met in the Straits, do you remember? That schooner of yours, going like a bat out of hell. Freeboard a bit low, bet she's pretty wet …"

"Yes, of course I remember. Do you still have *Pegasus*?"

"I do, and she should be out looking for Froggies, eyes of the fleet and all that, but that fool is going to have her carrying lobsters to Narbonne, or some such place. I hope Nelson doesn't find out about it, as you know he's not an enthusiast for Jameson. You know, Snowden, I must say I'm astonished you don't have your own frigate after all you've done."

"I'm surprised as well", said a marine in his red coat, "but he's probably offended too many people. It was enlightening to hear from our esteemed admiral that our efforts in Brittany were

– what did he say? – 'small-scale stuff'."

"Wain", said Snowden *"Major* Wain now, I see. Congratulations – very good to meet you again. Are you recovered? How did the Frogs treat you?"

"Completely recovered, Snowden, and the Frogs treated me tolerably well."

He thought, and then added, "Unlike your brother sea officer, Jack Stone. It was an evil day when he was hauled off from the hospital."

"It was, but he seems to have come out on top."

"So I've heard, in America no less. But he had a nasty wound. He wouldn't have made it but for the French surgeon, a brilliant man, and being nursed by Dominique did him no harm at all. Probably doesn't make up for a spell in the Temple, though."

"I shouldn't think it did", Snowden shuddered, "I've come across Monsieur Fouché. And Stone's wife, Dominique."

"A wonderful woman, Snowden. Jack did himself proud there ... Thank you," he said as a glass was set down on the table beside him.

Snowden was surrounded by a noisy group of officers, and one said, "Now, Snowden, what do you think of this raid that Jameson has concocted? After all, you're the expert on this sort of thing."

Despite the drink and the comradeship of his brother officers, Snowden knew he must be careful. "As Admiral Jameson said, I am to make a diversion."

"A diversion is only a diversion if it diverts the enemy," said a naval captain. "We assume the enemy's headquarters are in Marseilles and he will hear of your efforts before the real attack begins. What if that is not correct? Suppose the French headquarters are further west? Come on, Snowden, you must have an opinion?"

"No, Chester, I have not, and, Gentlemen, I think we should speak no more of this in public." He raised his glass. "Here's to Boney's downfall."

# CHAPTER 39 - FAREWELL

Snowden did not particularly enjoy the following morning, and in the afternoon he was dozing in his cabin, which was his own again, free of passengers, when there was a knock on the door and the marine announced that the boatswain would like to see him.

"One moment," said Snowden; and when Rubert came into the room he had managed to straighten himself out somewhat.

"Yes, Rubert, what can I do for you?"

"I'm sorry, Sir, but I have to leave *Oleander*, and indeed the Navy."

"That's a great shame. Why must you leave? It will be a loss to the ship, and to the Service more generally."

"I have accepted an offer from the Conde de Premià to act as his aide."

"Does Senor Vilar not perform that role?"

"He does, but his heart is not really in it. He is an engineer and he wishes to return to Merthyr or perhaps some other place of industry to work in that profession."

"Well, Rubert, I will be sorry to lose you, but I believe the Conde could not wish for a better aide, and one that can splice a rope as well. Will you join me in a glass?"

***

The 74 *Invincible* was moored just off the Gibraltar dockyard, in the final stage of her preparations for departure. To Snowden, used to the confines of *Oleander*, the ship seemed huge, and solid, but he knew that appearances were deceptive and that she was actually wormy and rotten, unfit for duty.

"I just hope the Frog doesn't try and interfere with the convoy," said Captain Fearns, her commander, as Snowden came aboard from *Oleander*'s boat. "We'll be lucky to survive the Bay in any event, and I dread to think what would happen if we fired a broadside. The sooner she's on the dry side of the dock gates in Pompey, the better!"

Snowden smiled. Fearns was undoubtedly correct about the condition of the ship, but he knew the man's reputation and suspected that any Frenchman attempting to interfere with Fearns' convoy would regret it, rot or no rot.

"Anyway, Snowden, you'll excuse me. I have to get her underway and organise this rabble of merchant ships into some sort of order. The passengers are in the cabin." He raised his voice to a passing midshipman, "Jones, if you please, take Commander Snowden to the cabin."

The passengers rose as Snowden entered the great cabin, and Rubert came towards him, smiling. It was a shock to see his former boatswain dressed as a Spanish gentleman, but, Snowden reflected, Rubert was a surprising man. Snowden shook his hand and then that of the Conde.

"I apologise for stealing your boatswain, Snowden, but he is a very able man and I know that I will always be able to trust a Puyol. Senor Vilar is resourceful, but his heart is in engineering, not politics, and England is the place for an ambitious engineer to prosper. I have no doubt that he will make his fortune, and I cannot stand in his way."

The Conde paused for a moment, collecting his thoughts.

"I wish to thank you, Snowden, from the bottom of my heart, for all you've done. My only regret is that I did not take up your offer of rescue as quickly as I should have done."

The conversation continued for some time until Snowden, recognising the shipboard noises, said, "The ship will be underway shortly. I must leave."

Isabella looked at him. "Lucia, would you like to come and see Senor Snowden get into his boat?"

On deck, as they leaned on the rail, watching as *Oleander*'s boat was brought alongside, Snowden turned to Isabella and saw her eyes were full of tears, and thought that, perhaps, his might be as well.

"I am sorry to part from you, Isabella."

"We have no alternative, Percy, but I will always treasure my time with you."

Snowden hardly dared to ask, "And the Conde?"

She looked at him. "He is an understanding man, Percy."

A midshipman approached them. "Sir, your boat is alongside."

Aboard *Oleander*, Snowden watched as the 74 sailed out of the harbour, thinking of what might have been.

# CHAPTER 40 - THE PLAN

Snowden continued to read his orders, futility and helplessness building in him.

"... *in outline, the attack will comprise two elements, the raid itself and diversions. The landing party will disembark from* Pegasus *at Valras, one mile west of the mouth of the Orb.* Oleander *and* Daisy *will undertake the diversions.* Daisy *will land a party at Maguelone, and* Oleander *will attack Sète from the sea ...*"

"... *the first diversion will commence simultaneously with the landing of the raiding party and the attack on Sète on the following morning. It is expected that news of the diversion will reach the headquarters of the French before news of the raid itself ...*"

The admiral's reputation with Nelson, the Admiralty and the public was not high, and Snowden believed that, instead of concentrating on his main task, watching the Strait of Gibraltar and Cadiz, Jameson had been influenced by the success and glamour of Snowden's own raids and thought that he could restore his image by conducting his own, though, because of his rank, the scale would have to be much larger. The Malpas Tunnel and the Fonserannes Staircase, strategic targets and worthy of an admiral's attention, were close together and only a few miles from the sea, and the premise was that the French had not realised this and had taken no steps to protect them.

Snowden's own raids had been opportunistic, with small-scale, flexible forces personally led by him. Taking advantage of the enemy's momentary weakness was entirely different from a meticulously planned, large-scale operation which relied on both the enemy's stupidity and accurate timing.

Snowden knew it would not work.

# CHAPTER 41 - KENNEDY

Snowden was in his cabin when Kennedy entered.

"A word with you, Sir?"

"Certainly, Ken, what is it?"

"I have orders, Percy." He held them out for Snowden.

Snowden smiled as he read. He had been preoccupied in the last few days and had not looked at his own correspondence, in which this news was undoubtedly buried.

"Ken, this is not only promotion but a great honour as well, one you thoroughly deserve. *Victory* – you must be very pleased. It seems that Nelson himself has need of your services."

"It is a great honour, but I've turned it down, or rather postponed it. I hope Lord Nelson, or rather Captain Hardy, will be understanding."

"Why on earth have you done that, Ken? It's not something that's likely to advance your career."

"It's this business with the raid, Sir. If we're to go dodging about again just off the beach in the Gulf of Lions, and with Pascoe in *Daisy*, I'll be needed in *Olly*, especially if you're up to your usual tricks ashore."

Snowden was touched by this. "Well, *Oleander* and I could certainly do with your help. Thank you, my friend."

# CHAPTER 42 - THE DIVERSION: DAISY AT PALAVAS

The ships sailed in company from Gibraltar, passing to the west of Ibiza, but keeping well off the coast. About fifteen miles off Narbonne, in a strong southerly wind, *Pegasus* hove to, while *Oleander* and *Daisy* continued eastward. As the distance widened, Snowden, watching from *Daisy*, saw Clasby, on *Pegasus'* quarterdeck, lift his hat in farewell. Snowden doffed his own.

*Oleander* and *Daisy* kept well offshore, clear of any observers from the land. Aboard *Oleander*, Kennedy was worried by the southerly wind. It would not hamper his own activities, but it would make landing on the exposed beaches of the Gulf of Lions difficult. Kennedy was not an enthusiast for the Gulf – *nasty, windy place*, he thought.

In the morning, *Daisy* had left *Oleander* idling off Sète and had sailed further east, before Pascoe, busy with sextant and compass, had taken her inshore in the almost pitch-black night.

"Here we are, Sir", said Pascoe to Snowden, "just about half a mile off the beach, exactly where we were before. I can just about see the outline of Maguelone Cathedral, over there, Sir."

Snowden looked in the direction indicated and saw it himself, faint against the slightly lighter background of the sky.

"Thank you, Pascoe, excellent work to get us here. I shall

start for the shore directly."

"Be careful, Sir, I can see a good deal of surf on the beach."

"I know, Pascoe, but the landing party are counting on a diversion. That's what we will give them, but I want you to be very cautious. It's not worth risking the ship or lives for."

Not an inspiring message, Snowden knew, but he did not want any heroics.

Pascoe, who felt very strongly about what they were proposing to do, burst out, "This is damned stupid, Skipper. Just a waste."

Snowden smiled. "Pascoe, I advise you to keep those thoughts to yourself." He patted Pascoe's shoulder. "Do your job, and we'll be back in Gib in no time!"

He turned. "Come on, Watton, let's have our run ashore. You have the ship, Mr Pascoe."

As Snowden got into the boat with Watton, a difficult task with the sea running as it was, a wave of depression came over him. Left to his own devices, he would never have been off a beach in the Gulf of Lions, attempting to land through the surf to create a diversion for an operation that he thought was probably doomed. He had wanted to go alone, but the task was too great for one man and so he had decided to take Watton. He refused to risk any more men on this overwhelmingly stupid operation, but he could not do it alone.

The trip through the surf was as bad as he imagined it would be, and he was very glad they had brought dry clothes packed in waxed canvas bags. He could only hope that the kegs of powder and the fuses had similarly stayed dry. How he hated this windswept beach!

He knew he must control his thoughts, or his judgement would be affected, and, with an effort, spoke to Watton. "Let's get off this beach."

"Good to be back," said Watton, and Snowden, despite himself, smiled.

They made their way across the sand and onto the path that led past the Cathedral mound to the canal. They moved quietly, stopping every few paces to listen, but they heard nothing but the wind in the bushes and the occasional complaint of a bird, and were not disturbed. Eventually, after about a mile of slow going, they saw the canal in front of them, with two barges tied up alongside the bank. Snowden knew the barge crew, often a family, would be sleeping aboard. He found that, in this desolate place, he could not bring himself to bring ruin and possibly even death to such people, so he pointed at the ferry, a large, flat-bottomed craft used to carry people and animals across the canal, which at this spot was perhaps a hundred and fifty yards wide.

"That'll do, Watton, let's get the powder aboard the ferry."

\*\*\*

Pascoe, with the aid of Soares, took *Daisy* three miles or so to the east. Pascoe had noted prominent marks ashore during the previous expedition, and there was sufficient light for him to take bearings from them. They moored the ship fore and aft, a quarter of a mile from the entrance to the Lez River, and adjusted her heading finely with a barber hauler on the stern anchor cable.

Satisfied with her heading, Pascoe went forward to where Appleby, a jovial gunner on loan to the ship, was standing over his charges, a pair of Congreve rocket launchers.

"As far as I can tell, Appleby, the ship is pointing directly at the fort. The range is 1,290 yards. Fire as you please."

Appleby made adjustments to the launcher's elevation, and when he was satisfied, fired a pair of rockets. The rockets hissed loudly as they left the ship, and *Daisy*'s crew, spellbound, followed their fiery passage across the sky and the loud explosions that followed their impact with, hopefully, the target. *Daisy* fired rocket after rocket, and they must have had some effect, as large fires were soon burning ashore.

And then, two things happened almost simultaneously. There was a large explosion from the vicinity of the canal.

"That'll be the Old Man", said Pascoe to Soares, who nodded, just as there was a shout from the lookout: "Boats leaving the harbour."

Pascoe looked, but his night vision had been severely limited by the rockets' flames and he could see nothing.

"Big guns they got", shouted the lookout, helpfully, "in their bows, there's about five of them, heading towards us."

"Christ", said Pascoe, "gunboats."

"Soares, get the sails on her. Cut the cables, quick."

They were quick, but not quite quick enough, and the two leading gunboats, their crews straining at their oars, fired at *Daisy*, whose own armament was not in a state of readiness.

Balls smashed into *Daisy*'s hull, splinters flew, and Pascoe heard men scream. *Daisy*, her anchor cables cut, drifted broadside onto the wind while men ran on her deck, bumping into each other, cursing. The gunboats continued to fire, but in the rough sea they scored no more hits, and in the darkness the mainsail was set and began to draw.

"Course south-west," shouted Pascoe. "Get her going as fast as you can!"

*\*\*\**

The powder kegs were in position on the ferry and Watton was working on the fuse when Snowden nudged him.

"Look at that," he whispered, and the marine looked up and saw the trails of rockets in the eastern sky. He saw the flash as the rockets landed, and shortly afterward he heard the noise of the explosions.

"Ready?" asked Watton, and when Snowden nodded, lit the fuse leading to the powder kegs. He made sure it was burning properly and said urgently, "Let's get away", and they ran off the ferry.

They had not gone far, only a few yards, when the powder exploded in a huge, blinding flash, lifting Snowden up and then violently knocking him to the ground. He lay, unable to move, shocked and winded, as the world went dark. When he came to, he was lying on the ground, with an impossibly painful headache in a completely silent world. He turned his head and saw Watton lying on the ground a few feet away. After a few minutes he felt slightly stronger and struggled to his knees. He crawled slowly to Watton, but, to his horror, he realised that the young marine's head was at an unnatural angle, and when he touched Watton's chest tentatively, he could feel no breathing, and the man's, *boy's really*, thought Snowden, face and hands were cold. Snowden lay back down on the ground, thinking of Watton's infectious enthusiasm, his musical talent and the waste of it all. He gave in to the despair washing over him, aware that consciousness was slipping away.

He awoke to see figures standing by the canal, probably bargees, but it was possible the military had responded quickly and they were soldiers. Briefly he thought he would lie where he was and allow himself to be captured, but something prompted him to stand, shakily, and to slowly make his way along the path towards the sea.

At the end of the path, he turned right and found the place from where Vilar and Luciani had observed the canal, it seemed so long ago. The cathedral on its mound was silhouetted against the fires burning from the direction of the fort as he lay down on the cold ground and drifted back into unconsciousness. When he awoke, in his still silent world, he saw the flash of gunfire out to see, off Palavas. The flashes illuminated the outline of *Daisy*, surrounded by gunboats.

*Get some sail on her, Pascoe, for God's sake*, he thought, and it was clear that Pascoe was of the same mind, as subsequent flashes revealed the ship under sail, heading away from the gunboats.

*\*\*\**

Before long, *Daisy*'s remaining sails were hoisted, and the ship made good progress, until, just after dawn, the wind died, and the xebec lay rolling in a dead calm. They watched as the gunboats, perhaps a couple of miles away, lowered their little sails and shipped their oars.

Pascoe went round the ship, talking to the men, making sure the guns were as ready as they could be, but though the cannons were bronze, they were small and did not inspire much confidence. He went below and visited the wounded men, and when he returned to the deck he looked up at the brilliant blue sky, knowing that the Mistral was starting to blow. He thought of Snowden and Watton ashore and the disappointment they must feel if they could see what was happening at sea.

# CHAPTER 43 - THE RAID ON THE MALPAS TUNNEL

The operation was, as Admiral Jameson had said, on a large scale. Not an invasion, but more than a raid, and Major Wain, waiting on the windy beach, knew it was too big and unwieldy for a nimble night operation. Their target was too far inland, they were late after the chaotic start, and the men were wet, cold and demoralised.

Clasby, captain of the frigate *Pegasus*, had wanted to postpone the operation. "Wind's from the south, Colonel Masterson, and there's quite a swell already, and it looks like surf on the beach. We'll have trouble getting you ashore as it is, and if it comes up any more, getting you off may be impossible."

Clasby's protestations had done no good, no good at all. *Pegasus* had anchored close inshore just after dark and disembarkation had started. The men, soldiers as well as marines, had only once practised disembarkation, in daylight and in the calm of Gibraltar. In the darkness with the ship rolling in the swell there had been a good deal of confusion.

The swell had been a further complication when the boats had reached the shore, and many of the men had got thoroughly wet in the surf. With only a weak moon for illumination, it had taken a very long time to get everyone ashore and lined up, and there had been a plenty of cursing, which had now died down to a sullen silence.

Colonel Masterson (Clasby had heard junior officers unflatteringly refer to him as 'Mastermind') approached him across the sand.

"Are we ready to go, Major Wain? We are decidedly late. The sooner we get these men moving, the sooner they'll warm up."

"I believe we are ready, Sir."

"Very well, I will lead the column to the first objective, the Tunnel, Major Wain."

Wain did not feel cheered by this announcement.

"Let us proceed," said the Colonel.

\*\*\*

The watchers smiled to each other. "You are sure you know what to say?" asked the leader.

"Of course, Citizen Sergeant Barras."

"Then go."

Morlaix and Odile were about to retire to bed when there was a loud knocking on the door. Morlaix knew instinctively what it meant before Badeau burst into the room, accompanied by a rather travel-stained man.

"They've come", said Badeau, "as you predicted. Tell them, Dumas."

Dumas collected his thoughts and recited, "Citizen Admiral, Sir. An English ship, a frigate, is anchored off the beach at Valras. The wind is southerly and there is a moderate swell from the south."

Odile said, looking at the large map Badeau had brought, "It would be better if we went to the kitchen, the table is larger there."

In the kitchen, with the map spread before them, Morlaix

asked Dumas to point to where the frigate was anchored. "A moderate swell you say, Dumas?"

"Yes, Sir. I would say it is quite heavy, myself, but Citizen Sergeant Barras is always one for understatement."

"I am sorry to interrupt, please continue."

"A number of boats have taken men ashore from the frigate. We estimate there are several hundred men. Many of the men were submerged in the surf, and it is possible that some have drowned."

Morlaix gestured for Dumas to continue – he realised he had made a mistake by interrupting him previously.

"The men were lined up on the beach and have now started to march northward, on the track away from the beach. We are continuing to watch them and will report as they progress. They are making a great deal of noise and some are dragging carts. That is the end of the message, Sir."

"Thank you, Dumas … You have seen service, I believe. Can you perhaps give your own impression of what is going on there?"

"I have seen service, Sir, a great deal of it. My impression, Sir, is that the landing was not a smooth operation. I was at Boulogne when the Emperor insisted on a demonstration of landing from boats. This operation is on a much smaller scale, but it reminded me of that disaster."

"Thank you, that is a most valuable observation. What is the road like from the beach? I seem to remember it as only a track."

"It is only a track, marshy on either side, so they'll have to move in a narrow column." He pointed to the map.

"You have done very well, Dumas. Badeau, I do not think this operation is one of Snowden's – he would not attempt to land through the surf. Anyway, let us go to the headquarters and set things in motion."

***

Wain marched, uneasily, at the rear of the column with a picked section of marines under Sergeant Wilson. It was dark, but he could see the men ahead of him, their black shapes visible against the white of the track. They doubled along for several hours, occasionally pausing when the leaders at the front of the column stopped to ascertain the route, before the column turned onto a different track or road. As soon as they stopped, Wilson stationed marines at the sides of the track, about two hundred yards behind the column, to guard against surprise. The country was almost flat and Wain knew it was quite barren. They passed isolated dwellings, but, though the occasional dog barked, there were no lights showing and no sign of human life.

Eventually, they saw the black outline of a hill ahead of them, and the column halted. The rearguard was deployed, and a messenger arrived.

"Major Wain's presence is required at the head of the column," he announced.

"I think we've arrived," he said to Wilson. "Watch out."

***

Messengers arrived at the headquarters and delivered their reports, verbatim, before being closely questioned. The column was making steady progress northward. Its destination was obvious, the Malpas Tunnel.

Morlaix knew that the English column was doomed, but he badly wanted the frigate, though he realised defeating it would rely on a good deal of luck.

And then, another messenger arrived.

"Where are you from?" asked Bandeau.

"From Palavas, Citizen Captain."

"Your message …?"

\*\*\*

Major Wain went to the head of the column as the first traces of dawn appeared in the sky, arriving in time to see the sappers, pushing barrows carrying barrels of powder, leave for the Tunnel, the eastern portal of which was to their left, along a narrow track. The sappers were accompanied by a strong escort. The remaining troops knelt with their muskets by their sides.

The Colonel was in an ebullient mood. "Ah, there you are Wain. Caught 'em napping, slow on the uptake, your Frog. We're six miles from the beach, right inside their country, and we've not heard a thing."

Wain had been thinking very hard about the six miles separating them from the sea. He started to reply, "I hope you're right …", but as he spoke, the unthinkable happened. There were shouts of alarm from the sappers' party ahead, and then a cannon roared from the front, and then another, apparently from the side. Now there were musket shots as well, and, as Wain turned, the Colonel, without a word, dropped to his knees and collapsed onto the ground, a pool of blood spreading out from him. There was an enormous explosion, which lit up the scene with an orange flash. *A demolition charge*, thought Wain as the men near him threw themselves flat on the ground and then scrambled off to the side of the road. Wain lay on the ground, balls whistling above him.

There were more screams, and men from the demolition party began to run back in ones and twos. Wain grabbed one of them and stopped him, a middle-aged sergeant.

"What's happened?"

The sergeant looked at him in the gathering light. "Ambush", he said, "a trap. There's an earthwork across the track with a cannon in it, and another gun enfilading from the side. Hundreds of men. One of our charges exploded. The officer's dead."

"Stay with me," Wain said to the sergeant. "We must fall back."

Wain and the sergeant got the nearby men to their feet and they ran back down the track under heavy but luckily ineffective fire. When they reached Sergeant Wilson, Wain stopped and the two men stood in the road shouting, "Halt, Halt." Wain pulled out his pistol and fired it in the air. Slightly to Wain's surprise, the running men stopped.

Sergeant Wilson said, "The only way is back, Sir, back to the beach."

Wain was inclined to agree with him, but just as he was about to give the order to retreat, firing came from the rear and a cannon ball crashed into the bushes nearby.

"Jesus, Sir, they're behind us as well," said Wilson.

By now, it was fairly light, and, rising over the road, Wain could see the hill through which the canal tunnel ran. There was only one thing to do to avoid a massacre on the road, and Wain did it.

"Up the hill!" he shouted.

# CHAPTER 44 - D'ENSÉRUNE RIDGE

In the gathering daylight, the remnants of the British column scrambled up the hill, with Wain at their head. There was curiously little firing, but Wain knew this was only a temporary lull. At the summit of the hill, he halted, and the men with him stopped as well, most throwing themselves down on the coarse vegetation. He could see a small town to the east and to the north a huge bowl or depression in the ground, with crops growing in a pattern of fields radiating from its centre. He knew the canal ran in its tunnel through the hill below him.

With the assistance of Sergeant Wilson, Wain got the men into a rough circle, lying down with their muskets at the ready. He knew, as he suspected every man there did, that the game was up.

They heard the noise of approaching troops, and then a French officer walked along the road towards them, a white shirt tied by its arms to his sword, which he held above his head. A man next to Wain, without a word of command, took off his own shirt and handed it to Wain.

The Frenchman stopped and Wain walked towards him, white shirt in hand.

"Wain", he said, in a low voice, "Major of Marines." He held out his sword, hilt first, and the Frenchman took it and said, "I am Francoise Renault, of the $4^e$ régiment de chasseurs."

As more Frenchmen appeared, the British troops stood and handed over their weapons.

# CHAPTER 45 – THE DIVERSION: OLEANDER AT SÈTE

They loitered through the day, and when darkness fell, worked the ship into the land. Kennedy was sure of the position he had started from, but he knew there were likely to be onshore currents in the southerly wind, and the ship proceeded very slowly, with several lookouts at the crosstrees and men calling the depth every few minutes.

Sète, their destination, was a port built specifically as a terminus of the Canal du Midi. Luciani knew it, as he had been there in his father's ships, but it was unfamiliar to Kennedy. When the drum beat the ship to quarters as dawn was breaking, Luciani pointed out the dark outline of a hill.

"That is Mont St Clair, just behind the town, and yes, I can see the town itself now. There is the mole, and the warehouses at the end of it. To quote Mr Pascoe, I think we're …"

Kennedy smiled, and completed the phrase: "just about where I thought we would be."

As the sky lightened, *Oleander* was sailing fast, parallel to the coast, towards the mole of Sète. They were close to the land, less than a quarter of a mile off, and they could see people ashore walking in the direction of the town.

As they neared the mole, Kennedy said to Luciani, "Let

us commence our diversion, Mister. Slow her down, but keep enough way on to tack."

The ship came upright as sail was taken in, and Kennedy could see they were very close to several ships moored to the mole. He ran forward and shouted to Gunner Trott, "Let 'em have it, Guns."

The guns along the port side of the ship fired, one at a time, at the moored merchant ships, the chain shot causing masts on two of them to collapse. Ashore, men started to run on the quay as *Oleander* continued to sail slowly along the mole, firing the port broadside as she went.

They were close to the end of the quay when Kennedy shouted, "Helm down, tack her."

The great Carrons on the fo'c'stle roared. There was a pause, and a warehouse wall collapsed slowly in a cloud of dust, and then *Oleander* turned to port, the starboard guns firing their heated shot into the warehouses.

"Sir", said Luciani ,"the fort on the hill is firing."

Kennedy looked up and saw the stone fort above them, very Vauban looking, wreathed in smoke, but he could not see the fall of the shot and dismissed it from his mind.

The starboard battery was now firing into the ships on the mole, which included, to Kennedy's surprise, a warship, a sloop of war. He was briefly tempted to try to cut it out, but a few better-aimed shots from the fort, which hit the water uncomfortably close, decided him against it.

"Get some sail on her", he said to Luciani, "let's clear out."

With *Oleander*'s task completed, Kennedy had decided, on his own initiative, to take the ship eastwards – to, as he said to Luciani, "See how the Old Man and Pascoe are getting on."

And now *Oleander* was becalmed about three miles east-south-east of Sète, her sails slatting uselessly as she rolled in the swell.

"What do you think the prospects for the raid are?" asked Luciani.

"I don't think they are very good, and if they have any sense they'll have postponed it. You saw the surf on the beach at Sète this morning – it will have been the same where they were landing. If they tried it, there could have been a disaster. And there we were, risking the ship like that, and the Old Man going ashore like as not. All for nothing."

The lookout shouted: "Boats leaving Sète, headed for us."

"Christ", said Kennedy, "and us becalmed. Up and have a look, Giotto", and then, "Quarters. Boarding Nets."

He spoke to Sergeant Riley. "Get all your riflemen up into the tops. Aim for the gunners on the boats."

At the foretop, Luciani steadied his telescope against the rigging and trained it on the harbour entrance of Sète. He could see that large rowing boats had left the harbour and were heading directly towards *Oleander*, the crews pulling strongly, a large bow wave ahead of each boat. In the bow of each boat was a cannon, looking disproportionality large. The lookout nudged him, pointed, and he saw that the small warship, the one they had seen that morning moored to the mole, was being towed out by four or five boats.

All they could do was wait. Kennedy walked round the ship, visiting each part of it, encouraging the men, joking with them, but there was a sense of foreboding which he could not alleviate.

The sun beat down from a merciless blue sky. Luciani looked at it and remarked, "The Mistral is coming."

"Sooner the better," replied Kennedy, judging the distance between *Oleander* and the approaching gunboats. "They'll be here any minute."

*Oleander* fired first, a ranging shot which fell short of the boats, but the gunboats checked their rush and, under the now-continuous fire of *Oleander*'s port broadside, fanned out until they half surrounded her in a rough semicircle and began to fire themselves. One of the boats was hit and then another, but the French guns had found their mark and balls crashed into *Oleander*'s hull or screamed over the heads of the men on deck. Sensing an advantage, the gunboats came nearer, and, under Sergeant Riley's steady supervision, the men with Baker rifles stationed in the tops began to fire. Men in the boats fell and their fire slackened. *Oleander* was wreathed in smoke until, suddenly, she wasn't, the smoke had drifted away.

"A breeze", shouted Kennedy, "a breeze!"

"The Mistral has arrived," said Luciani complacently. "I told you."

*Oleander* was moving now, just ghosting along, but the gunboats realised what was happening, and to keep up, turned so that their courses were parallel to the ship. The guns in their bows could not bear, and, side on, the boats made a much larger target.

"Get them, boys, get them!" shouted Kennedy, entirely unnecessarily, as the gunners realised their opportunity and fired shot after shot at the boats, hitting two of them. The wind was increasing quickly now, from the north, and *Oleander* really started to move, leaving the boats behind.

Kennedy saw the French warship, probably half a mile away, drop her towlines and set sail, slowly, as though she had been in port too long and her crew were unpractised.

Afterwards, Kennedy thought perhaps that he had been unwise, but his blood was up and he was a product of the Royal Navy, which had a tradition of aggression, and confidence bred from a long record of success.

The gunboats were pulling quickly back into the port, but

Kennedy ignored them, instead directly following in the path of the sloop. *Oleander* was sailing fast now, close hauled on the starboard tack, her canvas taut and straining, her wake foaming along her sides. The sloop had realised that *Oleander* was after her and had set more sail, heading towards the port.

"She's trying to get under the guns of the fort", said Kennedy to Luciani, who was standing near the helm. "It'll be a close thing."

*Oleander* was now close to the French sloop, directly astern of her. He saw the guns of the fort fire, but the splashes were short, and in any case the gunners ashore could not fire at *Oleander* without hitting the Frenchman. Closer and closer came *Oleander*, sailing almost twice as fast as the sloop, until Kennedy could make out the faces of individual Frenchmen aboard her, watching in horrified fascination as the great mouths of the Carrons on *Oleander*'s foredeck were trained on their ship.

*Oleander* was no more than fifty yards astern of the brig when the Frenchman put his helm down and turned to starboard.

"FIRE!" shouted Kennedy, and the starboard Carron fired, sending its huge ball smashing through the stern of the sloop to cause a trail of destruction and horror as it travelled the length of the interior of the ship. "Luff her", he said to Luciani, and, as *Oleander*'s head came up into the wind, the port Carron could bear, and it fired, sending another huge ball into the stern of the sloop. The French ship had now turned, and as *Oleander* came about, she surged past the sloop, almost touching, and *Oleander*'s broadside fired, deliberately, one gun after another, without any reply.

Kennedy, through the smoke, saw the sloop's tricolour hauled down. He shouted, "CEASE FIRE, CEASE FIRE," and *Oleander*'s guns fell silent.

"She's sinking," said Luciani, and as they watched, the French brig settled lower in the water.

"The Smashers got her", opined Luciani, "very effective point blank like that."

A ball from the fort hit the water just ahead of *Oleander*.

"South-east if you please, Mister," said Kennedy to Luciani "I think the French have been sufficiently diverted!"

# CHAPTER 46 - AFTERMATH

By the time the gunboats arrived within range, a small breeze, almost northerly, had started to blow, and the ship was moving slowly. The sky was brilliantly clear, and Pascoe believed that the breeze was the beginning of a Mistral, the cold northerly wind which dominated the weather in this part of the Mediterranean. The boats fired and *Daisy* fired back, but no damage was done to the ship and, as far as Pascoe could see, they scored no hits on the gunboats. There was a lull in the wind and the gunboats closed the distance, firing as they rowed. The wind returned and *Daisy* was underway again when a ball smashed into her stern, a hard blow, and the helmsman shouted, "She won't answer."

Pascoe looked at the whipstaff, and then went below and saw that the ball had smashed into the rudder stock, damaging it and detaching the tiller. He was about to shout for the Carpenter, or rather the young Carpenter's Mate currently filling that office, when the man arrived of his own volition.

"Cut the whipstaff away from the tiller", said Pascoe, "and lash the tiller directly onto the rudder. Bang some nails in for good measure. Tell me as soon as it's ready."

The man, assisted by several others, set to with a will, but when Pascoe got back on deck the gunboats were close.

"Get the sweeps out, Mr Soares," he said. "We'll control her by sheeting the sails and backwatering with the sweeps if we have to. Three men on each oar."

"*Oleander's* coming," shouted a voice from forward, and Pascoe looked up to see the schooner ahead of them, heeling under a press of sail, perhaps three miles away. The gunboats saw her too, and turned, heading towards the shore.

Pascoe thought his system for steering the xebec worked well. When the ship luffed up in the northerly breeze, they released the mizzen sheet and the men at the sweeps on the port side dug their blades in the water. When she bore away, they released the foresail and backwatered with the starboard oars. Progress was not rapid or very straight, but progress there was, and when *Oleander* came up with them, Pascoe thought they were getting the hang of it.

*Oleander* tacked, in the way, thought Pascoe, that only *Oleander* could, and lay hove to on the starboard tack. They saw a boat lowered from the schooner, and soon Kennedy was standing on the xebec's deck, surveying the damage and inspecting the rudder.

"Signal for Chips to come aboard. He'll know to bring his tools."

With *Daisy's* rudder repaired and the Mistral blowing strongly, the ships sailed in company on a south-westerly course, knowing their progress would be observed from ashore, until it was dark, when they parted company, with *Daisy* continuing to the south and *Oleander* heading back into the wind, towards Maguelone.

\*\*\*

Snowden, ashore, saw the flashes of gunfire diminish and then cease, and he slept again until dawn was breaking. The wind had dropped and, to his horror, just offshore, he could see *Daisy*, becalmed, with the gunboats in pursuit. He watched, transfixed, as the gunboats came close to the ship, firing, and then in relief as the breeze filled in and the ship drew away, sailing an erratic course with the sweeps on either side steering her. *Well done, Pascoe*, he thought, realising what must have happened – *who needs a rudder?!*

The Mistral had set in properly when Snowden saw the unmistakable outline of *Oleander* sailing fast from the west and heaving to as she came up with *Daisy*. He felt a slight surge of hope – perhaps after all they would be able to get him off – but this ended in utter disappointment when he saw soldiers on the beach, and the gunboats, quite secure in the offshore wind, anchor in a line in the shallows just off the land.

Snowden, working as quickly as his weakened state would allow, dug himself desperately into the sandy soil, until he thought he would be if not invisible, then quite inconspicuous to any searchers. Later, he lay on the sparse vegetation, warmed by the sun, drifting in and out of consciousness, waiting to be discovered, but the searchers did not come. He had some biscuit and a flask of water in his pouch and managed to consume a little of each, despite his headache and nausea and the horrible raw feeling that afflicted him after a blow on the head. In the night, he kept watch, and at about midnight there were muzzle flashes from the beach and he surmised that *Oleander*, or her boats, had attempted to close with the land, but had been surprised by the French. He hoped there had been no casualties. Fires were lit on the beach and he could see men gathered round them, eating.

He became conscious, slowly, that his silent world was becoming a little less silent, and was briefly thankful that he was not permanently deafened. About three, he realised his position was impossible. The French would begin to seriously search for him in the morning and there was no possibility of *Oleander* picking him up from the beach. He could not escape overland – he was on a narrow bank of sand separated from the mainland by saltwater lagoons and the canal – and there was no succour for him in France, anyway.

# CHAPTER 47 - PEGASUS

In the dark of night, Captain Clasby had waited impatiently on the quarterdeck of his frigate, *Pegasus*. She was a beautiful ship, almost new, and he had lavished much of his own money on her and her crew. He knew he was a good commander, and his ship was efficient and the crew cheerful and willing.

Almost in despair, he wondered how things had gone so wrong. Here they were, anchored off a lee shore, waiting to retrieve an expedition that was manifestly foolish. He had no faith whatsoever that the venture would be successful, but he knew that his duty was to wait. He blamed himself. He should have stood his ground and refused to be browbeaten by that fool Masterson into anchoring here and landing the troops through the surf. Masterson! It went further than that. He had argued with Admiral Jameson, vehemently, but in the end he had backed down. It was either that or resign his commission. He wished to God now that he had resigned.

And here he was, awaiting the dawn, with *Pegasus* anchored off almost a dead lee shore, the beach only half a mile away, the white surf beating on it visible even in the darkness. He could get her off when the time came, he knew, unless there were shallows between the ship and the open sea. He went through it once more in his mind – he wished he could discuss it with the First Lieutenant and Master, but they were on the maindeck, with much of the crew, trying to keep the boats from damaging themselves as they crashed against each other and the ship, despite the booms they had rigged to keep them away.

He made his mind up. He had had enough. If he did not get underway now, he would lose the ship. He would heave the cable in and, when it was short, cut it, get her sailing – either tack would do – and claw her off until she was a couple of miles offshore, and wait there. When the shore party returned they would launch the boats from there and take them off the beach.

He heard a shout from above, "On deck, boats on the port beam, close", looked and saw, against the paling eastern sky, the dim outline of several large boats, with guns at their bows, but he did not hear the boats' guns fire, or feel the ship slew sideways to the wind as her cable was cut, or even the ball that ended his life as it hit him square on the chest.

As soon as Wentworth, *Pegasus*' First Lieutenant, who was working desperately on the maindeck, heard the shout from above and then the gunfire, he rushed to the quarterdeck. He saw the remains of his captain, felt balls thudding into the ship's side, and realised that the ship was broadside to the wind.

"They've cut the cable," he shouted to the Master, who had followed him from the maindeck. "I'll get the topsails on her," the man yelled, and blew his whistle. The speed with which the crew released the topsails, braced them round and sheeted them home was a tribute to the way that Clasby had worked up his ship, and, for a moment, as the ship gathered way and came under control, Wentworth thought that escape was possible. He was urging the ship forward – *come on, my love, you can do it* – when there was another barrage of shots from the French boats and the main topsail yard, with its sail attached, came crashing down onto the deck. The halyard, he thought as the ship fell off the wind.

"Quarters", he shouted, and, as drums beat and whistles blew, "Get rid of the landing boats and get the mizzen on her."

Dawn was breaking as the mizzen was set, and the ship came back up into the wind and started to forge slowly ahead, her progress slowed by the boats alongside. The shore was very close now and she bumped on the sand, heavily, once, twice, and stopped, aground, the pressure of the wind on her rigging and sails and the waves building up under exposed bilge, heeling her towards the shore.

The French boats were close now and Wentworth shouted, "Stand by to repel boarders." Whistles blew and men staggered across the wet sloping decks to grab weapons, but the French boats did not approach any closer, labouring as they were in the waves.

"That's done it," said the Second Lieutenant, pointing towards the shore, and Wentworth saw soldiers, a great many soldiers, arriving at the top of the beach, with horses pulling guns. As Wentworth watched, the guns were unhitched and men worked feverishly to set them up and aim at the frigate. With the ship heeled as she was, *Pegasus'* guns could not reply. He knew he could wait until the guns ashore, firing at their leisure, reduced the ship to a mangled wreck and then surrender, or ...

"Strike the colours," he said, bitterness welling up inside him.

# CHAPTER 48 - THE BEACH AT MAGUELONE

Kennedy took *Oleander*, gently, very gently into the shore, against the Mistral blowing out to sea, listening intently to the calls of the leadsman. When he could stand it no more, he dropped the anchor on a short scope of cable, the outline of the shore with the white surf breaking on it clearly visible. They brought the longboat, which had been towing astern, alongside and men climbed aboard. Luciani stood beside Kennedy.

"Do your best, Giotto, but get out at the first sign of trouble. If there's any resistance on the beach, the Old Man and Watton won't be able to get down to the boat anyway."

"I'll try, Ken."

The boat departed, and there was silence for several minutes, until he heard, distinctly, an order in French, carried to him by the wind, and then firing, small arms and cannons. *The damned gunboats*, he thought to himself, *they've put the gunboats just off the beach.*

There was a shout from the forepart of the ship, "Longboat's returning", and then, as the boat come alongside, he felt a slight shudder run through in *Oleander*'s fabric as a ball hit her, somewhere forward.

"Bobstay's gone," came another shout. Kennedy knew

that the loss of the bobstay, which braced the long bowsprit against the loads of the forestays, would severely limit *Oleander*'s sail-carrying capacity.

"Cut the cable," called out Kennedy. "Let her fall off, and get the main on her."

He turned to speak to Luciani, who had just appeared beside him, felt a great blow on his shoulder, and fell to the deck.

Luciani, seeing that *Oleander* was making sternway, ported the helm, encouraging the ship to fall off onto the starboard tack.

"Get the loot into the cabin," he said to a passing seaman, and then supervised setting the reefed mainsail, hoping the mainsail would put less strain on the bowsprit than anything set on the foremast.

The Carpenter came to report. "The stem's damaged and the bobstay fitting is dangling in the sea at the end of the stay. I'll start work, but we'll have to keep the strain off it as much as we can."

Luciani thought quickly. There seemed to be very little chance they would be able to get into the beach to rescue Snowden – in fact, he admitted to himself, none at all. They had been very lucky to get away with the night's operation, but with the damaged rigging, the ship could not sail to windward to close with the land, and if they tried it the ship could be damaged or lost. He kept the ship on her south-west course and went into the cabin to see Kennedy.

They had cut off Kennedy's jacket and shirt, and he sat, pale faced, in a chair, with Butterfield and Cox attending to him, but to Luciani's relief there appeared to be no blood and Kennedy was conscious.

"How are you doing, Ken?" he asked.

Kennedy did not answer, but Butterfield said, "It was a musket ball, just about spent. It's bruised him and I think may have broken his arm, right at the top," He looked at Luciani. "He will be quite all right."

*** 

Suddenly, Snowden remembered the dinghy they had buried on the beach when they had attacked the barges, seemingly so long ago. The Mistral was blowing, strongly, offshore, and, if he could get into the dinghy he would be blown away from the land and would hopefully be spotted by *Oleander*. It was a faint hope, he knew, but it was either that or surrender. Surrender! He remembered Jack Stone's treatment at the hands of the French, and Sidney Smith's and Wright's. He was a serving officer, and should be respected as such, but he had been involved in clandestine work ashore, in league with people who could justifiably be called spies, and his successes had certainly annoyed the French. He thought of Fouché at the soirée in Paris, and the Temple prison, and, on the desolate, cold, windswept beach, made up his mind. He would try to escape, and he would do it now, before his resolve failed him.

He remembered where the markers for the buried dinghy were, probably only a hundred or so yards away from his hiding place, and he set out, crawling on all fours, bayonet in hand. He saw no soldiers – they seemed to be gathered round the fires, confident after their success at repelling *Oleander*'s longboat – and, though his hearing was returning, heard none.

He saw the posts that had been set up to point to the dinghy's location, and, with his bayonet, probed the sand. To his surprise, the wind had blown the sand almost entirely off the flat bottom of the dinghy and the boat was hardly buried. The dinghy was normally suspended in davits from *Oleander*'s stern. It was quick to launch and used mostly in harbour. It was not large, perhaps twelve feet long, built of cedar, and light, something Snowden was grateful for as he carefully dug with his hands along the almost vertical sides of the boat.

There was a shout from the sea and Snowden peered

in the direction he thought it had come from and saw the dim outline of a gunboat, riding to her anchor in the offshore wind. She was perhaps three hundred yards from where he was. He scanned carefully to the right and saw another one, lying a similar distance away in the opposite direction. *Lucky*, he thought, *you're in the middle of the gap.* The exercise of digging worsened his headache, until it was almost disabling. His arms felt leaden, but he forced himself to continue until the dinghy was pretty well exposed, and he fell flat on the sand, exhausted.

He knew it would soon be dawn and that he must leave immediately. Grabbing the dinghy under the port gunwale, he slowly lifted it up until the boat rested on its starboard side, vertical. Keeping the boat balanced, a difficult thing to achieve in the wind, he worked his way round it until he was on the opposite side. With infinite care, he lowered the boat to the ground so it was the right way up, pointing towards the sea. He saw the oars were in the bottom of the boat, under the seats, and, very slowly to avoid making any noise, he retrieved them and fitted them over the holes in the gunwale.

He made a final survey of the beach and then grabbed the boat's painter and began to drag it towards the sea, almost overcome by his headache and the nausea sweeping over him. The water, when he reached it, felt surprisingly warm, and he moved to the stern of the boat and pushed it out through the small waves until it was floating. He gave it a hard shove and then fell into it, over the transom, where he lay for a moment, collecting himself, before sitting on the thwart and picking up the oars. He did not attempt to row, but merely used the oars to steer the boat so that the wind was directly astern. He looked over his shoulder, provoking his headache, and saw to his horror that there was a gunboat ahead, riding to her anchor. He heaved on his port oar, and the dinghy responded so that it ran close down the side of the gunboat, not more than thirty feet away. He could see nobody in her, and the dinghy was soon past, out into the windy Gulf of Lions.

He felt an overwhelming urge to lie in the bottom of the boat and sleep, but knew he must not. It would be light soon and perhaps he would see *Oleander*, though he feared the Mistral was blowing him too far east, away from where she might be hove to after her night's adventures.

# CHAPTER 49 - BÉZIERS

Messengers arrived at Morlaix's headquarters. The first, at five in the morning, reported there had been an attack on Palavas, with rockets, and there had been an explosion ashore. There appeared to be a single attacking ship, an Arab-looking craft, and gunboats were pursuing her.

Morlaix and Badeau looked at the map, and Morlaix said, "A single, small ship, firing rockets. An explosion ashore. I don't believe this is a serious attack, it is perhaps intended as a diversion."

A second messenger arrived, and walked through a room which had become tense and silent, watchful as the man reported to the Admiral, but relaxing when they saw the smile break out on his face. He turned to address his staff.

"The English landing party has surrendered on the Ensérune Ridge. The ambush worked perfectly. The Malpas Tunnel has not been damaged", and as cheering erupted he shouted above the noise, "Well done, gentlemen."

Morlaix retired to his own room, apart from the general jubilation, waiting for the message from the beach. He had always known, barring some extreme circumstance, that any party landed to attack the canal would be defeated, but to really send a message to the English he knew he must destroy their ship. There was a knock on the door and Badeau entered, accompanied by an infantry officer. Morlaix knew, as soon as he saw their faces, that the news was good.

The soldier stood to attention and said, "Ensign Nissan, 12th Field Artillery, Sir."

"Go on," gestured Morlaix.

"Sir, I have the honour to report that the British frigate *Pegasus* was attacked by the boats from the Orb and covered by artillery from the shore. She has struck her colours and is ashore at Valras. She has been slightly damaged, but appears to be in no danger of breaking up. Efforts are underway to rescue her crew."

"Well", said Morlaix, "that is indeed good news. Can you add anything, Ensign Nissan?"

"No, Sir. The ship was in no position to fight – her guns could not bear because she was heeling. I believe the wind is dropping now. I believe the ship will be salvaged, and the rescue of the crew will be successful."

"Thank you very much, Ensign."

He turned to Badeau. "Tonight has been a success."

The news at one in the afternoon was less encouraging. Sète had been attacked by a single ship, thought to be Snowden's *Oleander*, which had sailed right into the harbour and damaged ships and warehouses. The ship had been pursued by gunboats and a sloop of war, but *Oleander* had fought them off and sunk the sloop.

By three, Morlaix' leg was painful, and exhaustion was setting in. "Badeau", he said, "I am going home. Let me know if there is any important news."

Morlaix limped home, flanked by two junior officers, clearly conflicted between their desire to prevent their admiral falling and fearful of touching him without being asked.

Odile met him at the door and looked at him quizzically.

"A success, Odile, not quite complete, but nevertheless an overwhelming success."

***

Through the night, Pascoe took the xebec slowly west-north-west, into the land. As dawn broke, they were about a mile and a half south of the beach where the main landing should have taken place, and Pascoe was standing on the forward yard, arm around the mast, telescope in hand. The wind was off the land, strong, but the waves were small.

He saw, to his horror, *Pegasus*, Clasby's crack frigate, lying heeled over just off the beach, clearly aground with a huge tricolour flying above a British ensign at her mizzen peak. French men and women, it seemed like hundreds of them, with horses and carts, were working round her, emptying the ship to make her more buoyant. Derricks were rigged and he could see a gun swung out over the ship's side. To seaward there were several boats, undoubtedly laying out anchors. At the top of the beach, artillery pieces pointed out to sea, and he could see gunboats, similar to the ones they had encountered yesterday, pulled up on the sand.

When he descended, the crew, almost to a man, were lining the rail, transfixed by the sight.

With a heavy heart, Pascoe gave orders and the xebec bore away, heading south, away from the shore, for Gibraltar, distant nearly a thousand miles.

# CHAPTER 50 - DAMAGED

When Luciani went back to the cabin a couple of hours later, Kennedy seemed slightly better, though he was pale and listless and his arm was in a sling. "How are things, Giotto?"

"The stem was damaged by a ball and the bobstay fitting has come off. There were no injuries apart from you, but the longboat was hit and we've cut it loose. Pretty well smashed. I'm heading a bit west of south with just the mainsail on her. We're quite a way off the land, should be clear of those damned gunboats."

Kennedy looked at him. "Can we go back for the Old Man, do you think, have another go?"

Luciani shook his head. "I don't believe we can at present. The ship cannot go to windward, and it would be very difficult to fight in her present condition. The place is …", he searched for the right English phrase, "a hornet's nest. We cannot even heave her to, all we can do is head slowly south with the wind behind us."

Kennedy sighed "Very well, Giotto, it seems we can't do anything for the Old Man and Watton until the repairs are finished."

*Oleander* jogged on all that night, under reefed mainsail, the men working on the stem fitting sometimes half submerged as the ship pitched in the waves whipped up by the north-westerly wind.

# CHAPTER 51 - THE FRENCH FLEET

The Carpenter, rubbing his eyes with exhaustion, shivering in his wet clothes, had spoken to Luciani.

"We've finished. I reckon it'll hold, at least until we get her into a dockyard. Would you like to come and have a look?"

Luciani had let out a sigh of relief. "I certainly would, Chips."

That was an hour ago, and now *Oleander* was hard on the wind, heading back towards Maguelone and the faint hope of rescuing the men on the beach, when the lookout shouted, "Sail on the horizon, starboard bow four points."

And then, a few minutes later, "And another."

And then, "It's a whole bloody fleet!"

As Luciani focused and steadied his telescope, he could see that the lookout was right, it was a fleet, or at least a powerful squadron. Ships of the line, frigates and smaller vessels, clearly heading to pass between Ibiza and the mainland. *Nelson*, he thought, *heading towards Gibraltar, same as us.*

He looked again, comforted at this demonstration of England's maritime power, and ordered a course alteration to converge with the fleet. He went into the cabin to speak to Kennedy, who was recovering well but who still looked white and pinched. He was starting to speak when he heard another shout from the lookout, and Iris burst into the cabin.

"They be Froggies", and then, seeing the dumbstruck expressions on Kennedy's and Luciani's faces, said, with great emphasis, as though talking to idiots, "Not Nelson, Froggies."

"My God", said Kennedy, "they've got out of Toulon."

There was no doubt about it, they had to get closer, to ascertain the strength of the French fleet, while avoiding capture, and to get the news as quickly as they could to …

Kennedy was in an agony of indecision. *Where?* Nelson was blockading Toulon, but the French were here. Nelson had either missed them in the heavy weather, or he had deliberately allowed them out and had set a trap for them. If that was the case, thought Kennedy, it would probably be very difficult to find Nelson to tell him the location of the French fleet, while *Oleander* simultaneously avoided the French. The French were heading just south of east, a course that would take them between Ibiza and the Spanish mainland, and their destination presumably was the Strait of Gibraltar, although there were Spanish ports along the way, notably Cartagena.

Kennedy made up his mind and spoke to Luciani.

"We'll have to tack, then edge in closer, count them, and then go as hard as we can to Gib." He swallowed hard. "I'm afraid we'll have to leave the Old Man and Watton."

For several hours, in the brilliant Mediterranean sunshine, *Oleander* ran almost parallel to the French fleet, edging ever closer, until, about three in the afternoon, Luciani believed he had a good idea of their numbers, and reported to Kennedy in the cabin.

"Looks like eleven battlers, Ken, and a number of frigates and sloops. There might be one or two more, but probably not."

"My word, Giotto, that's a fleet and no mistake. I'll probably not see its like again, so if you'll give me a hand I'll come on deck and have a look for myself. Can you carry my glass?"

Luciani and Cox the steward got Kennedy on deck, where

he stood leaning on the port rail, looking at the French sails.

"My God", he said, "that's an impressive sight. Have you noticed…"

He was interrupted by the lookout's shout: "One of 'ems altering towards us, I reckon. Frigate. Just setting her t'gallants, she is."

"Get all the sail you can on her, Giotto, we have to get to Gib before the French. I'm sorry, but there's nothing we can do for the Old Man."

*Oleander* heeled, the spray flew, but the repair to the stem held, and the frigate, for all her t'gallants, fell steadily behind, until, as darkness fell, she slid below the horizon.

# CHAPTER 52 - GIBRALTAR AGAIN

*Daisy*, two days ahead of *Oleander*, after an uneventful trip, arrived in Gibraltar on a blustery morning, and Pascoe, in his dress uniform and clutching the despatches he had written, went ashore to deliver them. After a long wait, he was shown into the Admiral's office, where Jameson was making a show of attending to other business. To Pascoe, Jameson looked exhausted.

"Ah yes", he said, "Mr Pascoe from that Moorish thing."

"Yes, Sir", said Pascoe, "*Daisy*."

"Very well, Pascoe, you seem to have made a diversion, as ordered, but were nearly captured and have lost your Commander and a Marine ensign. Do you have any news of Snowden? I fear he had no business going ashore like that."

"No Sir, I have no news, but I must say ..."

"That's enough, Mr Pascoe. If I want your opinion I'll ask for it."

"Yes, Sir."

"And this intelligence about *Pegasus*. You are sure? You saw the ship yourself?"

"I did, Sir, we took *Daisy* in pretty close. *Pegasus* seemed fairly undamaged, I expect the Frogs will have her off by now."

"Just the facts, Pascoe, if you please."

"Yes, Sir", and then emboldened, "the facts are, Sir, that there is a fine British frigate on the beach and the French are making a highly organised effort to get her off. She'll be afloat …"

"Was there any sign of the landing party?"

"None at all, Sir, but I expect …"

"That will be all, Pascoe."

"Yes, Sir," said Pascoe, and left the room.

***

As *Oleander* approached Gibraltar, she fired guns to draw attention to the signals she was flying, and Kennedy was ashore even before the ship had anchored.

He did not make it as far as the Admiral's room, as Jameson met him at the dock, and, after a short conversation, the admiral boarded his barge to rejoin his squadron, patrolling to intercept the French.

# CHAPTER 53 - THE DINGHY

When the dawn broke, Snowden knew he had lost his gamble. The dinghy was floating in an angry sea, covered in whitecaps, but there was not a single sail in sight.

*Oleander* would not rescue him, he was on his own, in a small boat, with the wind blowing him – he looked towards the rising sun and estimated – as far as he could make out, towards distant Sardinia. It was cold and he was wet. His head ached terribly and suddenly he knew he was about to be seasick. With a shiver, he lay down in the bottom of the boat, as miserable as he had ever been in his life.

From time to time, to start with, he bailed the boat, but as night fell, he felt too lethargic to even lift himself from her bottom boards, and the bilge water which rushed from side to side kept him completely wet. As he shivered in the darkness, the wind still blew, and he drifted in and out of consciousness, thinking of Isabella, or perhaps Julia, they seemed to run into one another. Later, dimly, for a moment, he was aware of voices and of rough handling, but he believed himself dreaming and lapsed back into darkness.

He dreamt. Sometimes the dreams were pleasant - in Gibraltar with Isabella; playing at cards, and sometimes they were hard and violent – the exultation he felt in battle; the desolation of the beach at Maguelone. One persistent dream was of lying in a narrow bed, with people feeding and talking to him, though he could not understand what they were saying. Eventually he realised that this was not a dream, and that he was aboard a ship, a ship at sea. The air was warm, and the ship rolled rhythmically. A small ship, he thought. He could hear the creak of ropes, the occasional slatting of sails and the sound of feet on the deck above his head.

He lay there, half conscious, trying to remember. He recalled the dawn in the dinghy, the crushing disappointment of the empty sea, but that was all. A man came up to his bed, perhaps a surgeon, and sat on a chest which was lashed to the deck beside the bed.

"Good afternoon," the surgeon said, in heavily accented English.

Snowden tried to speak, but only a croak came out, and he was given some heavily diluted wine.

The surgeon repeated, "Good afternoon. Can you hear me? Nod your head if you cannot talk."

Snowden nodded.

"You have a severe concussion, monsieur. You must rest."

He looked for a response from his patient, but there was none, Snowden slept. The surgeon felt his pulse and left.

Snowden, drifting in and out of sleep, had no idea of the passage of time, but he was aware of the surgeon's occasional visits, and of the motion of the ship, an unceasing, deep, rhythmic roll.

Occasionally, there were shouts of 'rafale', and the rolling was replaced by the sharp heel of the ship, and the gentle creaking of timbers with the scream of the wind and the flogging of sails, as whistles blew and men ran on deck, fighting to reduce canvas in the squall.

Slowly, his mind seeming to hardly function, Snowden

assembled and processed these pieces of information: The soft warmth, the squalls, the rolling ...

"Trade wind roll" he muttered to himself, and opened his eyes to see the surgeon, accompanied by an officer, standing by his bed, swaying as the ship moved under them.

"Good afternoon," said the officer, in almost perfect English. "You are correct, a trade wind roll"

Snowden nodded

"Ship?" he whispered.

"*Herault, frégate. En flûte.* For Martinique"

# NOTES

I have tried to make the novel as plausible and as historically accurate as possible. There was a great deal of anti-French sentiment in Spain at the time, which culminated in the uprisings of 1808, hauntingly depicted by Goya, and eventually the Peninsular War. Captain Wright is a historical figure. An associate of Sydney Smith, he died in suspicious circumstances during his second incarceration in the Temple prison in Paris. The French fleet broke out of Toulon in 1805 and passed through the Strait bound for Martinique, an operation which culminated in their defeat at Trafalgar.

The canals described in the book were very important to the economy of southern France. The Canal du Midi effectively joined the Atlantic Ocean to the Mediterranean – it was the first large scale summit canal, an astonishing work of imagination and engineering. It's creator, Riquet, had to overcome enormous challenges, including providing a water supply and huge differences in level. I may have been guilty of slightly advancing the opening date of the Canal du Rhône à Sète, which connects the Midi Canal to the Rhone allowing vessels to bypass the hostile Gulf of Lions.

The Sally Rovers, much feared in earlier times, had ceased to be a significant force by the time the novel is set, but independent actions by individual reis are not improbable.

I have cruised to all of the locations in the book, either in our 31' motorboat 'Mitch', or in our 40' aluminium yacht, 'Kadash'.

'Mitch' overwintered in Lezardrieux, where Snowden cut out 'Blonde', and then went along the Breton coast, avoiding the Libenter reef to visit Aber Wrac'h, before transiting the Chenal du Four and the Raz de Sein. We visited the Basque Roads, where Commodore Parkinson came to such an unfortunate end, and passed through the Pertuis d'Antioche on our way to the Gironde. We went along the Midi Canal, marvelled at the Malpas Tunnel, and at Sète, joined the Canal du Rhône à Sète. Like the Spanish barges, we moored for the night against the bank near the Maguelone Cathedral, and even spent some time on the beach, in rather more pleasant circumstances than Snowden. More recently 'Kadash' has taken us across the Bay of Lions, and then along the Catalan coast, spending time in Palamos, walking the same country as Snowden and Puyol. We had a very windy west bound trip through the Strait of Gibraltar, as 'Oleander' did, working the tides and hugging the Moroccan coast, though the wind was behind us, and we had Raymarine to tell us exactly where we were. We visited the astonishing city of Rabat (Sale), and like 'Daisy', had a rather unpleasant experience on the bar, before experiencing the "trade wind roll" on our way to the West Indies.

# GLOSSARY

74 - two decked warship, larger than a frigate, nominally armed with 74 guns.

AB - Able Bodied seaman.

ancien regime - the former Royalist regime of France overthrown by the Revolution.

Armée d'Angleterre - the army assembled by Napoleon at Boulogne for the purpose of invading Britain.

Barbarossa – most famous of the Moorish corsairs.

Billy Ruffian – 'Bellerophon', famous British warship.

blockade – during the French Revolutionary Wars the Royal Navy closely blockaded the entire French coast for many years, winter and summer – an outstanding display of seamanship and determination which had the side effect of making the Navy extremely efficient, in contrast to its French counterpart which was bottled up in port.

Board of Trade – department of the British Government which became responsible for enforcing the Merchant Shipping Act later in the nineteenth century.

bomb, bomb vessel - a small ship built for the bombardment of shore targets, armed with a mortar and rockets. The most famous bombs were Erebus and Terror.

bosun (boatswain) – senior seaman.

braces – ropes to control the yards which support square sails; hence 'lee braces' are braces on the side of the ship away from the wind.

Brittany Canal - canal which links the Channel and Biscay coasts.

Bumboat – small boat selling goods to the crews of ships.

Canal du Midi – (Midi Canal, Royal Canal) - a remarkable summit level canal, completed in 1681, which connects the Garonne at

Toulouse with the Mediterranean at Sete.
Canal du Rhône à Sète – a canal which connects the terminus of the Canal du Midi at Sète with the Rhône at Beaucaire, thus avoiding the passage across the notorious Gulf of Lions
Ça ira – French revolutionary song
capstan – winch with vertical axis, on sailing ships driven by men pushing wooden bars as they walked around it.
Cardouan lighthouse - a huge lighthouse which marks the entrance of the Gironde.
careen – to haul a grounded ship down so that her masts are nearly horizontal.
Carron (carronade) – a gun manufactured by the Carron Ironworks of Scotland. The company was founded in 1789, and now manufactures domestic sinks.
Carteret – port on the western side of the Cotentin Peninsular noted for its exceptional tides and vast sandy beaches.
chasse-marée – literally 'tide chaser', a heavily canvassed French vessel used for smuggling and similar activities.
Chenal du Four (The Trade) – passage between the mainland coast of Brittany and the island of Ushant subject to extreme tidal currents
Chesil Beach – a long shingle spit which joins Portland to the mainland. With the wind from the west or south west it forms a lee shore, especially for vessels proceeding up the English Channel. The beach is very steep, and the undertow from the surf in rough conditions makes escaping from the sea very difficult.
Chouan - name given to the Bretons who violently opposed the Revolution
ci-devants - "former people" such as aristocrats from the Royalist regime
coasting – trading along the coast rather than 'deep sea'. In British ships coasting is traditionally limited to the area between Brest and the Elbe.
cockpit sole – the 'floor' of the cockpit.
Congreve rocket - a rocket with an explosive warhead, similar to

the familiar firework rocket but much larger.
Downs, The – anchorage off the east coast of Kent.
Eggs and Bacon – familiar name used by sailors for HMS Agamemnon. Several ships were given such names, including Bellerophon -"Billy Ruffian", and Temeraire, Turners "Fighting Temeraire", Saucy.
fall – rope system supporting a ship's boat.
famous victory - a reference to Southey's famous anti-war poem, "After Blenheim".
Fontainebleau – royal palace, formerly a hunting lodge, about 20 miles from Paris
fo'c'stle – (abbreviation of 'forecastle') accommodation at the fore part of the ship where the crew lived 'before the mast', as opposed to the officers living in the aft end of the ship
fother, fothering – to stem a leak below the waterline by stretching a sail over the hole.
Fortuneswell – a village near on the north west part of Portland.
Fouché - minister of police, responsible for massacres during the Revolution.
Frégate en flute – a warship modified to carry troops or stores with reduced armament and sail plan
Gironde - the estuary of the Garonne and Dordogne rivers, connecting Bordeaux with the Bay of Biscay.
Genoese tower – round forts built by the Genoese, very common around the coast of Corsica. The one at Myrtle Point was the prototype for the British Martello Tower
Godoy – Spanish politician
Hard Times of Old England – English folksong.
Hawke's squadron - in November 1759, in a rising gale, a British squadron under Admiral Hawke chased a French fleet into Quiberon Bay and won a famous victory.
Heart of Oak – official march of the Royal Navy, composed by William Boyce in 1759 with lyrics by David Garrick.
heaving line – thin rope used for throwing from one vessel to another.
helm down – turning the ship's head into the wind.

helm up – turning the ship's head away from the wind.

high water at Dover - tides are governed by the phases of the moon. The time of tides in the Channel are often referenced to the time of high water at Dover.

hove to - a sailing ship is sometimes stopped in heavy weather by backing one or more sails, and keeping the ship close to the wind by putting the helm down

in irons – ship stationary and pointing directly into the wind with the sails flapping.

Iroise – Royal Navy frigate which had been captured from the French. French ships captured by the Royal Navy generally continued to use their original names.

jib boom - spar extending from the bowsprit.

ketch - a small vessel with two masts, the after mast shorter than the forward one

King – In Weymouth Bound, Not by Sea, Cape Corse and Gulf of Lions, the king referred to is George III, 'Farmer George'. George was very fond of Weymouth and spent long periods there. As described in Weymouth Bound, he was renowned as an early riser.

landing – smuggling contraband ashore.

Le Petit Neptune Français - an eighteenth century pilot book describing the coasts and ports of France.

leach, or leech – the aft side of a fore and aft sail, or the lee side of a square sail

Leave Her Johnny – chanty with improvised derogatory words about the ship and officers traditionally sung when the crew is about to pay off at the end of a voyage. Perhaps the most authentic version was recorded by Bob Roberts.

Leghorn – Livorno, a major port on the coast of Italy near Pisa

Levanter – easterly wind in the Mediterranean

Lilli Bulero – satirical ballad about Ireland. Signature tune of the BBC World Service.

lugger – a vessel, generally a small one, propelled by a lugsail, rather than a gaff mainsail.

luff – to turn the ship into the wind so that the 'luff' or fore part of the sail flaps

lunars – method of determining the ship's position in the absence of a chronometer, considered to be a difficult technique to master.

main topsail – upper sail on the main mast.

maintop, foretop - platform for a lookout at the top of the mast.

Marins - marines of the Imperial Guard.

Martinique - an island in the West Indies

midshipman – trainee officer in the Royal Navy.

Master - non-commissioned officer responsible for navigating the ship. A smaller ship might be commanded by a commissioned lieutenant who would combine the roles of master and commander

Mistral – wind which blows down the Rhone and into the Mediterranean.

mizzen – aftermost mast of a ship.

Nore – a shoal in the Thames Estuary where a guard ship was anchored

painter - a rope attached to the bow of a small boat used for towing etc.

pawl – ratchet.

Pool of London – part of the River Thames below London Bridge where ships worked their cargo.

Popham – Royal Navy signal code devised by Admiral Sir Home Riggs Popham KCB, a naval officer who led a varied and interesting life.

port (starboard) tack – ship sailing so that the wind is coming from the port (starboard) side.

port wheel - when ships were steered by tiller, "port helm" meant moving the tiller to port, steering the ship to starboard. When wheel steering became widespread, this lead to considerable confusion.

Post – promotion to captain

privateer – a privately owned ship with a 'letter of marque' from its government permitting it to attack and capture ships belonging to enemy nations prize money – when an enemy ship was captured the value of the ship was assessed by a prize court and the proceeds shared between the officers and crew of the capturing ship.

Quiberon - peninsular in Brittany.

queue - ponytail

race (tide race) – an area of confused breaking seas caused by the tidal stream running strongly over obstructions. Several races feature in the books: the Portland Race, an area of confused breaking seas off the tip of the Isle of Portland, the Race of Alderney, between Alderney and the adjacent coast of France, and the Raz de Sein in western Brittany, a narrow rocky channel which divides the English Channel and the Bay of Biscay. These races are extremely dangerous in some states of wind and tide. In the Race of Alderney, off La Foraine beacon, the tide can run at up to nine knots.

Rance - river, now dammed by a hydrogeneration scheme, which enters the sea at St Malo.

Raz de Sein – narrow rock strewn channel on the western extremity of Brittany through which the tide flows with great violence.

reis - corsair captain and shipowner.

renegado - westerner who has "gone Turk" and embraced Islam.

revenue cutter – small ship used to suppress smuggling.

St Peters - or St Pierre, the main town of the island of Guernsey.

Salé (Rabat) – city and now the capital of Morocco, located on the Atlantic coast at the mouth of the Bouregreg River, with remarkable architecture and history

Sally Rovers – corsairs who operated from what, at its height, was the Republic of Salé. They roved widely, as far as Iceland and Ireland.

scandalised mainsail – reducing the power of the mainsail by lowering the peak of the gaff.

scarfed - a joint between two pieces of wood, with the ends chamfered so that they fit snugly together.

schooner - a usually small ship, principally fore and aft rigged which has two or more masts, the foremast being lower than the mainmast.

sextant – instrument for measuring angles, most commonly between a celestial body and the horizon.

sheer - the curve of the deckline of a ship or boat, so that the bow is high and able to ride above waves.

squall (rafale) or line squall – intense weather event prevalent in tropical latitudes characterised by the sudden onset of rain and often violent wind, frequently from a direction different from the prevailing wind.

staysail – sail set on a forestay.

steep to – a coast is said to be 'steep to' when the sea bed rises quickly near the land

swivel – gun supported on a mount which allows it to be aimed easily.

tack – turn the ship through the wind.

tartan – small lateen rigged vessel.

Talleyrand - cardinal and foreign minister of France.

Temple – a prison in Paris used for housing political prisoners, including the royal family. One of Napoleon's last acts was to order its destruction. As a superstitious Corsican, he was unnerved by a letter Sidney Smith had displayed in the window of his cell there, prophesying that Smith would end up in the Elysee, and Bonaparte in the Temple.

thwart - a seat running "athwartships" or across a boat.

tiller – lever attached to the rudder which is used to steer the craft.

trade wind – steady easterly winds which in the North Atlantic blow in a band between about 19 and 6 degrees north

tramontane – westerly wind, often violent, which enters the Mediterranean at the end of the Pyrenees

trenail – a wooden dowel driven into a hole bored through two pieces of timber to fasten them together.

Ushant – a large island surrounded by smaller islands and rocks on the north western extremity of Brittany. Tidal streams run fiercely through the channels.

Vilaine - Breton river which flows into the Bay of Biscay. It is now dammed by the barrage at Arzal, and is navigable as far as Redon.

William – third son of George III. He spent a considerable time in the Royal Navy, and was a friend of Nelson. The Duke of Clarence, he later became William IV, nicknamed 'the Sailor King'.

Wright, Captain RN – associate of Sidney Smith, escaped with him from the Temple. Captured by the French for a second time in Brittany, he died mysteriously in the Temple.

xebec – vessel of Arab origin, often lateen rigged in full or part

# ABOUT THE AUTHOR

## Paul Weston

www.paulwestonauthor.com

Paul Weston's writing is informed by his career as a merchant seaman, on tankers, offshore oil support vessels, and on ferries, as well as his experience in business and engineering. A prolific inventor, he has several patents to his name. He has been sailing since childhood, initially in the family's converted fishing boat 'True Vine'. In his his teens he crossed the Atlantic in a home designed and built 26 footer, and in his twenties raced to the Azores and back on another 26 footer. He owned 'Mitch', a 31 foot Mitchell Sea Angler, for over twenty years, and during an intermittent four year voyage with his wife Sally, took the boat to the Mediterranean and back by sea, river and canal. They have now reverted to sail, and own 'Kadash', a 40 foot aluminium lift keel yacht which they bought in France and have sailed via Spain, Morocco and the Canary Islands to the West Indies.

# BOOKS IN THIS SERIES

*Paul Weston Historical
Maritime and Naval Fiction*

Books in this series have plausible and fast moving plots, are historically and technically accurate, and are informed by Paul Weston's knowledge of the sea and ships. In these complex novels, the author evokes the era of the Napoleonic wars, set as they were against the background of scientific progress and the nascent Industrial Revolution.

## Weymouth Bound

The merchant ship 'Cicely' is captured by the brilliant and ruthless Captain Morlaix of the French Navy. Apprentice Jack Stone's life is changed forever. Apprentice Jack Stone's life is changed forever, and he determines to do what he can to survive and to frustrate a French plot which will strike at the heart of the British establishment

## Not By Sea

Napoléon knows that if he is to win the war, he must invade England, but the Armée d'Angleterre is blockaded in Boulogne by the Royal Navy. Frustrated by British sea power, Napoléon entrusts an alternative scheme to the brilliant Captain Morlaix which if successful, could lead to the subjugation of Britain.

## Cape Corse

Britain is at war with Napoleonic France, and Lieutenant Snowden RN is sent to Bermuda to commission a fast cedar built schooner, 'Oleander'. In the Mediterranean, the short lived Corsican Republic has been defeated by the French, and Pasquale Paoli, the Republic's leader, is in exile in London. Snowden and 'Oleander' are sent to Corsica to support a delicate and dangerous operation which could be of considerable assistance in defeating Bonaparte.

## Gulf Of Lions

Though Spain has entered the war against Britain on the side of Napoleonic France, the causus belli provided by the Royal Navy's seizure of its treasure fleet, the Bonapartists are unpopular with the Spanish people. This will eventually lead to the uprisings and brutal repressions depicted by Goya, and the defeat of the French in the Peninsular War, but in 1805 Lieutenant Snowden RN is sent in HMS 'Oleander' to the Mediterranean on a secret mission to encourage the Spanish opposition. Snowden's gift for seizing opportunities takes 'Oleander' on a wide ranging cruise from Brittany to Spain, France and Morocco.

Printed in Dunstable, United Kingdom